Mossycoat

THE BAND OF UNLIKELY HEROES BOOK 2

DAWN FØRD

scrivkids

Copyright © 2024 by Dawn Ford

Published by ScrivKids,
an imprint of Scrivenings Press LLC
15 Lucky Lane
Morrilton, Arkansas 72110
https://ScriveningsPress.com

Printed in the United States of America

Paperback ISBN 978-1-64917-399-7

eBook ISBN 978-1-64917-400-0

Editors: Erin R. Howard and Linda Fulkerson

Cover design by Linda Fulkerson - www.bookmarketinggraphics.com

To the child who reads this and then dreams in stories. I believe in you.

CHAPTER 1

"What are they doing out during the day?" Princess Horra Fyd whispered to Balk, her mercenary companion. They sat at the shadowed edge of a forest between the magical Weald and the old witch lands. Though elves eradicated witches in a long-ago war, their half-breed offspring with orcs remained.

Balk pointed at the group of six ugly worqs. "And since when have they become civilized enough to roast their meat?"

The elf's lethal spell had left the land poisoned, creating a mostly dead zone. The extensive area, which from its center out was a day's ride in every direction, lay flat and open, leaving no way to get around the worqs without being seen.

"This was supposed to be the easiest way back to the castle." Horra couldn't help the whine that crept into her voice. She'd been on the run for weeks, hunted by an evil elf called the Erlking, and then taken captive and thrown into her own dungeon.

"A well-versed warrior troll princess would know what to do in this situation." Balk's teasing reply made her frown. His stubbly face, however, was more somber. Not that she blamed him. The worqs, under the Erlking's control, had held them both prisoner in her castle, and they'd suffered the same maltreatment from them. "I told you we should've went back through Bough Valley. It's faster and safer."

She ground her tusks together. "You know why I didn't want to go that way. It isn't safer." However, turning around now seemed to be the smartest course, even if it would take them half of a day out of their way. "This is the Erlking's fault. You never saw worqs like this before he tried to take over Oddar. His dark music magic is affecting creatures in strange ways."

Balk grunted a laugh. "Like the giantess beast knocking a bridge to pieces?"

His reference to Grendel, the bookish girl giant turned monster, made her cheeks flush. "You know I'm right. A giant girl doesn't turn furry and start throwing boulders around for no reason. You're the one who told me about your daughter, Floke, and how you believe the Erlking is responsible for her disappearance." Horra would've said death, but Balk had become obsessed with the idea she was still alive.

Balk shifted in his saddle. "Aye, I did. But I didn't realize you were such a scaredy mouse. The girl was only a little wooly around the edges. If you're going to fill your warrior foremother's shoes, you'll need to work on your bravery."

Her frown deepened to a scowl. "Nothing about Grendel was little, though she was smaller than she had been when I first saw her." Thoughts of that event still made Horra shiver. "I'm not the only one scared here," she hissed back. "I don't see you rushing out there to battle the worqs."

One of the worqs pinched off a piece of the meat from the sizzling chunk. The cook punched him, which started a fight that four of the six worqs joined in.

Horra grimaced at the display of violence.

The look Balk sent her left no doubt why he wasn't facing off with the brutish creatures. Neither of them could take on one of them, even on a good day.

Their animals both danced nervously in place.

Horra took a deep breath to calm herself and almost choked. She stuck her tongue out and gagged. The worqs reeked worse than a stagnant swamp on a humid summer eve. Nimble, her pet gulgoyle, sniffed and snorted, smoke curling from his nostrils.

"Don't you worry about those big, bad bullies. None of them will take a whip to you again." She patted her pet's neck once and stopped, surprised at how hard, almost rock-like, that it had become.

Nimble had been her mother's pet, saved from a group of dwarfs who had mistreated him. Horra had taken on the responsibility of caring for Nimble after her mother died. After she'd witnessed the worqs beating him, she vowed to rehabilitate the gulgoyle so it could defend itself if it ever needed to again. He was more than a pet to her.

As a half-dragon and half-gargoyle breed, turning to stone wouldn't be uncommon. However, Nimble had never shown signs of doing so. She wasn't sure if it was good or if she should be worried about her immediate safety.

She played with the leather reins to disguise the tremble in her claws, the memory of the worq's brutality toward her still vivid in her mind. "Let's turn back. There's no way the two of us can take on a half-dozen of them."

"You know what that means." Balk gave her a meaningful look.

Vinegar and beans! She didn't want to go back across the damaged bridge—if it still stood. But she knew he was eager to get back, fulfill his oath to her kitchen maid, Sageel, who had helped save them both, and return to hunting for Floke.

She wrinkled her nose at him. "I know, but we don't have a choice." She flicked the reins, and Nimble responded immediately, acting desperate to go back the way they'd come.

Balk, on her father's massive Stempner steed, followed her lead.

Crack! The sound of her companion's horse stepping on a dead branch shattered the silence. Surprised shouts exploded from the group they were trying to avoid.

Horra stiffened in her saddle and jerked her head around.

Balk's face reflected a desperate apology. He mouthed, "Go!" and slapped his reins across his horse's flank.

Her heart hammered as she coaxed Nimble into a run. They tore back through the forest. Balk veered away from her to draw the worqs' attention. It was a plan they'd made as they traveled to the Weald in case of trouble.

The gulgoyle's wings were up and open, a sign it wanted to fly. Unfortunately, Nimble's first owners clipped its wings, rendering them useless for flight. But the gulgoyle was swift and its eyesight keen enough to avoid obstacles and trees as they raced.

She glanced behind her, losing sight of Balk in the dense forest. However, she caught sight of the worqs splitting up—four going after Balk and two coming after her.

The lessons she'd had about them being unintelligent were far from correct. Either they were evolving or someone was training them. Like the Erlking. Horra's heart pounded as hard as her gulgoyle's feet struck against the forest floor.

The ground rumbled, distracting her attention and skewing their path. Nimble bounced off the trunk of a thick stringy pine tree. A ripple moved across the gulgoyle's hide and was gone.

She jerked the reins left toward the Weald and a denser section of trees. Horra knew if Nimble could get through the thicket, the worqs could as well. However, she had no proper plan and was going by instinct only.

Several birds exploded in the sky as she passed beneath the trees. Their distressed cries added to the racket, making her more tense.

Crack!

Pop!

Rumble.

Horra jerked her head around. Nimble's strides were more frenzied, making it harder for her to catch what was going on. At the last moment, she noticed a movement in her peripheral vision.

Were the trees moving?

Nimble dodged something on the ground, tossing her sideways. Her claws were slick with cold sweat, and she almost tipped out of the saddle, managing at the last minute to secure her hold on the pommel.

Thwack! A crooked arrow sunk into a tree to her right.

Horra squealed and ducked low.

Something else whirred by her head. Nimble bellowed. When she glanced up, she saw a fresh arrow sticking out of the side of her pet's shoulder. Anger churned in her gut. Those worqs would pay for that!

Nimble dodged and bounced off trees in a fierce effort to escape their enemies. No help was in sight. Horra yanked on the leather straps, jerking her pet left and then right, not daring to be an easy target. Fear pounded a drum in her chest as a prayer for safety sprang into her mind.

The acrid scent of dragon fire drifted to Horra's nose as her pet careened forward, accompanied by hot, belching breaths.

The gulgoyle was tiring. Blood trailed down its side where the arrow still protruded.

If only she hadn't gone this way back to her castle, Nimble wouldn't be injured now. If only she could reach the wooden-cloak, tucked inside her knapsack belted to Nimble's side, she might've hidden them in plain sight.

Too many doubts and should-haves bombarded her mind until she thought it would explode.

Crunching and more rumbles echoed around them. Hair raised on Horra's arms. Steeling herself, she darted a glance behind and found only trees. She didn't have time to question anything when Nimble collided with another tree. But this time, they didn't bounce off.

Horra went sailing over Nimble's head, the reins still in her claws.

Leaves scattered and floated in the surrounding air before she hit the ground hard, landing on her back.

Above her wasn't a tree. It was an enormous orange giant.

No, two enormous giants. In the middle of the Wilden Lands, far away from their northern home in Giborham.

Horra screamed.

CHAPTER 2

"Don't scream, deary! You'll reveal our position to those vile creatures following you." The woman bent down toward her. Horra recognized the woman from when she'd gotten lost and taken by the giant child, Galumph. Now, all she needed was a blown-up version of a catterwump and a torentula to make her nightmare complete.

She squealed and scrambled back—against her boulder of a pet. Of all times for the gulgoyle to turn to stone.

"Troll princess?" the man asked, reaching for her.

She raised her arms over her head. The last time a giant had grabbed her, the girl had nearly shaken and strangled Horra to death. "Don't!"

"You're scaring the poor girl, Grint. Have some manners." The woman's voice was admonishing.

Horra glanced up at them.

The woman smiled, creating crease lines at the ends of her flecked eyes. "You're the troll princess, aren't you? We've been searching for you, hoping you can help us."

7

Help them? Taken aback, Horra was speechless for a moment. Jewels sparkled from the sides of the woman's shaved scalp. A tuft of bright red hair wafted on the top of her enormous head.

"I-I am Princess Horra, yes." She flipped over to her knees. The boulder she braced herself against to stand was hot to the touch, making her flinch back and stumble.

The giantess caught Horra before she would fall over, steadying her. "Oh, my. We're so glad to have found you! Have you seen our daughters? They've both gone missing. We believe it might have something to do with your visit to our lands."

Horra stared. Visit? It wasn't a visit if she was kidnapped, was it? She'd never look at a torentula or a catterwump the same again.

Sensing Horra's reluctance, the woman moved back, giving her some space. "Please, we're desperate to find them. First Grendel disappeared. Then, shortly after, Galumph went missing. When news about the coup at your castle spread to us, we realized the dolly our youngest daughter referred to was you. We're right, aren't we? It was you?" Tears filled her brown eyes, trailing down her orange cheeks.

"It's not only our daughters. Many other children have gone missing from Giborham. It's happening as far up as the shores of the Burly Sea." The man, looking earnest despite his disheveled clothes, referenced a unique area of the giant lands.

From what Horra recalled of her geography knowledge, that encompassed a large area of the southern giant region. This land bordered the mysterious elflands and was northeast of the Riven.

"No one can find them, orange hide, nor red hair." He snuffled and wiped a handkerchief across his bulbous nose.

Sympathy overtook her. She hadn't had time to warn

anyone. Even Balk hadn't completely believed her when she told him about what happened with the music and the giant girl—hence his teasing. Horra inhaled a deep breath, letting it out slowly, before recounting her encounter with their daughters. She started with getting lost and ended with Grendel's strange behavior on the bridge.

"So, you're saying this Erlking has a magic flute that does strange things to different creatures?" The giantess wrung her hands and glanced uneasily at the man. "How is that possible?"

"The same way he mesmerized the trolls. I'm not sure what kind of music magic he has, but he's able to bring even the biggest troll under his control." Horra shrugged, knowing the giants would understand that trolls were famous for their immunity to magic. "As for Grendel, I'm not sure what happened after we escaped the bridge."

The woman nodded. "The villagers contacted our leaders about the destruction. It's why we came—to restore the bridge and find our daughters. But then word about the coup at your castle reached us. We'd hoped you might know something that would help us locate our daughters." Tears flowed down the woman's flushed face.

"It should be easy to locate a giant in your lands," the man continued. "But we haven't had any luck. Do you know of any large place she could hide away?"

Horra considered his question. "She wasn't the same size as before. Like with the contracting candy, she'd shrank. The Iron Mountains have many enormous caverns and canyons, but nothing I could point you toward off the top of my head." A terrible thought struck her. "And there are many hidden doorways into the lower dwarf mountains. With her new smaller size, she could've easily fallen in."

Their eyes widened, and the woman's face twisted with more grief.

Dwarfs were not a welcoming bunch. Even giants tended to give them a wide berth.

The man handed the woman his handkerchief, which she used to mop her face and blow her nose—a very wet and disgusting sound.

Horra tried not to grimace. "Possibly you should send a search team to the lower Iron Mountains?"

"Or storm the Riven?" the man stated, anger replacing the sadness in his voice.

"No one enters the Riven and returns." Horra couldn't help the disbelief in her tone. On a scale, giants couldn't rival elves—especially dark elves—in magic and power. "I don't think —" Horra started but stopped when the man spun around and took the woman's hand.

"C'mon, Giga. She's of no more use. We have all the information we need to start searching. Let's go find our daughters." Hands interlaced, they strode out of the forest in a swift march without so much as a glance back at her.

Horra stared blankly after them. Woodsly had never taught her how strange giants were.

Noises of something moving startled her back into her own dilemma—the worqs. With a frantic search, she found nowhere to hide, and Nimble was still a boulder. Because of her pet's condition, she couldn't get to her woodencloak.

With no other recourse, Horra unlatched her dagger from the sheath at her side and stood, readying for anything. Vague recollections of her old instructor Woodsly's admonishment, "If you have no better option, run," flashed through her mind.

Before she could do that, Balk, on his steed, blasted through the trees. He caught sight of her, his face frantic. He jerked on the reins, and he and his horse slid to a stop beside her. "Where's your gulgoyle, Princess?"

She slapped the boulder. "The giants scared it."

"Giants?" He shook his head. "You don't have time to explain. We need to go. The worqs are hot on my trail."

The Stempner sniffed at Nimble's rock hide. It shimmered, then cracked, and then broke into pieces. The gulgoyle shook its head and gazed at Horra with its dark eyes. Flakes of rock and dust fell to the ground. The arrow was gone. Horra touched the space where the wound should be, but it was completely healed.

Balk grunted. "Get on. Let's go before they catch up."

CHAPTER 3

The Weald ~ The same day

Merrow, woodgoblin seedkeeper of the Weald, scraped a crusty patch of fungus from the sapling's periderm, the light outer bark on the druid woodgoblin's stick-like trunk. "Oh dear," he grumbled to himself, fearing the worst.

If the seed failed to thrive, the Honorable Order of Druids would come to an end. Caring for the seeds, which would become the balance holders of the Wilden Lands, was his life's work. His charges, the woodgoblins chosen to become druids, were anointed by the Creature God to keep evil in check and balanced with the good of all creatures.

His mind returned to when the troll princess arrived with the seed. It had suffered damage from a trip through a poisoned forest and an errant curse. She was young and impetuous, not coming to the Weald immediately. She'd lingered to save her kingdom and her father from the Erlking's nefarious hold. Her mentor, Master Kryk, had made it far too easy for the girl to choose which was more important to her. She'd chosen her kingdom over the safety of the entire Wilden Lands.

"Such is the folly of youth. Fickle to the roots," Merrow spoke out loud. He was used to talking to himself or talking to the roods—the dead druid spirits that lived in the trees. Merrow understood why she did what she did, but her actions made his work much more complicated.

He placed a hand on the ancient Yew tree in the center of the garden and closed his eyes, seeking his old friend, Woodsly. Though he hadn't taken up his final resting place in one of the Yew trees, he was nearby.

"It had to be done. I had to use some of my energy to help keep her safe." Woodsly's ghostly voice traveled up the tree and into Merrow's mind. *"I trained Princess Horra on all things she'd need to know, just in case. But her father had coddled her after her mother died. Possibly rightly so, since her mother's dying wish had impaired her. What she needed was experience, something you can't train into a warrior. She was bound to go headfirst into emotional reactions. She got my seed here before it was too late. Have no fear, my friend, it will survive. I sense his life force strengthening. In the end, the troll princess will help this new druid find his way around the world. She will become a magnificent leader one day."*

Merrow patted the tree trunk. "One day, perhaps," he agreed. "Until then, we are all at the mercy of a small troll girl to keep the darkness at bay long enough for us to complete our mission."

Murmurs rumbled from the ground—the roods speaking to one another of more curses and danger throughout the Wilden Lands. Merrow hobbled over to a wooden bench and planted himself on it with a heavy sigh. Arthritis made his roots swell and his limbs creak.

Darkness was creeping across the land too swiftly. It would

take weeks at the least to unroot the seedling. Then he could start his druid training. But the Erlking could do much damage in that time. They, he and Woodsly, had been far too unprepared for the dark elf's arrival, thinking they had more time before he came.

If only the first plague hadn't taken so many of his kind—the Seventeen Wise Men of the Yew Order. Merrow stared off into the canopy of leaves above him. He was the only one left. Fourteen had fallen to the first Erlking's plague. One had died in the War of the Warts. The last, Woodsly, was the one that grieved Merrow the most. They'd come from the same forest and had shared a childhood before entering the Order. His death by this, the second Erlking's hand, had been especially shocking.

"Do the elves know malevolence grows at their border, invading the lands they once ruled?" he asked the tree spirits. "Surely their Sylvan Counsel knows. Where else would the dark elf have come from if not from Endwylde?"

Hints of agreement traveled along the roots. He wasn't the only one to think so. The elves had joined the old viken wizards, drawing up an impenetrable wall of magic spells. Because of their combined powerful magics, no one knew for sure what to believe. None of the roods could penetrate their complicated shield that went deeper than roots could grow. They had cut themselves off from the rest of the Wilden Lands as promised.

"It's unconscionable for them to have created the Riven," came the voice of a long-dead elder.

"He could be a murderer," spoke another of the older roods eagerly, referring to one of Sylvan Counsel's seven unpardonable sins. *"Or he uses dark magic."*

"Aye, we know he does from his use of music magic." Merrow frowned at the obvious answer. Some roods were well

14

over four hundred years old in their spiritual form and were losing their sharpness. It was only a matter of time for some to forget altogether who they were and leave their Yew tree behind for their heavenly home. That, among other reasons, made Merrow anxious about ancient knowledge disappearing before the next druid came into power.

Merrow shook his leaves, discarding the thoughts and worries of which he had no control. His cane tapped as he made his way back over to the sapling. He only had one job, something he'd dreamed of since he was a sprout—growing and training the next druid warrior.

Glimmerbugs danced around Merrow's leaves as he rubbed tingleroot paste to the area on the trunk he'd just scraped. The sapling moved.

Merrow clapped his stick-like hands. "That's it, my boy! Wake up!"

A breeze born of the land's gladness rippled through the giant old Yew trees that made up the Weald. Roods exclaimed in joy. Whimsy birds sang and bobbed the long feathers on their tails. Hope, in the form of sunlight, sparkled down on the rocky path around the garden. The ancient protection symbols etched into the path and on the trees glowed and hummed.

The sapling moved again, as if stretching, and his eyes opened and blinked. He let out his first clackity croak. With shaking limbs, Merrow held the bottle of lifesap to the lips of the newborn druid, and it suckled. Sap seeped out of the corners of his splintered mouth as he dragged in deep gulps of the liquid.

"I shall name you Rowan." Merrow wiped away the excess sap.

When Rowan finished, he slept. Merrow was almost certain Rowan visibly grew before his eyes, though it could just be his own eagerness. Light-green buds spread across the youngster's reddish crown. The thin periderm on his trunk had thickened and darkened from a taupe to a nice chestnut color.

The color of life.

"Thank the Creature God. It won't be long now, my boy." Pleased, Merrow took the bottle and refilled it. Rowan would need to eat every two hours now until he had grown enough to unroot. Normally it took weeks of careful tending, but Rowan hadn't sprouted as expected, so it might take longer.

Merrow didn't mind. He'd been waiting two generations to be the Master Seedkeeper to the next druidborn. With four hundred and ninety rings under his bark, he was more than ready for the challenge.

After Rowan unrooted, they'd immediately begin their training. With the Erlking on the move, there wasn't time to spare.

There was only so fast a sapling would grow, though, even in the best of circumstances. Merrow prayed for a miracle.

CHAPTER 4

"Is it safe to go over that?" Horra asked Balk. Hobgoblin Pass's bridge leading to Bough Valley looked whole, but the waning sunlight showed it was patch-worked. It had taken them the rest of the day to travel out of the forests around the Weald, find the main road, and get to where they were now. Her shoulders ached, as did her bottom, from riding so long.

She scanned the bridge for any weakness. Many of the smaller hobgoblins and imps moved easily over the structure, but all of them weighed less than her on her gulgoyle and Balk on the Stempner.

Balk grunted. "You go first, and I'll follow shortly after."

She spun around in her saddle. "Why do I have to go first? If it's unsound, I'll fall to my death, and you'll break your oath to my father."

His face puckered in a scowl. "Fine, I'll go first, and you follow shortly after me." He kicked the horse into action, scattering a group of gnomes as they trotted past.

"I don't know why he's such a grumpy gus," she muttered.

After waiting for him to make it halfway across, she ambled Nimble onto the bridge, being much more careful to avoid the other travelers.

Angry glances turned her way as they moved slowly across. Why was everyone so irritable today? Balk made it across as she hit the mid-section of the bridge.

"What'd'ya think you're doing crossing this bridge?" A redcapper pointed a thin cane at her while standing on a section of the unbroken side. He sneered at her.

Horra ignored the creature. Redcappers hated trolls because they controlled the largest section of the central Wilden Lands. As such, redcappers were under her kingdom of Oddar's rule. And redcappers were always in trouble. They made up the majority of her Goblin Court's cases.

"Heh. See how this high and mighty princess ignores her citizens? It's time to overthrow their tyranny! Down with the trolls!" the redcapper shouted.

Its voice sounded familiar to Horra. She dug around in her memory and recalled the moment she'd been caught right after she and Pidge, her pet pudge wudgie, had escaped the castle after the Erlking had taken over. It had to be the same one. She glared at them.

Several on the bridge ignored the outburst. Others glanced at Horra, then raised their fists in support of the redcapper's screed. The crowd turned into a frenzy of spewed hatred toward her, her father the king, and her kingdom.

Horra signaled Nimble to move faster. Shouts accumulated into a loud united shout of 'down with the trolls' and 'imprison the princess.'

This couldn't be happening. Since when had the public turned against her? But she recalled the crowd in the castle when the fairy queen had sentenced her to years in her own dungeon for crimes she hadn't committed. Could it be these were some of the same witnesses, and they didn't know she was innocent? Or was it something else?

A crowd gathered in front of Nimble. They held their arms out in an ineffectual barricade. Hide on the gulgoyle's side rippled once more, sending a zing of fear racing through Horra. She couldn't get stranded on this bridge right now. Though she had no love for redcappers, Horra didn't want to hurt anyone. She just wanted to get back to her castle—uninjured, if possible.

With a nudge, Nimble's rumbling walk turned into a trot. "Get out of the way," she implored the blockade.

A few realized she wasn't kidding and stepped aside. Several of the bolder imps and spriggans remained, grins on their faces.

Woodsly's voice in her head, warning her of the repercussions of any actions she took, flitted through her mind. *Sour grapes!*

"It is unlawful to detain a member of the monarchy in such a manner. Unless you want to be hauled into the Goblin Court to meet her father's wrath, let the Princess through." Balk's voice was loud and brooked no argument. He marched his steed into the back of the gathering, his horse's hooves motivating them to move aside.

Rocks and debris flew, hitting Horra and Nimble. With the way finally cleared, she ushered her pet to move swiftly past the protesters. Once on land, Balk caught up to her, his head swiveling.

"What was all of that about?" she asked.

"Your guess is as good as mine. The only thing I can think of is the Erlking is sowing discontent among the lesser creatures. None of the hobgoblins, gnomes, or goblins joined in the fray. I was going to insist on camping outside of Bough Valley. I think it might be safer to travel through the night."

Aches from running from the worqs and then riding all day nagged at her, but she agreed with his assessment. With a nod, Balk indicated a smaller trail, which would be adequate for smaller creatures. It was almost too narrow for their animals, but it was better than having more face-offs with other angry critters.

"Are you sure about it?" Horra knew the mapped roads, not the side paths from deeper forest burrows that smaller creatures would use. She vowed to review more maps when she got back to the castle.

"I see track marks, so someone's used it lately, though they appear to be from a smaller creature's conveyance." He glanced ahead of them, down the road. "I recall taking a shortcut once past the Deep Barrows. The gnomes there don't bother you unless you bother them."

At the mention of the Barrows, Horra cringed. "Gnomes won't. But the spriggans might. They've been trying to assume control of the Barrows since before I sat in on my first Goblin Court."

Dwarfs had tossed the spriggans out of their wattle homes along the Dunder Mounds after too many spriggans had stolen from them. Her father had very little patience for their complaints. Lately, they'd become a general thorn in the king's side. Horra recalled a few who had cheered the fairy queen when she'd sentenced Horra on illegitimate charges.

Balk grunted. "I'm not afraid of any spriggans." He nudged his horse into a slow canter. It was just wide enough for the Stempner's feet to fall where the small wagons created two bare treads.

Irked by his retort, Horra sent him back a haughty glare. "I never said I was afraid of them."

His chuckle floated to her on the breeze, annoying her more.

She refused to speak to him any further until they got to the castle.

Stars shone through a bluish-purple sky when they came upon a large, downed tree on a curve blocking the path. The Stempner stamped, sending dust into the air. It must be as eager to get back as Horra was.

Balk swung down from his saddle to get a closer look at the tree.

Horra did the same and walked through stickery weeds to get to the base. "What do you think caused it?" She kicked at the trunk with a booted foot. It was sturdy, not rotted. And instead of an uneven break such as wind would cause, it had an even split. "That's chopped on purpose. And this looks like something lived in it recently." She picked up a teapot, without the lid, in a thicket of weeds. Some amber-colored liquid remained inside the container.

Balk bent over to examine the cut. "Would they have cut their own tree down?"

A rustling sounded, startling them both. "Oh, no, you don't. You i'nt blaming us for this mess." A red-faced gnome man with a dark object held in his hand broke out of the brush and darted right at them.

CHAPTER 5

Horra backed away from the man as Balk moved in front of her, his dagger in his hand. "Whoa! That's close enough."

The gnome stopped a couple of strides in front of them and pointed a curved-handled pipe at them. Smoke curled out of the bowl. "What're you two doing here and not traveling on the thoroughfare? You come to set the final nail'n our demise?"

Horra scrunched her nose at the smoky odor. She never liked the scent of any kind of tobacco, especially the uncured kind this gnome smoked.

Balk's face didn't reflect any emotion. "We just got here, so clearly we had nothing to do with your house being toppled."

"That don't answer why you're here'n the first place."

"We prefer less-traveled roads," Balk snarled at the man.

"I'nt likely," the gnome said, shoving the mouthpiece into his mouth, his teeth clattering against the smooth, clay object. He stood with his arms across his chest, staring at them.

Balk's face changed, and he shrugged. "Doesn't matter.

C'mon Princess, there's no getting around this. We'll have to go back the way we came."

"But that's hours' worth of riding." Horra fought the urge to stomp her feet. They'd already been detained longer than she wanted. She knew she was being unreasonable, but she was tired and hungry, and she longed to sleep in a real bed for a change. "Can't we go around it?"

The gnome wheezed out a laugh. "Unless you like gully climbing on t'other side, you i'nt going around it."

Balk stopped and glared at her. "Can you move this tree? This extremely large tree that even a giant would have trouble moving?"

Horra sniffed back the frustration. "No, of course not."

"Then what do you suggest? We use our wings to fly over this forest to get back home?" He crooked his arms like wings, flapped them, and danced around in a circle. "Why didn't I think of that?"

"That's uncalled for. Sounds like you two need some grub." The gnome man shifted the pipe from one side of his mouth to the other without touching it. "Ain't no tempers like those of someone whose wranglin' with hunger. C'mon then. The missus has cooked every'n'thing we had stashed for winter since we now need to move."

Horra blinked at the man, astonished by his instant change of mood. "So, what happened here?"

The gnome's brown hat bobbed as he turned and walked away. "Them spriggans came while we was gone this morning to Bough Valley t'sell our wreaths. It was down by the time we returned home."

"So, how do you know it was spriggans?" Balk followed reluctantly behind me. "It could be anyone."

"Who else bothers us gnomes? Nobody I tell you." He stabbed the pipe in the air to stress his last sentence.

Horra didn't say so, but she thought it could have been the worqs, though they would've probably destroyed more than just the one tree. And they wouldn't have waited for the gnomes to leave to do so—they would've attacked them when they were home.

"I'm so sorry. You need to let my father, the King, know. He'll make sure—"

The gnome stopped, spun around, and leveled a death glare at Horra. "He'd make sure what? They're punished? Tossed out of the Barrows like the dwarf's done? We've complained about their mischief for years. And the king i'nt made them leave the Barrows yet."

Surprise and anger warred for dominance in her gut. Her father was a fair ruler, but lately there'd been so many problems, it had been hard to get a handle on all of them. She should know. They forced her to sit through all the Goblin Court sessions. "That's not fair. I've never seen your fellows bring enough evidence to act on."

He narrowed his eyes at her, red blooming across his pale cheeks. "Spriggans are sneaky, conniving vermin. Common sense would tell you—"

Balk stepped in front of her. "Common sense would tell you that anyone could've downed that tree, including any of the halflings that live within a day's ride from the Barrows. Unless you have proof, there isn't anything anyone can do for you."

The gnome stood with his rounded nose in the air, his glare taking them both in now.

"He's right, Yosnan." A woman appeared out of a bush. Her cheeks were also flushed, but it probably had more to do with the food odors filling the air than anger at Horra and Balk. "We i'nt able to say a hundred percent whodunnit. I'm Ymeni, by the by."

Yosnan stomped up to the woman and stood nose to nose with her. "You'n I both know twas them spriggans. They been sniffing around for a fortnight now, trying to get our measure before attacking."

"Can't bring it to the courts n'less you gots proof like these kind folk here said." She turned to Horra and clapped a hand to her chest in salute. "Welcome, princess, to our humble piece of land. I thought we'd have to waste our meal, but thank the Critter God you've come to help us out of that predicament."

Critter God? Was that the same as the Creature God? Horra wasn't sure, and she didn't want to cause any more ire from Yosnan. She placed a claw across her heart. "Thank you. I appreciate that." To Balk, she murmured, "It's already dark. It won't hurt anything to delay another hour."

Balk grunted before speaking in a low voice. "Thought you wanted to get going before." She sent him a side-eye but couldn't draw his attention to see what was bothering him so much.

The gnome's food was plain but tasty, and Horra was hungry. She cleaned her plate despite the smacking noises Yosnan made while he grumpily ate and the lateness of the hour. A small fire lit the area enough to make it warm and seem cozier than just a dark forest.

A yawn tickled the edges of Horra's mouth. "Thank you, Ymeni. If you ever pass by our castle, know you are welcome to stay and break bread with us." She stated the traveler's blessing Woodsly had made her memorize for just such an occasion. Her mind flicked to Woodsly's seed. She sent a silent prayer that whoever it sprouted into would be half as intelligent as her late instructor had been.

She stood and Yemeni took her claws into her smaller hands. Though the gnome woman had sat next to the fire, her fingers were like ice. "Blessings upon your house, Princess. Until we meet again."

Yosnan frowned and looked off into the darkness. It seemed nothing would make the man happy, except possibly a successful court case against the Spriggans.

Horra had pity on his wife. "Until we meet again."

She and Balk walked in silence to their sleeping animals. It was a shame to wake them, but they needed to get back, and it was getting close to sunrise now. "What made you so inhospitable?" she asked in a low tone.

"We were not alone, Princess. I believe there to be at least two, maybe more, somebodies watching us feast with the gnomes. I didn't want to make a scene or worry you."

She blinked at him, her claws hovering above Nimble's head. She trusted his mercenary instincts. "You think they're troublemakers?"

His glare was hard. "They didn't reveal themselves, did they?"

"Are the gnomes safe?"

"Safer that you or I."

Horra rolled her shoulders, positive an invisible target had taken residence on her back.

CHAPTER 6

Horra and Balk's ride back to the castle in the bleary morning hours had been uneventful after they left the gnomes. Relief had been sweet upon viewing the gray stone mountain in the midday sun.

She opened the castle's side door to the kitchen and instantly choked on the dirt clogging the air. Eyes watering, she rushed past the cloud coming from the dungeon's stairway.

"What is going on?" she inquired of a maid in passing as she rubbed the dirt from her eyes. They were already gritty enough without any help.

The hobgoblin *tsked* and planted fists on her hips. "It's them fairies, Princess! Determined to redeem themselves, they are. All them cleaning spells have made it impossible to use the kitchen today. Yesterday we couldn't do anything with the dining room or throne room." A grin broke across her creased face. "I'm so glad for your return, though. I'm sure the king will be as well. Are you hungry?"

"Famished." Horra glanced at the icebox hopefully. Though

the gnome's food had been filling, it was well past their noonday meal.

"Oh, Princess! There you are. I was hoping to run into you. I just spoke with Balk." Sageel, the hobgoblin maid who had saved Horra from the Erlking himself, hurried over to Horra. She, too, dodged a dust cloud rushing toward the door. "My apologies. I was avoiding our guests."

Horra squeezed the old hobgoblin's gnarled hands. Another dust cloud flew up the stairway from below. She couldn't help but roll her eyes at the display of magic. "If they're so powerful, couldn't they gather it all up and get rid of it in one fell sweep instead? And why are they cleaning the dungeon, of all places?"

"Who knows why fairies do anything?" Sageel hefted out a laugh. "Glad I'm leaving. Those three, well, two really, will be the death of me." She leaned over and whispered, "The injured one just sits around and stares into space."

Horra nodded as though she agreed, but she sympathized with the disfigured fairy princess's plight. At least the Fairy Queen still had her daughters, unlike the giants. "It's quite sad."

Another whirlwind of dirt and debris whipped up the stairway. The door opened to the courtyard and the cloudy mess flew out, startling a horse. It whinnied, and someone yelled before the door slammed back shut.

Exhaustion pulled at Horra's patience. "When do they leave?"

"Not soon enough," the other hobgoblin murmured. She handed Horra a basket. "There's all of your favorites except the spruce juice. I think it got poured out during the coup. I made you some tart berry juice instead."

Horra dug into the contents, breaking off the end of the

bracken bread loaf and dipping it into a crock of bacon grease. "*Mm.* Thank you."

The maid nodded and strode away.

Sageel waited for the other hobgoblin to leave before tugging on Horra's shirt. "This way, Princess." Using her cane, she led Horra to the storage room. There on the shelf was a tray holding a plate full of pickled squall eggs, braised frog's legs, and another decanter. "Sour spruce juice," she muttered, sounding quite pleased with herself. "I tucked it away for you. Since I'm going to be gone for a fortnight, I wanted to be sure you ate well. You're growing now, you know."

Horra licked the bacon grease off her claws, blinking back the tears the woman's concern brought her. "Thank you."

Tinkling laughter floated into the dark space.

"Best you stay here. I'll try to distract them." Sageel pattered out of the storage room, her cane clacking against the stone floor.

Horra removed the contents of the basket onto the tray, waiting for the voices to die down. When they did, she pulled the hidden lever and entered the secret passages.

She locked the door with the heavy pin and sat down to eat. The passage was eerily quiet, devoid of the vermin that usually darted back and forth. Pidge had done a wonderful job of ridding the castle of the extra rats and mice. Hopefully, someone had returned her pet to the Conservatory.

After eating her fill and yawning a great deal, Horra took the remains on the tray and headed to her room.

A quick peek at her hole sent elation through her. Her room was no longer frilly and glittery. The fairies had reverted it to the dark space it should be. Horra couldn't believe it, but she wanted to kiss them for it.

She entered the room, shut the doorway, and set the tray on a side table. It wasn't completely back to its normal clutter, but that would happen soon enough. Her boots were the first to be removed, her pack set beside her lumpy bed, and a soft nightgown—free of prickly powder—donned last. She was asleep before her head hit the pillow.

HORRA DREAMED of shadows and reflective eyes watching her as she slept. A noise woke her. She jerked up in bed, unsure where she was. It took her a moment for the wool to disappear in her mind to realize she was in her room.

"Woodsly, is that you?" she muttered groggily while scrubbing a claw across her weary face. Her uneven, hard-as-flint nails scratched her thick hide. She flopped back down, memories of the last couple of days coming back to her. Her arms and legs were sore, and a nasty flavor lingered on her tongue— she'd forgotten to brush her teeth before falling asleep.

"*Umph!*"

Clatter.

Whispered voices.

Horra reopened her eyes and scowled. "Who is it? What's going on?" she yelled at her door. With her night vision, she couldn't see anything inside her room, and the muted noise came from behind a wall. Unless someone was inside her secret passages, it had to be coming from the hallway.

"Hello?" she called out.

No answer.

Frustrated, she threw her blanket aside and stalked over to the door. She yanked it open to find her father, Torren, and another classmate carrying her father's bedroom furnishings outside in the hallway.

"Oh, sorry, Daughter. Did we wake you? We were trying to be quiet." He dropped his end of the stone couch, catching

Torren's foot. Startled, the other troll jumped back and dropped his corner. Torren screamed in pain as his end fell on his foot. Her father raced to lift the heavy object and mumble an apology to Torren.

At her raised eyebrows, her father sent a contrite shrug. "I told the fairies I would reset my own rooms." He rubbed his dark green hair. "There aren't many worker trolls left since—" He hefted his shoulders in another shrug and let out a deep breath. "Since the Erlking."

"How many are left?" Horra asked, still rubbing her eyes. Grit from her trip and the dust cloud she'd walked into in the kitchen had crusted in the corners.

"Not enough." Her father's voice was weary. "But it's not for you to worry about. Get your rest. We'll be more careful. I'll see you at a late dinner." Dim light came in from the windows above their heads. No cobwebs clung to the stone walls. No dirt ground beneath their feet. The fairies had done an admirable job cleaning the castle.

Having peeled the last of the eye crust away, she studied the group. How bad off were they if one of her classmates had assumed a door troll position? It always went to the biggest trolls in their kingdom for obvious reasons—the doors were thick, too heavy for just anyone to handle.

Resolve settled in her gut. "I'm up now. Let me help you."

Her father tried every excuse he could think of to get her to go back to bed, but she was more stubborn than he was at that moment. It took much less time with four of them than it would have with three, and soon they had his bedroom and sitting room put back together.

King Divitri dismissed the other two and turned to her when they'd left. "Thank you, daughter. You'll make a great ruler when you're old enough." He sat down heavily on his rock couch, positioned across from his immaculately clean fireplace. No sign of fire or soot remained. He gave her an appraising glance. "Which, to my dismay, won't be much longer. How'd your trip go? I take it nothing bad happened since you returned so quickly?"

It was Horra's turn to plop down on the furniture. "Actually, it did."

CHAPTER 7

W orry furrowed the king's forehead as Horra told him all that had happened after she left for the Weald. From the giant girl monster on the bridge to the gnomes, she told him everything the best that she could recall.

"You're unharmed?" he growled.

Though her father's face was dark and stormy, his concern warmed her. She squirmed, still trying to get used to her father's new show of emotions. "I'm a little sore from riding Nimble, but I'm fine." She stifled a yawn. A couple of hours of a restless nap wasn't sufficient to curb her fatigue.

King Divitri grunted as if he didn't fully believe her, but he didn't challenge her on it. "This is not at all what I'd hoped to hear." Her father stared up at the ceiling, his tusks grinding. "The giants have never been involved with the smaller creature's affairs before."

His shoulders dropped. "It seems as if our kingdom is at war, but I'm unclear of why. I know Oddar's history with the first Erlking and his final curse. But even if that were true, why involve the giants?"

"You don't believe it to be true?" Horra's eyes roamed his sitting room. Mostly how clean it was—leaving the gems exposed. She'd have to check to ensure the hidden passages were secure again. Meanwhile, she enjoyed the easy conversation she was having with her father.

"If you're asking if I thought it would ever come to pass?" He fiddled with his clawnails, not something her father normally did. Was he nervous? "I never knew what to think. I was a poor, swamp boy whose parents had been too old to fight when the withering warts curse came upon the land. It didn't really reach us until the end. Pa had already passed by then, and Ma had a heart condition. There wasn't much talk of the war or the curse. Life was more normal for us. It was only after I'd met your mother that I learned of the realities of what had happened."

Horra's brows furrowed. "I never knew that. You don't talk about anything from before. I don't think you've ever shown me a picture of your family."

He slapped his claws together unexpectedly. "I don't have one. The earliest picture of me is when I went to Knight School. Ma made sure I got in before she passed. It was her last wish for me to become an honorable knight. I often wonder if she'd be proud of me."

Horra almost gasped. "Why wouldn't she be proud of you? You married well. And you've been a good ruler for Oddar."

He looked at her then, his clay-colored eyes a bit on the watery side. "She would've boxed my ears if she knew I fell under the Erlking's spell. Ma was an extremely proud swamp troll." He glanced away. "Your mother was proud as well."

He stood and moved to the shelf where a portrait of him and Horra's mother, Terra, rested on the top shelf. "Your mother had the best tutors, the strongest military training. She was incredible to watch on the field." A chuckle rolled from his chest. "She would've bested me right away, but she played with me before beating my hide into the ground. She told me later she was having too much fun to let it end right away."

Horra grinned, her heart swelling. "She fell for you that day."

He grinned back at her. "As I did for her." He became serious. "She believed in the death curse. I accepted it was because her family had been on the front lines and had scared her into believing it. Now I'm not so sure. And I don't understand this Erlking's reasoning and motivations. Until I know those, I don't know how to fight him." He ran a claw over her mother's face in the picture. "She would know what to do," he muttered so low Horra almost missed it.

Even though she'd witnessed her father being incapacitated during the coup, it was terrifying to hear him so unsure of himself. Was he scared too?

"Father?" She stood to go to him, but he turned around, stopping her with a claw.

He swiped away the wetness dripping down his warty green cheeks. "I'm supposed to be the strong one for you, not the other way around." His laugh was weak. "We'll figure this out. I promise you. Now, it's almost dinnertime. Go and change. I'll see you in the dining room." At her hesitation, he straightened his figure. "Go on. I'll be fine. Even strong trolls have moments of weakness. It will all look better after a good meal."

Horra gave him what she hoped was a convincing grin. She turned and strode from the room, closing his door quietly behind her. Though it was silent, the weight of his fear and grief sat heavily on her own shoulders. She'd almost rather face a half dozen worqs than see her capable father and king cry.

She placed a claw on Woodsly's door. "I wish you were here to instruct me. I miss you, you gnarled, old stick."

After a moment of grieving, she sucked it up and went to her room and changed.

———

DINNER later that evening was a somber affair, with only a portion of trolls in attendance where there would've once been full tables. Even with Balk and the fairies present, the discussion was stilted and forced.

The only highlight for Horra was the fact she didn't need her special 'booster' chair anymore. She could sit, albeit with a cushion, at the table like a normal troll her age would. She couldn't help the small smile that stayed on her face after her father said grace.

Conversation was quiet, mostly bare, as many diners were not very inclined to talk. Finally, the queen, seated in the third chair and next to Horra, turned to her. "Princess, we have finished our task of restoring your castle as penance for our offenses. I hope you find it acceptable?"

Horra didn't have to look around to know they had polished every room from top to bottom. The castle was cleaner and more refreshed than it had ever been—probably even during the first queen's rule. Trolls were not known for their tidiness. She also knew it was high time they returned to their own kingdom. The space for the injured fairy princess remained empty, with the queen making the excuse that she was 'feeling under the weather.'

Memories of the poor pink fairy's disfigured face popped into her mind and compassion filled her.

She dug into her etiquette training to reassure the woman. "It is more than acceptable, Queen Stella. You have gone over and above anything expected of you, and I am grateful to you for it." She waved her claw in a show of traditional fairy honor.

The queen returned her compliment with a dazzling smile. "Then we will take leave of your welcome first thing in the morning with the greatest wishes for your kingdom's welfare." She dipped her head and returned the gesture.

A pinging sounded as the king hit his water glass with a silver fork. "I want to make a toast to Queen Toppenbottom and her daughters." He waited while everyone took hold of their glasses and glanced back at him. "We have been very fortunate to have had their company for this temporary visit and wish them well on their return to their Shining Kingdom. Speed and safety be yours as you travel. Oddar's welcome mat will always be rolled out to greet you." He lifted his glass and took a drink.

Horra hesitated a moment before drinking. Despite the fairy's best efforts at amends, it would be a while before she wished to welcome them back again.

Possibly the queen understood this was diplomacy, for her smile was thin—not as bright as it had been to Horra's response.

A disturbance at the doorway stopped the discussion at the tables.

Horra's heart raced, and alarm instantly zinged through her veins.

The young door troll stumbled into the room from the front of the castle, his uniform askew. "Your pardon, King Fyd. We have a situation."

CHAPTER 8

Balk was immediately on his feet, followed a moment later by Horra's father rising. He motioned to the door troll to go back the way he came and moved to join him.

Horra stood to follow, but her father stopped her. "He's new. It might be nothing. Please finish dinner, and I'll let you know if there's anything to be concerned about."

She hesitated. Ever since the fairies came and took over her castle, she'd been the decision-maker. The one taking charge. It heartened her that her father would keep her informed of what was going on. He'd never done that before. Still, it stung to stay behind.

She dipped her head to her father and sat.

Balk, however, joined her father without being turned back.

The queen laid a gentle hand on hers. "Being a parent, I know the lengths we go to in order to keep our children from the worst strains of our jobs. I don't believe he meant offense, nor do I in speaking to you about it. You have shown yourself quite adept in difficult times, and your father has spoken highly of your actions. I can tell how proud he is of you. I'm certain he is just trying to be sure whatever it is would be worth diverting your attention."

Horra's cheeks heated. Woodsly's admonishment of 'diplomacy' rang in her head. "Thank you, Queen Toppenbottom, for your reassurance."

The rest of her meal tasted like sawdust. Her father hadn't returned before the end of the meal. A hobgoblin added some more food to her father's half-empty plate and set a wooden topper over it to keep it warm.

That wasn't a good sign. If her father were returning, the servants would leave the plate as is.

"Where is my father?" she asked a maid as they hustled around.

"In the throne room, miss," she replied without stopping.

Everyone except Torren had left the room. He scraped the last dregs of gravy into his mouth.

She stared at him. Mixed feelings raced through her. She knew the Erlking had mesmerized him as well as the others. However, the fiend had used Torren to search for her. And he'd almost found her once. She'd been able to set her feelings about him aside when her father and the door troll had been with them. But now that just the two of them remained, the pang of the betrayal rose inside her.

Hobgoblins raced around, clearing everything off of the table and putting things away.

Torren glanced up and noticed her staring at him. "What?"

"What was it like when the Erlking mesmerized you?" She hadn't meant to ask him. It came out without her thinking it through. She didn't apologize, though.

His face screwed up, and his shoulders drooped. "Blurry. Like I was there, but I wasn't there at the same time. It was weird and scary sometimes. I don't enjoy thinking about it."

Her chair scraped across the stone floor as she scooted it back under the table. "Do you recall the time you were hunting me? You turned right toward me and stopped, but because I was wearing the woodencloak, you shouldn't have seen me."

He frowned, and his cheeks darkened. "I remember they beat me once or twice. There was lots of strange music. Each time it bombarded my mind, I wanted to do something terrible, like my life depended on it or something. There were odd voices in my head speaking words I didn't understand. But other than that, I don't really know what I did or said."

She didn't know if she believed him, and he must've read that on her face.

"Really, there's not much there." He motioned to his head. "It's all foggy, and I don't know, grim. Like I was walking around in the dark."

"Torren?" Her father's voice startled them both. "I need you to come to the throne room. Now."

Torren stiffened but wiped his mouth and left the table without glancing at either of them.

"You can come too. But it's not good news." The king spun and followed Torren.

She let out a breath and hurried after them both.

Torches hissed and lit the throne room with a wavering light. Shadows danced at the edges of the ceiling and corners, making Horra shiver, though she wasn't cold.

The door troll and a couple of other trolls were in the center where most of the defendants stood when the Goblin

Court was held. Her father sat on his high-backed quartz throne. Her own granite throne sat empty beside the king's. He motioned for her to sit.

As Horra walked past Torren, she eyed Sorsha Rindthorn, her classmate's mother. Confusion creased his face. His glance went back and forth from Horra to the king, like a game of swamp ball. Horra couldn't blame him. Sorsha always wore pressed suits. Her thick hair tied up neatly. Her current appearance was far from what she normally looked like. She was not only untidy, but harried-looking.

When Hora settled into place, the king twisted his neck, stretching it. "Ambassador Rindthorn has informed us that Goren, her husband, has gone missing." He nodded to the woman.

Torren gaped.

"He was home this morning. We had breakfast before I went to the market. When I returned later, he was gone, but he'd taken nothing. It was as though he walked out of the house and just kept walking." Her claws remained clutched tightly in front of her.

Horra detected a tic on the woman's cheek. As an ambassador, their training included de-escalation, setting aside emotions to get the job done. Clearly, she was pulling from that training at this moment.

"How can that be?" Torren asked, his voice cracking. "Did anyone see anything? I mean, wasn't everyone home? The Council hasn't been convened since before the Erlking."

His mother twisted her lips. "It was market day. I had much to restock since the worqs had stolen some of our supplies." She didn't glance at her son, making Horra wonder if he had somehow been involved in the taking of their food. "Those who didn't go into town to get the last of the farmer's wares were doing other things to get ready for winter, like chopping wood."

The community normally stocked wood in the spring and summer, but Torren's father was large and strong and would have firewood cut in no time. The question was why he had to cut it now. "What about his horse?" Horra asked, trying to be helpful but feeling utterly helpless. "Did he take it for a ride, perhaps, and just got delayed?"

"His horse is gone. Besides, he always leaves me a note." She sent a loaded glance toward the king. "Goren isn't the only one missing. Prother, our neighbor, is gone as well. It's also not like him to disappear without telling anyone. His wife is beside herself with worry." She loosened her claws and tossed her arms out. "It's not like either of the men to do this."

Her father sat up on his throne. "You don't have to convince me. I know Prother to be a studious troll, generous to a fault, and having a wicked sense of humor."

The smile on Sorsha's face was tenuous.

"For now, go home and wait for him to return. Come back on the morrow if he hasn't returned, and we'll form a search party. We'll do everything we can to figure this out." He waved his claw, dismissing them.

Torren's face turned dark, and he walked, hunched over, next to his mother as they left the throne room.

"What do you think happened?" Horra asked her father. "And why was everyone so untidy?"

King Divitri sat with his chin resting on his palm. "Redcappers and imps blocked Sorsha from coming into the castle. There was a bit of a scuttle, but our ambassador was top of her class in Knight School. She cleaned them out before they became too big of a problem."

"And the door troll?"

Her father hesitated. "He's young, and he hasn't had to

detain any creatures yet." He sent her a side glance. "Give him a chance. He's the best we have at the moment."

The best they had? Times were dire indeed, then. "Has this entire kingdom gone mad?" she asked.

A grim frown tugged her father's mouth down. "I wish I could assure you it hasn't. But it certainly feels like it has."

CHAPTER 9

Pidge's squeal greeted Horra as she stepped inside the Conservatory. After the strained meeting with Sorsha Rindthorn, she hoped to find some solace in her favorite place with her favorite pet pudge wudgie. Pidge nudged her claw, which held a jar of torrentula eggs.

"Hold on! Let me get it opened first." When opened, Horra tossed an egg in the air. Pidge darted up in a black blur and caught it before the foliage hid her. In a matter of seconds, the whole jar was empty, and Pidge nattered at her.

"Poor girl!" Horra said with laughter in her voice. "The fairies have cleaned us out of spiders and all the other creepy crawlies, huh? There haven't been many signs of vermin since I've returned. Something tells me you're not as hungry as you let on."

The bird screeched her annoyance and, with a turn, flew back up into the trees.

Horra leaned over the thorny henbane and poison persimmon bushes, examining the new plants. A gift from the fairy princesses. These replaced the ones they'd destroyed.

Horra plucked a leaf from the henbane, twisted it in her claws, and savored the crushed green scent.

She ambled around the garden, most of which was new, thanks to the fairies. Because of that, the space was bare. In the center were benches that had been hard to get to before. Horra sat on one next to the only Yew tree inside the Conservatory.

Wood creaked, and a face appeared. "Princess?" Kryk's clackity voice spoke from the tree.

Once again, longing for her former instructor Woodsly hit Horra. Concern quickly followed. "Kryk. What are you doing here? I'm not in trouble again, am I?"

"No more than usual, Princess." Kryk's face creased in what she assumed to be a smile. "I came to give you an update on the seed and give you a warning."

Her heart dropped. "Glad I'm sitting down."

He clattered, the wooden mouth moving as if coughing. "The seedling has awoken."

"What does that mean, exactly?"

"You were successful in your mission." The tree moved, leaves drifting to the ground. "Evil is on the move, however. It petrifies our roots, interrupting our vital communications. I come to warn you that my brethren may be hard to reach."

Horra's gut tightened. "So, if I need you—?"

"We may not be able to respond. Please take every precaution." His woodenish words trailed off, the face disappeared back into the bark, and silence remained.

"Kryk?" Horra couldn't help the note of desperation that made her voice crack. Fear for the roods settled into her gut. They were the backbone of balance between good and evil in the Wilden Lands. "What kinds of precautions? Kryk?"

There was no answer.

Horra waved goodbye to Sageel and Balk as the horse and cart Balk steered took Horra's faithful housemaid back to the Halflands to visit her family. It rattled out of sight, past the fairies' faint blue magic tracks. Thankfully, the queen and her daughters had left at first light.

Her father strode back into the castle for an early breakfast, leaving her alone in the watery orange sunrise. She detected the scent of an impending snowstorm. As a young troll, she loved to frolic in the snow. There was no lightheartedness to be found for her today.

Kryk's warning had made her restless. So, instead of sleeping, she dug through her old coursebooks to pour over maps, battle strategies, and other useful survival information. Despite the direness of the warning, Horra was eager to jump in and start planning her next move. Too bad Balk had to leave with Sageel, or she'd have discussed it with him.

She turned to follow her father when Torren surprised her. "What're you doing up so early?"

His head hung low, hidden beneath his long, green hair. His rumpled clothes were the same ones he wore yesterday. "Couldn't sleep." He yanked on the heavy, stone door, opening it easily.

"I know the feeling." Not that she couldn't open it. She could, it just took more effort. However, it established her thoughts about him making a terrific door troll. She strode in ahead of him, liking the fact that for the first time in her life, she didn't have to tilt her head so hard to look him in the face when they walked together. She was only a couple of inches shorter than he was now.

"I can't stop thinking about my dad. This isn't like him." His tusks clicked as he spoke. He stood rigidly. She'd never seen him as wound up as a coiled mugwort vine.

"I take it he hasn't shown up yet?"

He grunted.

"Well, I agree. But what can we do?"

"We need to go out and search for him." He turned his face her way. His mud-brown eyes were dark-ringed. "If you could convince the king to let us help—"

Horra held up a claw. "Hold up. You think *I* can tell my father what to do or how to operate a search party? You're nuts!"

Torren's lip twitched. "I knew you wouldn't help me. You always think it's a competition between us. I'm not trying to best you in combat training, or at how fast we can establish a campsite. My father is missing, possibly mesmerized, like I was. I have to find him. Save him."

Horra stopped and faced him. "Whoa! I didn't say I wouldn't help you. But the king has enough on his plate without worrying about us going off all commando and getting into trouble. Besides, you haven't been out there like I just was. You don't know how dangerous it's become." She waved her arm toward the door. "If we're going to sneak out to find your father, we have to be smart about it."

CHAPTER 10

Two weeks later, Horra held out a clawful of juniper berries to the stone wall in front of her. Smoke curled from a hole in the surface—a hopeful sign. If she and Torren were late getting back to the castle, all their sneaking around would be for nothing.

Her father thought they were out gathering mushrooms and hunting swine in the swamps—which they had done twice since the snowstorm had passed a week ago. It had taken every ounce of acting Horra had to convince her father to let them out again.

However, one whiff of old worq flesh had scared her pet gulgoyle into its boulder form. At least, Horra hoped it was old, otherwise they were in more trouble than she was prepared for. The air still held the chill of the storm, though the snow had already melted into a dirty mush.

"C'mon, Nimble, you can do it. There's a good gulgoyle," Horra crooned to the frightened beast. She didn't blame her pet. The odor of worqs had increased as she and Torren entered the remote swamplands their forefathers abandoned years ago.

Besides the foul stink, the dreary area had a menacing aura to it. As if it were a predator waiting for its next victim. "I never should've let Torren talk me into coming here. We should've stayed closer to home."

Pidge, her pet pudge wudgie, had already eaten anything that moved in this bog, and they'd neared the far edge, covering the whole of the area. The king had insisted she bring the wudgie, a known master huntress, to seek the swine. Though Pidge couldn't eat the animals like she did rats, she could find them. He was looking forward to swine stew with root vegetables.

"C'mon, Nimble. Pidge has our back. We're safe. You can change back." She hoped the beast could return to its normal shape. There was no documentation on gulgoyles, as Nimble was one of a kind. Though gargoyles had no issues switching forms, this was unfamiliar territory, and they were miles from the castle.

Horra lifted her palm filled with berries once more, trying to appeal to her pet's baser instincts. It worked so well with Pidge. "They're delicious, I promise."

"Who are you talking to?" Torren, atop an older steed, plodded up to her. The horse nickered softly and nudged the boulder.

A thick cloud of smoke wafted from the top of the rock. The stone popped and then cracked, breaking apart to reveal the gulgoyle hidden inside. Nimble stretched and shook out its wings and the stony exterior transformed to feathers and flesh.

Horra jerked back to keep from getting trampled. "Vinegar and beans, Nimble!" Juice from the berries dripped down her wrist as she clenched her claw. She tossed the smashed pulp to the ground and wiped her claws on her pants. Pidge darted for them, snapping them up and then crying out for more. Horra ignored her pet bird. "Okay, food does not calm the wayward beast." She wiped her arm down her royal tunic that was already smudged with mud and muck.

Torren snickered. "The laundresses are going to starch your clothes again."

Horra held back the urge to stick out her tongue at him. Obviously, everyone already knew about the redcapper's revenge for Horra's infamously soiled clothes. Luckily, the redcappers had quit in protest after the one on the bridge confronted her the other day. Unluckily, a group of goblins had taken over until her father could regain control of the redcappers, and they were bigger and meaner.

"It's better than having the king find out about what we've been doing." Horra swung up onto the gulgoyle's massive back just in front of the wings. The saddle had been her mother's and almost fit her perfectly now. She patted Nimble's neck. "Let's keep tracking. We have miles yet to go today. And so far, the only thing we've found are bones and one missing royal horse." The horse didn't really count. They'd found it two fields from the castle first thing that morning and had taken it back to their stalls.

She nudged Nimble into a canter, leaving the other troll behind.

A dark shape flickered at the edge of the forest a couple hundred feet away and then disappeared into the dense thicket beyond. Fear slid down her spine as she recalled a similar figure—the Erlking. Horra glanced at her pet pudge wudgie flying between her and the thicket.

Pidge squealed as if she'd also spotted the strange presence.

"Did you see that?" she asked Torren. She braced to run, either to or away from the figure. She wasn't sure which way to go. On one claw, she wanted to catch the evil elf. On the other, his magic frightened her.

Torren jerked his head back and forth, oblivious to her turmoil. "See what?"

Horra scanned the perimeter. No sign of anything appeared. Finally, her fear dissipated, and she knew what she had to do. "Follow me," she yelled over her shoulder as she kicked at Nimble's back, urging the creature to run. They followed Pidge, who dodged into the trees above a wall of brambly bushes.

Nimble tucked its wings tightly against Horra's legs as they dashed into the trees along a wider path. Horra ducked as they scraped between the trees, realizing too late the drawback of having a dragon crossbreed dashing through a thick forest. Horse clomps from behind assured her that Torren was on their tail.

Ahead, she spotted a couple of dark objects moving on the ground. Dappled sunlight revealed buzzards with their pink, bald heads and large feathered bodies.

Pidge attacked, taking on all three of the scavengers.

"Pidge, no!" Horra screamed, knowing there was no way to stop the wudgie from her mission.

Feathers flew.

Birds squawked.

The battle of three-on-one continued.

Pidge held her own magnificently. Nimble drew near, finally chasing off the buzzards for good. Their cries were angry and mournful as they left their meal behind.

Leaves and feathers drifted down around bones on the ground. Pidge poked at it, but the bones were a gray-white and picked clean. The odor of worqs, however, was distinct.

"Did we interrupt the buzzards in their feast or were they the remnants of a worq's hunt?" Horra mused as she dropped off a sitting Nimble, sloshing in the muck a few feet in front of the unsightly mound. Closer, she identified dirty clothes, crusted with dried mud, blood, and she dared not think too hard about what else.

With the tips of her claws, she flicked a tattered piece of cloth and gasped. It was an Oddar uniform. The green turned to grayish-black. It was their kingdom's seal on the coat's chest that gave it away. And they only had a clawful of Oddar Council members who would've worn this—one specifically, who was missing, who would've worn this size of a jacket.

Horra's stomach plunged to the ground. Before her brain could fully process things and stop Torren from coming near, he was there by her side.

"Father!" A keening wail broke out of Torren. He grabbed at the fabric before Horra could stop him from contaminating it.

Not that she blamed him. She would've done the same. And there might not be any identification to find since it looked to be ruined.

Horra wasn't accustomed to consoling anyone. She placed an awkward arm over Torren's heaving back. He choked on his sobs. Pidge fluttered up into the air, scared away by the guttural sounds her classmate made as he bent over the remains of his father.

Remembered pain from her mother's death burst in her heart and tore at her soul. It was awful to lose a parent.

Especially one in this gruesome a manner.

CHAPTER 11

The Weald

A week later, Rowan tottered across the stone path toward Merrow. A wide grin split his wooden face as he fell into Merrow's waiting branches. He was growing stronger, faster than any of the druid textbooks indicated would happen.

Merrow laughed. "Well done, young one." He stood Rowan up and waited for him to get his twig-legs beneath him once again. Like a newborn unicolt, he was all branches and no balance.

Concentration furrowed Rowan's wooden face as he learned to walk. It hadn't been a clean unrooting since radicles of the roots remained on the bottoms of his lower limbs. Dark, sooty mold covered his lower outer bark. It had still been soft the last time Merrow had scrubbed Rowan's trunk down. Nothing he did kept the mold from returning. However, thankfully, nothing had stopped Rowan from learning and growing.

"Just a few steps farther, and we'll rest," Merrow encouraged Rowan.

"Step?" Rowan clacked out.

Hope soared in Merrow's heartwood. "Yes. One more step."

Rowan's last step was stronger, surer. He was becoming more aware with each day. A good sign. Graduated from the bottle when he unrooted, Merrow handed the sprig a cup full of mineral rich sap—a double dose to spur his growth.

Rowan made a face at the oversweet confection but drank obediently. He closed his eyes and, with a heavy creak, fell asleep.

Wind whipped through the Weald, a sign of the rood's presence. He waited patiently for one to come speak to him, but lately, the roots had been silent. Without the dead druid spirit's presence, it was lonely. He wasn't used to the void of voices that traveled along the root systems. It made his bark shiver.

Rowan's snores were the background of his prayers to the Creature God to work against the evil plaguing their world. Sorrow increased in his heartwood. He had no choice but to focus on the bigger picture. Druids were not born for peaceful times. That's why one hadn't been born in so long. Oh, no—druids were born for times of tribulation. He added a prayer to be up to the task laid at his trunk.

A WEEK AFTER FINDING HIM, Goren Rindthorn's funeral had been dismal. The skies threatened snow that never seemed to materialize, leaving the land in a cold, gray stupor.

After the service, Horra wandered over to the simple mound nearby that held her former instructor's kindling. At the head of the mound stood a carved wooden cross with

Woodsly's name. It also listed his date of death, and his druid rank: His Royal Highness Archdruid, Honorary of the Hazelwood Clan, Magi General of the Third Troll Army.

"Thank you for burying him for me." Horra placed her claw on the ground, careful not to dirty her dress pants in the moist dirt. The sun had come out, but the mornings were still chilly and dew coated everything with a moist layer.

Sageel sniffed, a scrap of a kitchen towel held to her nose. "Of course, your highness. What with you fleeing the castle and your father mesmerized, there was no one left to pay him any mind." She blew her nose and snuffled wetly. "Woodsly was always kind to us maids. He even lent the younger maids some of your used textbooks so they could learn how to read and write. He was an honorable woodgoblin."

"Yes, he was." The more Horra found out about Woodsly's hidden actions, the more she admired the crotchety old piece of timber. Horra glanced up. Torren stood by the hole dug for his father. The service being complete, the small crowd walked back to the castle for the mourning feast.

He hadn't spoken to her on their trip back to the castle. He'd ridden with his father's bones tucked carefully inside a sheath of fallen bark tied with the ropes they'd brought for errant horses. Horra remembered being numb, uncommunicative, after her mother passed. She hadn't pressed him to talk. That would have been too cruel.

Lacking a cleric since Woodsly's death, King Divitri headed up the ceremony. He had blessed Goren's soul into their Creature God's eternal hands. Did it count since her father still held a grudge against their Sovereign for her mother's death? Would Torren's dad rest in eternal peace?

If Woodsly were here, he could tell her. Horra's shoulders slumped. There was so much her instructor still had yet to teach her. Moments such as these made her grief more acute.

Though she'd been avoiding it, Horra was glad to have finally been able to visit his grave. It gave her a sense of closure, something she never fully had after her mother's death.

She walked over to the empty chairs beside the Goren's grave. Torren's mother and grandparents had left him alone to mourn. Too many times Horra had sat at the foot of her mother's grave, alone as well, grieving her loss.

The metal chair creaked when Horra sat down. Torren lifted his head slightly but said nothing. They sat together in silence for several minutes before he turned to look at her. Tears pooled in his clay-colored eyes. "When does it stop hurting?"

Horra's nose stung, but she willed the tears away. Her lips, however, didn't cooperate. She bit the inside of her cheek to keep from crying. "It doesn't."

He blew out a breath, and his face twisted. He swiped a claw across his running nose. "You could at least try to lie once in a while."

"What good would that do? Make you feel good today? What about tomorrow? Or the day after that?" Horra held his stare, unflinching and unapologetic. "If you want sugar-coated anything, you'll have to visit the fairies."

The corner of his mouth curled upward. He strode over and sat in the chair beside her. It sank beneath his weight. "This is the Erlking's work, isn't it?" He stared off into the ashen sky. Birds chirped in the surrounding trees, making it seem like a normal day.

The day was far from normal. Guilt niggled her insides. She hadn't had the guts to tell him about the shadow she spied before she entered the forest where they found his dad. She knew it was the Erlking. But Torren had been too distraught at the time for her to mention it. And afterward, it wouldn't have changed anything.

"Yes," she replied in a low voice. Their lab had found no proof on the fabric, the bones, or any of the debris they'd taken from the forest. Balk, having returned from his trip with Sageel, had even tried a spell the fairies had recommended, with no luck. It wouldn't have even mattered if Horra hadn't spotted the shadow in that forest. She knew it was the Erlking's work. He left destruction in his wake.

"We're going to find a way to stop him?" Torren turned back to her, desperation drawing his features tight.

Grief, she knew only too well, came in stages. Perhaps it wasn't wise to indulge this part of his healing.

She shouldn't make any promises. She'd never swear a blood oath on it. But she would do whatever she could to bring justice for Woodsly, to Torren's family, and for a fractured Oddar. "We will."

CHAPTER 12

The Weald

Two months later, sunlight filtered through the Yew trees upon Rowan's bark as he sat on the carved oak chair with an attached desk. Merrow watched as the boy filled out the last questions in his History of the Wilden Land test. It was the hardest exam so far, but the sapling had passed everything with an ease that surprised Merrow, given the slow growth the seed had had begun with.

Rowan stretched and handed Merrow the parchment, his twiggish arm spanning the distance between them. He'd grown to five feet in height, good for a sapling, but his limbs remained scrawny. He should be filling out now, but lichen and moss continually covered his bark. It seemed to hinder his ring growth.

"Well, my boy. Let's see how you did on the test." Merrow perused the questions as his ever-thirsty student went to the well for a drink.

Every question on the parchment had an inordinate

amount of detail. More than he recalled giving the twigster. Merrow wondered if it were the roods at work, yet they hadn't informed him of any special gifting to the young sapling. Merrow got to the last question. "You got one wrong," he murmured, his head bent.

"That's impossible." Rowan's voice creaked. Pollen from the flowers adorning his crown scented the air.

"The question was, 'What started the War of the Warts?'" Merrow glanced at a confused Rowan. "It was a plague of warts that the first Erlking cursed the land with. You put down it was an Elven scourge."

Rowan's face twisted in concentration. "I distinctly remember it being Elven."

Merrow frowned at him. They weren't into elf history yet. And he hadn't included them with the lessons on the War of the Warts since they hadn't learned until the end of the war what type of creature the Erlking had been. Only the roods could have given him this information.

Or had Woodsly retained some of his memory in the fibers of his seed?

Merrow smoothed the paper, bringing his thoughts back to his student. "I haven't taught you anything about elves or scourges yet."

Rowan tapped a twig finger to his wooden lip. "I'm not sure. The answer just came to me like everything else you've taught me. So, did I get it right?"

Merrow hesitated. "You've passed. That's all that matters."

He'd have to summon the roods to inquire of their counsel. Even so, his next step in Rowan's tutoring was clear. Merrow would train the new druid woodgoblin on the elf's complicated history. At least, what had remained to be taught. The elves had done their best to destroy all information about them when they'd seceded from the Wilden Lands.

A glance up revealed a still confused Rowan. Merrow had already discovered the lad didn't like to be wrong about anything. What happened if the boy grew too intelligent for him to train? It wasn't something he'd considered before. He shook his leaves. They'd cross that bridge when they came to it. He cleared his throat. "It's time to clean you up. Tomorrow, we'll start with the history of the elves and their lands."

After Rowan left, Merrow placed his hand on the central Yew tree. "Woodsly?"

"*Yes, old friend,*" the creaking voice came as if from far away.

"What did you do to your seed? The lad has knowledge he shouldn't have. Things I haven't taught him. What is happening with him?" He couldn't help the frustration that seeped into his voice.

"*I was a druid through and through. I won't apologize for any impressions left in my heartwood. It was bound to carry over.*" The tree cracked as it moved. "Are you worried about yourself or the young druid?"

Merrow prided himself on his honesty. "Both. How can I teach someone molded after the greatest rood since Kryk? And why didn't you warn me?"

"There was no time to warn you. I barely had time to prepare the princess for the journey. And my spirit has only now settled into the Weald." The trees around Merrow grew restless. "You are more than up for the job, Master Seedkeeper of the Weald. And wasn't it you who used to tell me that the greatest warriors rise to their calling in times of unrest and tribulation?"

Merrow leaned his branchy head against the tree. "I did. But I'm no warrior."

"You are. You just don't see it." There was silence for many moments. "Take care, dear friend, and don't let doubt become your undoing." Woodsly's face disappeared, and his presence left the Yew tree.

Merrow didn't bother calling out his name. The spirits had been fickle lately, and he sensed a darkness trying to infest the roots. Surely, the Erlking would know by now the druid seed had arrived in time. Whether he knew the sapling had unrooted and was growing at a remarkable pace was anyone's guess.

If only he understood the Erlking's motivation, it might help figure out how to defeat him. And if only the elves didn't hide themselves behind an impenetrable magical veil, he'd know more about their elusive magics.

Merrow limped to the bench, his cane clicking on the stones. He sat down heavily. He'd grown so tired lately. Even his bark ached. Deep in his heartwood rested a suspicion that he would join his dearly departed friend sooner rather than later. He prayed that his work with the new druid would be good enough to keep the evil at bay.

But he'd never been so unsure of something in his entire long life.

CHAPTER 13

On the seventeenth day of Winterlude, Horra took her place on her hard granite throne. The stone seat was cold against her body. She'd been dragged from her warm bed by her father to attend an abrupt tribunal. Trolgar Oilgrum, their former door troll, who had been missing since Horra had broken the mesmerization spell, had finally been located and brought back to Oddar to answer for his treasonous actions during the Erlking's takeover of the castle.

Her side gaze landed on the spot where Woodsly used to stand, parchment in hand. A pang of longing hit her in the center of her chest. His absence caught her off guard, though it shouldn't have. He'd been gone long enough for her to know better. She chalked it up to sleep deprivation, but the feeling lingered.

She blinked back the tears. There was no time for them. They had a traitor to try.

Horra focused instead on Torren, who sat across from the thrones in the galley, a blank expression on his face. Sorsha, his mother, sat next to him. Her back was stiff. A hard glint shone in her mud-colored eyes.

Their gulpy herald with his overlarge, bobbing head stepped up and smacked a hand to his chest in salute to Horra and her father, disrupting her thoughts. "Trolgar Oilgrum, your majesties." The gulpy handed the king a rolled parchment containing the charges. The herald's huge head lolled back and forth as he stepped out of the way to let the shackled troll pass.

Horra winced at the memory of the gulpy handing the mesmerized fairy queen charges against her. She also remembered this particular troll's glee in watching her suffer. How the tables had turned.

Tall with broad shoulders, Trolgar the Traitor, as Horra deemed him, stepped up to the throne, a haughty tilt to his head. Massive chains wrapped around him, from his shoulders to his waist and down to his ankles, allowing him to walk, but do little else.

Had it not been giants who found him, Horra knew that there'd be no capturing this defiant troll. He was the only troll in their kingdom bigger than her father.

King Divitri, took the scroll and unfurled it with a frown. "Trolgar Oilgrum, you have been accused of treason toward the kingdom of Oddar by two giants, Grum and Grud Colossus. They found you in the Mires of Mulduff conspiring with four swamp trolls."

Trolgar grunted and smiled.

King Divitri continued without acknowledging the other man's rude behavior. "You and your band of dissidents intended to overthrow the rulership of Oddar. The giant witnesses also state you admitted to masterminding the disappearances and murders of other trolls." He rolled the parchment up, his eyes as cold as Horra had ever seen. "Along with treason, there are other charges. You conspired to imprison the princess, allowed access to the castle to an enemy, and revealed Oddar's secrets to said enemy. How do you plead?"

Trolgar stood straighter, the chains straining against him. "Not guilty. As for the Erlking, I was mesmerized, just as you were. As for the other, the giants you speak of are the ones behind the missing trolls and possibly their deaths. They were looking for mercenaries when they found me, your majesty," he snarled, his lip curled. "Maybe you should consider who would benefit most from the Erlking suddenly showing up and mesmerizing half of Oddar. If you ask me, the giants are behind everything."

Torren's mother gasped at his accusations. Her face puckered, a sure sign of her anger. However, a consummate diplomat, she composed herself and remained silent.

Horra narrowed her eyes at the calm and composed betrayer. He did not look mesmerized now. His mud-colored eyes held no vacant glaze. If he wasn't influenced currently by the Erlking, did he really believe this line of defense would sway her father? Had he not learned anything about the king while he worked as their door troll?

King Divitri stared at the troll for a long moment. "Besides the giants searching for mercenaries, what proof do you have of the giants being behind any plot to overthrow this regency?"

"Well, I—uh," the troll stammered before his eyes hardened. He nodded at the scroll. "I have just as much proof as you."

Her father shifted on his throne. The look he gave the former door troll should've shriveled any creature, yet the man stood there glaring at his king in utter defiance. "I see. So, it's your claim that you were mesmerized and that the giants are behind the rise of the second Erlking?" His cheeks moved as he grated his teeth together. "Do you really believe me so daft?"

"Yes," Trolgar growled, a scowl puckering his green face.

King Fyd nodded at the gulpy. "Record his plea and testimony." He turned back to Trolgar. "Please bring forth the witnesses."

Sageel walked to the center of the throne room. She stood no higher than Trolgar's knees. In Horra's eyes, though, the woman stood taller than the betraying brute.

"Your majesties." The hobgoblin struck her chest with a fist and bowed her head to both Horra and the king.

"Sageel, please testify with whatever knowledge you have of Trolgar's betrayal." The king's voice was steady, low.

"It's all lies. All them gobhoblins were enchanted," Trolgar sputtered, his face turning dark.

Sageel took out one of her hearing aids. "Pardon me, sir? I don't think I heard you correctly."

"But, she, wha—?" Trolgar fussed and stepped closer to us. A hook secured his chains, however, to the massive stone doors. They moved, but not nearly enough to let him close.

"Continue if you please, Sageel." King Fyd kept his eyes on Trolgar as he spoke, anger making his voice quiet and deadly.

"After I helped her royal majesty the princess escape, I kept my eyes *and* ears open. I hoped to catch some information that might be useful to help when someone came to free the kingdom from that evil wretch."

She brought out a notebook and read from it. "Night one, the kingdom is in disarray following the fairy visit." Sageel scanned the page with a crooked finger but stopped for a moment to look at the king. "Here it is, sir. The first eve, I snuck into the throne room and overheard the Erlking offer Trolgar an 'auspicious and commanding position' in his newly formed army. The only catch was that he had to do whatever the Erlking demanded, when he demanded." Sageel slammed the book shut.

King Fyd frowned. "And did you see or hear him agree? Did Trolgar follow through with the agreement?"

"Oh, yes, sir. Trolgar readily agreed. Said his talents were overlooked by you and the princess. Said he was good and tired of it. I watched from the shadows as he carried your prone body to the guest room and locked you in there. The Erlking muttered some nonsense about Trolgar being the only one strong enough to handle you on his own. He laughed about how easily swayed the big lunk was—his words, not mine—and that he didn't even have to mesmerize Trolgar, he was so willing." Sageel raised her head, looking down her nose at the massive troll in front of her.

Trolgar sputtered. "She's lying. No good gobhoblins. They're all liars! Every one of them."

"Thank you, Sageel. You may go." King Divitri waited until the door closed behind her. He reached down and pulled out two more parchment rolls. "These are the statements against you given by the giants. I've tested them for truth, thanks to some parting gifts Queen Toppenbottom gave me before they headed back to their Shining Lands."

Trolgar's eyes widened and his mouth opened, but no sound came out.

Horra gaped at her father as well. Trolls didn't use magical tools to rule. Her conscience pricked at that thought. She'd used the giant's expanding desserts and contracting candies, after all. Still, this was a first.

"Your sentence is death for treachery against the throne on several counts."

The gulpy gasped. Torren smiled leeringly. Sorsha gasped and gathered her claws to her chest.

Horra's ears filled with the sound of her blood pumping through her veins. Could this be happening? There hadn't been a lethal sentence since the War of the Warts. The last sentence had been the first Erlking, who'd cursed the land with a second coming. And now they were dealing with that sorcery's fulfillment.

"You'll not kill me. My master will free me. Together we'll bring your stone kingdom to dust." Trolgar twisted, jerking the door almost off of the frame. His eyes were wild, and his mouth frothed slightly in the corners like a rabid animal.

Horra shivered. Had it not been for the giant's magicked chains that tightened around the traitorous troll to keep him from rampaging, he would've gotten loose. Her mind whirled with what could've happened then.

Maybe magic wasn't so useless after all. She inwardly shook herself. Her belief in Oddar's motto, "Hard work is the bounty of a kingdom," remained firm.

As four trolls struggled to lift Trolgar to take him to the dungeon, an errand woodgoblin boy, the one whom Oddar used to order food for their kitchen in Bough Valley, barged into the throne room. "Majesties," he panted, out of breath, a hand on his chest in an exhausted salute. "I have news from the roods. It's time. Horra is to return to the Weald immediately."

CHAPTER 14

Later that morning, a knock on Horra's bedroom door interrupted her packing. It had to be Sageel, coming to help her. "Come in," she called.

Clothes lay in disarray around her room. Most of it was from normal life, but some were discards as she packed things she'd need to go alone to the Weald. After suffering through an unplanned trek into the wilds before, she knew what she'd need more now. The problem was that the necessary items didn't all fit in her knapsack. She smoothed the folded woodencloak as the door opened with a click.

"I'll need another pack for the rest of this and some food supplies. You know what I like. Add them to my saddlebag, please."

"*Ahem.*"

Horra spun at the masculine-sounding noise, holding the cloak against her like a shield.

Torren stood at the door, a contrite but slightly humored look on his face. "Sorry to disturb your epic packing session." He picked up a stiff sock from the floor with the tips of his claws and grinned. "I thought you had housekeeping service here."

Of course, it wouldn't be Sageel. Horra inwardly kicked herself. However, none of her classmates were allowed near their private rooms. She tipped her chin upward. "I can clean my own room." The urge to race around and pick everything up made her twitch. Instead, she turned and set the wooden-cloak next to her pack so he wouldn't see her embarrassment.

"Do you?"

Horra made another pile of the items that didn't fit in her pack, but her thoughts scattered like rocks tossed in a lake. "Do I what?" she asked, distractedly.

"Ever clean your room? Ma tans my hide if I don't clean mine once a week." His voice moved as he entered her room.

Her shoulders tightened, and she forced herself to relax. The hobgoblin maids had been too busy compensating for the missing trolls to get around to the menial task of cleaning her room. She was quite capable of doing the chore, no matter what the room currently looked like.

"What do you want, Torren? I'm busy." Her pile made, she straightened to face him. Her pile fell over onto the floor, and she swallowed a groan.

"Looks like you need some help. That's why I came. I want to go with you to the Weald." He moved to pick up her clothes, but she bent over at the same time. They bumped heads.

"*Ow*, Torren!" She rubbed her forehead. "I don't need any help for that."

He massaged his chin. "Didn't you tell me that the sprig-gans and redcappers almost stopped you from crossing the bridge? Since the bocan is gone, I thought I could step in and be a kind of bodyguard or something."

Horra picked the pile from the floor and set it more care-fully on her unmade bed. "A bodyguard or something? Look, last time Balk wasn't allowed entry into the Weald. He had to sit outside and watch the animals."

Torren shrugged. "Okay."

She stopped fiddling with her packing and faced him. "Why do you want to go so badly? You know it won't bring your father back. Nothing can ever do that."

Anger flashed across his face but was gone quickly. "I can't stay here doing nothing. It's ..." his voice dropped off. He let out a *whoosh* of breath.

Horra waited for him to continue, partly because she wasn't sure what to say, and partly because she could tell it meant something to him.

"It's too hard to stay here and not do something consequential to help. After we found Da, Ma doesn't want me to leave her side. It's driving me crazy. I need to be useful." He picked up a pile of clothes and put it next to the overflowing hamper in the corner.

Her heart went out to him. She remembered the agitation she experienced over losing her mother. If Woodsly were here, he'd put Torren to work on something. It's what he had done with Horra. She'd resented it at the time. Now she understood his motivation to keep her mind and claws busy.

"Fine, but you have to listen to me. You can't go off all angry or anything if I annoy you."

He thumped his chest. "I accept the terms."

She wasn't sure if she was relieved or not as she eyed his too-eager face. "Then go get packed. We have to leave right away—"

"I'm already done. My stuff's downstairs." He rushed over and took her by the shoulders. "You won't regret it. I promise." With a squeeze, he left her standing by her bed, her bedroom door still wide open.

"*Ugh.* What have I done?"

"What have you done indeed?" Her father stepped from the hallway and into view. "You realize you are responsible for him now, not the other way around. You are the leader. If something happens to him before you return, you will have to answer for it." His unwavering eyes held hers in a solemn gaze.

Horra sobered. It had always been the other way around. Woodsly had been in charge of her tutoring. Her father in charge of the kingdom's affairs. And then Balk had been in charge of her safety. The weight of her decision sunk in. "I can't tell him no now."

Her father stepped up and hugged her. "I know. I'd go with you if I could. But I have a kingdom to run." He squeezed her tight. "You'll do a fine job, Daughter. But you must be aware of the burden you carry. You will be queen one day. Each decision you make will have consequences." His warmth left her as he stepped back. "I believe in you."

Yes, but did she believe in herself?

A WINTERY weak light lit the castle's courtyard as Horra ran a claw over the fine, slate-colored feathers on Nimble's bony wings. They were filling in nicely, though she wasn't sure if they would ever really work. She'd already tied her two packs to the belt that held the saddle to the creature's body. It was a fresh addition, thanks to her father's insistence on her safety.

He himself walked over to them. "I recruited Murda to help you arrive safely at the Weald."

Murda, a novice KIT, Knight-In-Training student, stood brushing her sleek chestnut horse. Studious and quiet, she eyed the half gargoyle/half gully dragon mix uncertainly. "What is that?"

"Nimble? He's a gargoyle-gully dragon mixed breed. I

recently found out he's a he." She tossed a skeeze in the air. The gulgoyle gulped it down.

Her father grunted. "How? We've never known that for sure."

"I found an archaic reference in the *Legendary Guide for Rare Reptilian Species* book I found in the library last week. It said that only males can turn to stone, and they can only do so when they've fully matured, which would be approximately fifty years old."

It was her father's turn to eye the creature skeptically. "I guess the fairy's cleaning did some good if you found that old tome. We'll have to have the hobgoblins dust more often."

Nimble belched, and fire and smoke curled out of his mouth and nostrils. The scent of ashy sulfur filled the cool morning air.

"Good gulgoyle," she crooned to it though she scrunched her face against the odor. "As long as I'm not the one doing the dusting." She finished attaching her quiver and bow to the back of the saddle for easy reaching. Her father chuckled. He knew her too well.

Three hobgoblins rushed out of the side entry to the kitchen, carrying large bundles and several jugs.

"Oh, good! I got back just in time." Torren called out as he led his steed, not a Stempner this time, to her side. His saddle bags were overstuffed with items, some sticking out of the edges of the bags.

"What'd your mother say?" the king asked him.

The maids loading her saddlebags with food distracted Horra as Torren gave the king a clipped response.

King Fyd frowned at him. "I can't let you go without your mother's consent." He laid a claw on Torren's horse's neck. "She's been through enough after your father disappeared."

Torren sat higher in his saddle. "And so, you would allow

your daughter to ride into danger with only one escort? What if something happens to her? The future of the kingdom rests in her safety."

Horra walked over to Torren's horse. She hadn't planned on taking her classmate's side, but she knew he would sneak out and follow her, anyway. It would be better to go together than have him trail behind and possibly end up finding trouble with no one to help him. "What is he going to do if he stays here? We've gone out together several times without finding trouble."

"Until you did," her father's growl was cut short by him running a claw through his green hair.

She knew he referred to finding Torren's father. He hadn't punished her when he found out where they'd found Goren's body. But she knew he wasn't happy that they'd lied to him.

At her father's silent glower, she tried a different tactic. "Yes, but we handled it. We aren't children anymore, father. Torren, Murda, and I are the future of Oddar. We've no tutor left to train us. Dropout trolls run the Knights in Training program because they're the only ones left to teach. Where are we to learn the skills we need unless you trust us in small things?"

King Fyd's mud-colored eyes glimmered with the hint of tears. "It's still dangerous."

She nodded. "It is. But that's why it's better for three of us to go. I know my responsibility as the future queen. Three of us will be safer, I promise."

Her father glanced off into the distance as if contemplating what she'd said. "Don't take any chances. I don't want to give Sorsha bad news again."

Torren dipped his head, his fisted claw smacking his chest. "Yes, my king."

After the hobgoblins finished packing their supplies, her

father double-checked on her knots, giving her a grunt of approval when he got to the last one. "Now, be smart and safe, watching each other's backs." He spoke to all of them, but his gaze remained on Horra.

Her shoulders pinched with the weight of being responsible for two other troll's lives, even though she'd just begged him to trust her. She allowed her father to help her climb up into the saddle and settled in. She swiped a claw across her face and tucked pieces of her red hair back into her hood. "We will."

His smile was wobbly. "Be well until we meet again." The king laid a claw across his heart.

"And you as well," they all muttered the warrior's farewell words back.

Horra kicked Nimble and didn't look back, fearing the threat of tears.

Torren rode up next to her when they were out of the castle's sight. "Thank you for standing up to your father for me."

Horra blew out a breath. Did Torren really understand the sacrifice she just made? She doubted it. He was full of energy and vengeance. "I know what it's like to want to strike out against something, anything, you think did you wrong. After Mother died, I blamed magic for failing to save her life. I believed her wish at Norrow Lake didn't come true. What I was too young to realize was that Crud is fatal. She couldn't be healed."

"What does this have to do with me coming along with you?" An edge of bitterness made Torren's voice low.

She pulled Nimble's reins, coming to a stop. She turned in her saddle and stared down at Torren. "I know how you feel. You're devastated. You want revenge. I did, too, but there was nothing for me to fight. So, I grew angry, deeply hating anything magical as useless. I thought the fairies were frivolous and worthless creatures. Kryk warned me about that bitterness I felt turning into a darkness that can't be stopped."

Torren glanced away from her, but not before she saw the trail of a tear down his cheek.

"Don't let your hatred toward the Erlking distract you from what you're supposed to focus on. And don't make me regret sticking up for you."

CHAPTER 15

Winterlude, that special time between Wintertide and Springtide, glazed Bough Valley's straw-like grass in a crystal frost that crunched beneath their animals' feet. Bare trees created a dead pallor across their surroundings. There'd been little snow, just frigid temperatures that muffled sounds like cotton in one's ears. However, today, the air held a sweet hint of crispness, hinting at a snowstorm building.

Horra drew in a deep, icy breath of air, relishing it. With Nimble's warmth beneath her, she wasn't nearly as cold as she feared. Her booted feet were even on the too-warm side.

Murda rode up to her when she slowed Nimble down to a walk. "Pardon, Princess. The sun is setting. Shouldn't we set up camp?"

Though Bough Valley had an inn, Horra was reluctant to stay in it since her run-in with the redcapper on the bridge last time. Their travel had been much slower than she'd expected since they'd had to keep to lesser-traveled trails. They'd arrived hours later than they would've otherwise, but it couldn't be helped.

Horra glanced around the open area. "Scout out a place to stay, preferably out of the wind, while I search for water."

Murda nodded and raced off toward a grove of trees. Horra squinted at them. Was that a shadow among them? Or was it just that the setting sun making them look so dark?

She trusted Murda, who'd had more specialized training than she or Torren at this point. To pass time as they traveled, she had gone over several safety protocols, a kind of quiz that Woodsly would've done in their Wandering Wilderness classes. Their discussion had assured Horra of their readiness and knowledge of safety procedures.

Horra turned in the opposite direction to access Dragonfly Creek. It ran from the edge of Bough Valley into the Sterling River, which ran beneath the massive Hobgoblin Bridge. She'd not seen it when she was there before, but she'd studied maps after she'd returned. It wasn't a swift stream, so it shouldn't be hard to sniff out. Hopefully, it wasn't covered with too thick a layer of ice.

"Shouldn't someone be with you at all times?" Torren's voice from behind startled her.

"Did Murda tell you to get lost?" Horra teased him. Murda was very no-nonsense and probably didn't need his help.

"She's too nice to do that." His steed stamped, its flesh quivering against the chilled air. "Besides, she doesn't need any help, not with her organizational skills. Are you searching for water?" He didn't look at her directly, but gazed toward Bough Valley, which was now aglow with lamplights.

She pointed to where she'd been heading. "There's a stream round here somewhere close by. Nothing big, but enough that we should be able to fill our canteens without having to go into the village."

"I can do it." Torren reached out for her canteens. He'd become less intense as they'd ridden, possibly because of her speech. If so, at least that meant he was listening to her.

She handed hers over.

He nodded and led his steed off at a gallop.

Horra stared at his back and recalled all the years they'd spent competing in the classroom and on the archery green. Even in her anger when the Erlking mesmerized him and she'd thought he was betraying her, she would never have wished this grief upon him. The one thing she did know, however, was that no one could take the grief from him. It was something he had to learn to live with. Just like she had.

A few yards away, Torren cried out that he'd found the stream. So, she headed back toward Murda to help get their camp situated before Torren returned with fresh water.

A couple of birds shrieked and darted out of the trees ahead of her. The hairs along her hide stood on end. She nudged Nimble into a canter and whistled. It was a basic skills code asking for the all clear.

A shrill tone answered. A warning: stay away. The sound came from deeper into the forest than she expected.

Horra whistled a high-pitch warning for Torren, then kicked Nimble's side, her heart wanting to jump into her throat. She couldn't leave Murda in danger. The gulgoyle clomped toward the trees as she dug into her pack. Finding the woodencloak, she flung it on over her other jacket. They reached the edge of the trees and she yanked on the reins. Nimble dug his legs in, and they slid to a stop.

She dropped to the ground and flipped the hood over her head. It wasn't completely stealthy, but she didn't care as long as she got to Murda and figured out what was going on. She fitted the straps for her quiver of arrows with attached bow, shifting it so it was easy to reach.

A pungent scent of unwashed flesh hit her before Murda shrieked.

Horra ran, clutching at her mother's dagger she'd had in a sheath belted on her waist. The sky was getting dark, but inside the shelter of the trees, it was like night. She used her night vision to navigate around the trees. Still, saplings and bushes snapped at the woodencloak's exterior, possibly giving away her position.

Where had Murda set up their camp? Clear on the other side? Her classmate was smarter than that. A tingle of warning skittered along her nape a second before Piskies lit up the trees. The stench became noxious.

Worqs!

The light the piskies threw became misshaped, moving shadows against the unmoving outlines of the trees. Jerking her head back to discover the origins of the moving shapes, she found them. Three of them. They were hulking figures, bald, with chalky grayish-pink skin like they were on the verge of rotting.

Horra ground her teeth. Two worqs had captured Murda in a net. She thrashed about, but no sound came from her mouth, which was bound with something white and stretchy, like cobwebs. It looked flexible as it moved against her muffled screams. Horra shivered. Where'd they come from? She glanced around, but there were no spiders nearby.

Two worqs removed Murda from the net. They tied her claws and feet. One other worq stood watch, glancing about the trees and grunting.

Though they'd all talked about what they'd do in case of an emergency, her legs weighed her down with indecision. What was she going to do now?

CHAPTER 16

Horra considered whether she should go back and get Nimble, a more intimidating presence that might give her an advantage she didn't have on foot. The trees, however, were far too close together to get the gulgoyle through. No, she'd have to go on her own and pray Torren was smart enough to stay back.

Her promise to her father to keep Murda safe rang through her mind. Had it been one worq, she wouldn't have hesitated to attack. Frustration and anger warred inside her as she moved as quietly as possible toward them.

The worqs grunted and spoke low in the telltale hard consonants of their dialect in conversation. Did Torren still know Worqen now that he was unmesmerized? She'd have to ask.

A piskie flew over her, lighting up the area where she stood tree-still. It stopped as if sensing Horra for a moment before flying on.

She frowned. That shouldn't be possible, should it? The woodencloak had worked so well before. At least, except for the time she thought Torren had seen her. Another thing she had questions about.

One of the worqs jerked to look in her direction. Horra held her breath. It grunted louder and pushed the other two toward the far edge of the trees—away from Horra.

Stupid piskies!

Horra let out her held breath in a hiss and frowned. She had to get to Murda before they left the trees. She had a slight advantage there. In the open, the worqs would have the upper hand.

Horra kept a sharp eye on the two carrying a thrashing Murda. They moved too fast for her to get to them. In the blink of her eyes, they were out of bow range. "Dragon's fire!" she exclaimed softly as she snaked her way back to Nimble.

She swung herself up onto Nimble's back. The gulgoyle thundered around a curve in the forest, moving as Horra guided the reins. They rushed toward where the worqs were exiting with Murda.

Just as she found a straight stretch, Torren jumped on the first worq as it left the glade. His horse ran off in the opposite direction. Torren's screams held a note of insanity as he slashed at the creature with a wide-bladed sword. However, being so close, he couldn't actually do any damage with the weapon. He needed a smaller knife.

Horra slowed Nimble, grabbed her bow from the holder, and freeing an arrow, aimed. She let it fly, praying silently she didn't just kill her classmate.

The worq ducked to buck Torren off, and the arrow flew wide and wild.

"Vinegar!" Horra yelled while grabbing another arrow. She flicked off her hood, giving her an unimpeded view.

The other two worqs, alerted to trouble, swung around and headed up and away from her.

She kicked at Nimble, wanting to get to Murda. Torren seemed to hold his own for the moment.

A crack echoed as Torren's opponent caught him square on the side of his head.

Torn, Horra rode by them, aiming another arrow at the big nasty that was bent over Murda.

Her arrow sunk into the back of his right shoulder. Horra and Nimble slid past them as she tried unsuccessfully to stop quickly enough.

Something struck her shoulder. Pain exploded and Horra squealed. She clutched her injury with her other claw.

Startled, Nimble bucked and Horra lost her grip on the reins and slipped sideways. Blood slicked beneath her good claw as she tried desperately to cling to the saddle, and then the belt, but it was no use. Nimble had turned into a boulder again. She landed hard on her backside on the ground, her shoulder in excruciating, fiery pain.

Poison, she was sure of it, though it wasn't an arrow that had struck her. But she didn't have time to contemplate.

Torren's worq came for her. She glanced over at Torren, who was now an unmoving lump on the ground.

The other two worqs' strange chatter echoed from behind her. She moved to face the first worq and found her bow and two arrows dropped near Nimble's rocky form. She grabbed them, nocked the first arrow, and shot at Torren's worq.

It landed in his chest, right where his heart should be. He jerked backward and then staggered. He dropped to his knees and then to the ground—hopefully dead. Lively grunting sounded from behind her.

She swung around, aiming her next arrow at one of the two remaining attackers. However, the ache in her shoulder threw her off. That arrow landed with a *thunk* in one worq's leg. Its grunt wasn't so much a word this time as it was anger.

Horra rose, the pain making her vision swim for a singular moment. She blinked it away and headed toward them. However, they had a cart hooked to a horse and another horse beside it. The injured worq jumped on the unattached horse, and the other dumped Murda into the cart and mounted the horse hitched to it.

The brands on the horses' haunches proved them to be royal Oddar infantry horses. A third horse stood off to the side until the other two worqs steered their animals toward it, scaring it off. Glancing around, Horra couldn't see Torren or Murda's horses.

She ran for a few more feet before she stopped. There was no way she'd be able to catch them now. She couldn't even get near the cart, which was much slower than the unattached horses.

She'd just done the opposite of what she promised her father, the king, she'd do—keep Murda and Torren safe.

Some warrior troll queen she'd make.

She screamed until her throat was hoarse.

CHAPTER 17

Torren was coming around by the time Horra returned to his side. He had a nasty bump on the side of his head and a bleeding cut on his chin. "Are you okay? Can you hear me?" Horra asked as she kneeled in front of him to get a better look at his injuries.

He groaned and clutched his head. "Did they get Murda?"

"Yes," she spoke through clenched jaws. Her shredded throat closed up, and she struggled to swallow a ball of guilt. It stuck like a porcuvine in her windpipe.

"We have to get her back. Worqs are awful, violent." He stood and staggered.

Horra caught him awkwardly and helped sit him back down. "It will have to wait. We have no animals to ride on at the moment."

He grunted and shook his head. "How close are we to the Weald?"

Horra sat back and slumped over, willing the sharp pain and nausea away. "By my estimation, we're not quite halfway."

Torren glanced over at her. It wasn't a steady gaze—one of

his pupils was larger than the other. That was not a good sign. She hung her head in defeat, her shoulder sending a shard of agony at the action. Her stomach lurched, but she breathed through it. She didn't want to get sick in front of Torren. She had to be strong like her warrior foremothers would've been.

After a few minutes of silence, the roiling in her stomach settled. "We need to get you back to the castle to get treated. Let me see if I can coax Nimble out of his shielded state." Horra left Torren and headed back to her gulgoyle. There was no way she wanted to camp with the worqs running the countryside freely. Besides, whatever they had hit her with was making her more than sick. Her head was dizzy.

She walked slowly toward her pet, careful not to fall over. "Hey, boy. Come back, now. The big, bad, smelly beasts are gone." She ran a claw over the hard surface. After a few minutes of trying, Horra fell against the side of her pet, slipped to the ground, and leaned her head back against the hard surface. "Okay. I get it. You don't feel safe. Neither do I. If you change back, we can get you somewhere safer, I promise."

The rock rumbled. Smoke tainted the crisp air. It was dark now. She couldn't see the clouds on the horizon, but she knew the storm was building in the distance. It whispered on the night's breeze, which had been picking up since they'd stopped to camp. She needed to get them out of where they were and somewhere they could both be treated.

Instead of sitting around and waiting, she left to find where Murda had taken their supplies for the camp. Far enough away from Torren, she threw up in some bushes. Thankfully, it eased the sickness enough for her to continue on. She circled around the dim patch of trees until, at last, she found their packs. Farther out, she found Murda's steed, tied to a tree on the outside perimeter.

If this was the campsite, how did Murda get caught in the

middle of the copse of trees? Had they lured her in somehow? It wasn't like Murda to be so reckless. There had to be an explanation.

Horra untied the horse, gathered the scattered camp items, and tied them back to the steed. Torren sat hunched over, his head leaning on his knees.

She reached her gulgoyle mountain when the first breath of moisture fell on her cheek. "Oh, bother."

"What's a bother?" Torren asked, his voice stronger, but still groggy.

"Snow's coming." She led the horse over to Nimble, hoping it might entice the creature to change back. More smoke curled up from a spot on the stone. "There's a boy. Come back to me."

The rock rippled, moved, and then shook. Scaly shards of rock fell to the ground. With a great roar, Nimble lit the sky with a spout of flames. "You're doing it, Nimble! You're breathing fire." Horra scrubbed at the patchy skin on his belly.

Nimble nosed the horse and seemed to settle. He stretched his leathery wings and tucked in his legs before staring at them much like a watchful cat.

"I found Murda's horse. You can ride it back to the castle." Horra held the reins out to Torren. He rose and stumbled to her.

He rubbed his chin and took a deep breath. "That's a waste of time. Let's get to the Weald first. I'm just befuddled. Combat training injuries were worse than this. It'll be fine."

Horra disagreed. She'd been there, and now here, and he wasn't acting the same no matter what he claimed. This was by far worse than any training injury he'd had. She opened her mouth to say so when he cut her off.

"Look, if we go back now, the king will never trust us to go out again. And you're the one injured. I'll be all right. It was a good hit, and I'll shake it off in a few minutes. Let's just get to the Weald. I know they have healing elixirs there for you. We can figure all this out when we get there." He mounted the other horse and looked down at her. "Coming?"

"Fine, but if you start acting all coo-coo, it's not my fault." She climbed up the rope ladder and hauled herself onto Nimble's back. Her head swum woozily, but she didn't tell him that. She cleared her sore throat. "Try to keep up. It's going to take us all night to get there now."

The haze of smoke hit her nose before they reached the edge of Bough Valley again. As they grew closer, she could hear shouting. Flames lit up a shop. She squinted to get a better look and realized it was the butcher's shop. Her heart pinched, remembering the butcher's kind words.

Nimble slowed as she foolishly pulled back on the ropes. Hobgoblins raced around, dousing the building with buckets of water. One after another, starting from a line at the well at the center of the town to the shop, people hauled bucket after bucket of water. Smoke shadowed an already dark sky as snowflakes gently fell around them.

Though the building looked to be a loss, they seemed to have it well under control. Horra turned the gulgoyle left toward Hobgoblin Pass.

Torches led the way across the patched-up bridge. Timber blocked off several holes in the guard wall, but it seemed to be safe. This late at night, the town was void of any traffic, and Horra and Torren transitioned easily from one side to the other.

Horra's stomach growled, reminding her she hadn't eaten since that morning. Snow smacked her in the face as they continued toward the Weald. Glowing eyes gazed at them from the edges of the road, breaking the dense darkness. The air held a hush, like the waited breath of a coming storm. Had there not been the clopping footfalls of Torren's steed behind her, she wouldn't have known he was there at all.

They rode on until she became weary and then rode longer. The night dragged on, and the wind howled and spat snow at them. She hunched over as the pain became unbearable. Her mind wandered a bit more than it should have. Glad for the warmth Nimble provided, she rested her body back against her beast's back, and let him do all the work. She said a silent prayer that whatever instinct the gulgoyle had would lead them back to the Weald.

Nimble plowed through the storm without effort. Horra turned to glance behind, but pain sliced through her. She had to trust Torren was following.

Horra must've dozed because the next thing she knew, her hide prickled with magic, and the sun lightened the sky in the east. She slowed Nimble down to a walk and allowed Torren to catch up beside them. Snow blanketed the area in a pristine cover, which also clung to the trees in a dazzling white.

Familiarity rolled over her. "*Whoa!*" She stopped Nimble and slid off the beast's back down into a cold blanket, slipped, and landed on her behind. Torren was there to help her stand. She glanced around, sure this was a dream.

"Horra?" Torren's concerned voice brought her attention back to the present.

"Sorry." She found the oldest-looking tree, placed a claw on it, and whispered, "Kryk, are you there?"

The tree groaned and popped until a face took shape in the deep creases of the bark. "Hello, Princess and companion. We are glad you have arrived. Please enter." His voice was deep and clackity.

A long branch moved, opening a path to the right.

Horra glanced at a weary Torren before leading them all into the Weald.

CHAPTER 18

~ *ROWAN* ~

Rowan stared at the red-headed troll who stumbled into the forest, bleeding and incoherent. Behind her trailed a massive black-winged creature, a green-headed male troll, and a horse. None of them were what he expected, though he wasn't sure what to expect at all. Except for the birds and insects in the Weald, and not counting Merrow, they were the first creatures he had ever met.

"Ah, good. Kryk told us you were here. It doesn't look like it was an uneventful trip, however?" Merrow greeted them and, taking Horra's claw, led them to the center of the garden where Rowan waited. "Rowan, please take the animals to the stables."

Rowan hesitated before doing as his instructor asked him. He wasn't accustomed to taking care of animals. The large, winged creature was intimidating as he grabbed the reins. Keen eyes glowed gold as it studied him. It shook its head up and down and smoke furled from its nostrils.

"You better get a move on or Nimble will burn your bark." The red-headed troll spoke breathlessly.

"Fire?" he clacked out.

"Humor, Rowan. She doesn't mean it." Merrow put a hand on his shoulder and pushed him toward the outer edge of the glade where the empty stables stood. "If you'll get them to the stables, tie them down to the fence. I'll show you how to take the tack off and brush them down in a few minutes. Our guests need some attention first. Do as I instruct, and I'll be with you shortly." He turned and ushered both trolls to a sitting area beneath an ancient Yew tree.

Rowan had studied trolls in the books Merrow had given him. The female didn't look very princess-like. Besides the blood, she wore rumpled clothes, and her hair stuck out at awkward angles—more like a tree with branches.

The other one wasn't much better. In fact, he had a decided lump on one side of his head. Rowan dismissed the thoughts and tugged the reins. The animals *clip-clopped* on the flag-stones spread in a pattern across the ground of the garden.

Woodsly spoke in his mind, *"After you tie the ropes off, give them some water and hay, young druid."*

Rowan followed his instructions, which ended up being much easier than he thought. The animals sucked up the water and munched on the dry sustenance loudly. He stood and watched them, making notes about their behavior, until Merrow joined him.

"Worqs attacked the trolls. One of their companions is missing. I've attended to their wounds. They're exhausted and will need to rest. When they have recuperated, we'll discuss their lost companion and talk about their next mission. Now, let me show you how to remove the tack to make the animals more comfortable."

Rowan watched intently as Merrow showed him how to

remove the saddles and the other gear, which they stowed in a clean stall.

"Be careful of this one," Merrow said, as he patted the bigger of the two. "He's the only one of his kind, a gulgoyle. Part dragon and part gargoyle. He can turn to stone when frightened. He also breathes fire when he gets upset or angry. The princess mentioned he has been nervous and unpredictable. Do try not to make sudden movements around him."

Rowan finished brushing the horse as Merrow wiped the scales down on the gulgoyle. The animal groaned, scaring Rowan.

"It's okay, dear boy. He is just enjoying it." Merrow gave the beast another scratch and motioned for Rowan to follow him. "Now, we will need to wait while our guests rest. It would be a good time to prepare questions you have for the princess before you leave with her."

"Leave? With her?" Rowan couldn't help the crickety note in his voice. He thought they were simply to be introduced. He dug his roots down into the ground for comfort.

"Why, yes. I've done all I can to instruct you. It is now time for your next phase of learning—experience." Rowan placed a kind hand on his arm and led him back to the center of the Weald. "You have many adventures that lay ahead of you. You will get to put your knowledge to work and start your search for the Erlking."

His leaves shivered, the rustling noise joining the birds' calls in the shelter of their magic-laden trees. "But, I—."

Merrow interrupted him with a slim hand on his shoulder. "New experiences and adventures are always scary at first. It's all part of learning that you must do to become the finest druid warrior the Wilden Lands have ever seen. Most of your kind go out in the world on their own. You have an advantage, Rowan. You'll have the troll princess to help guide you. Lean on her understanding to help you grow, and you'll do just fine, my lad. Now, finish reading your book. Tomorrow will be a big day for you."

Rowan frowned at Merrow's back as he crossed the stone path to their sleeping quarters. This was the troll warrior Woodsly bragged about as being the greatest troll warrior to emerge for centuries? She didn't look like any warrior he'd read about, especially if she had gotten beaten by the worqs.

No, this troll princess wasn't an advantage. His bark quivered.

CHAPTER 19

~ *ROWAN* ~

That eve, after the trolls had rested through the day, Rowan placed a tray of food out for their two guests. He poured water into the glasses, adding some sap to his own glass. Though he didn't need it to hasten his growth now, he preferred drinking it over straight water.

Merrow nodded at Rowan, pleased with his show of hospitality. "Now that you've rested, can you retell what you told me earlier today?"

The princess recounted seeing the worqs, catching them by surprise, the fighting, and Murda's abduction. Rowan went through the facts in his mind as she spoke, waiting until she finished talking to speak as Merrow had trained him.

He started with what he knew. "Worqs, a half-breed mix of orcs and dark witches, are famous for their cruel nature and violence. Only the giants outrank them in strength." Rowan summarized his lessons. "As a troll, your odds for taking one worq down are minuscule, let alone taking down two or three. Why would you try?"

Horra raised ruddy brows at him and her cheeks darkened. "Because a troll who was under my care was being taken by them. It was my duty to keep her safe. Surely you, a druid warrior, would've tried to help." She said it to him, but her narrowed glance was at Merrow.

Merrow sat unspeaking.

The princess's question confused Rowan. "I would've weighed the benefits of attacking versus fleeing. That's what great strategists do."

Horra let out a sudden *pshaw* sound that startled the birds flying above them. "You're saying you would let one of those filthy creatures take me if we got cornered somewhere?" Her mud-brown eyes glittered like slick silt. Her cheeks expanded like a photo he'd seen in the *Dangerous Species to Avoid* textbook of a puffertoad when threatened. Female trolls, he reasoned, should be added to the list of dangerous animals.

Rowan considered why she was angry but could not come up with a reason. Discernment and judgment were obviously not this troll's strengths.

"I'm afraid Rowan has much to learn, Princess, and he's struggled to grow. His brain is mostly sapwood at this point. And there's only so much you can learn from books. Real-life experience is what you're here for, my lady. I cannot leave the Weald since I am the last seedkeeper. And surely you have some empathy for Rowan since you were recently thrown out into the world that you had to navigate on your own. I pray you remember that when you're training young Rowan."

The princess looked as happy about it as Rowan was. Ignoring the fact that his instructor had just apologized for him, he twirled the sap water in his glass around. He wondered at the soundness of Merrow's decision to pair him with such a rash, uncivilized troll.

~ HORRA ~

Horra was up with the sunrise the next morning in the former druid barracks bedroom. It was a sparse room with a bed, table and a chair, and one window that looked out into the Weald. The barracks itself was a long, stone building, with rooms on each side of a long, narrow hallway. Merrow had explained that it once housed all of the woodgoblin-born druids for training. Now, he and Rowan were the only occupants.

Though she and Torren had slept through the day yesterday, she'd still been exhausted when evening came. Merrow had warned her it would take a while for her to recover from the worq's poison.

Now she was being put in charge of a young druid who knew nothing of the Wilden Lands except for what he'd read. She'd already lost Murda to the worqs, and Torren was injured during the battle. Tears of frustration pricked her eyes. It was a wonder she'd been able to sleep at all.

She stretched, avoiding moving the arm on her injured side. It still stung. Was she up to training a green-behind-the-bark woodgoblin? She wasn't even sure if she could keep him safe, let alone teach him anything. He seemed to be as thick as an infomapedia, having no common sense. Her shoulders pinched as she combed her claws through her matted, unruly hair, knocking loose a stick or two.

The image of Woodsly coming to warn her in the dining hall flitted across her mind. He'd done everything he could to keep her safe. She would do anything in his memory to keep his prodigy safe as well. The truth of that sank in, and she realized it was why she so readily came back when Merrow called on her. She was honor-bound to help Rowan. It's what her old instructor would've expected of her.

"You were always after me to be more responsible, listen, and become a proper princess," she muttered to herself as she wove her thick tresses into two large braids. "You're probably laughing at me in the great hereafter, aren't you Woodsly?"

What did she really know about Rowan so far? He was mostly obedient. Droll in his humor. She smiled, remembering the rare, but important moments when Woodsly's humor showed. It had been priceless when it happened and usually bolstered her when she'd been ready to break. It didn't even matter to her now how many marks he'd given her when she hadn't lived up to his expectations. He'd been her friend as much as her instructor.

"*Gah*," she muttered. "I miss you, Woodsly. Rowan's a bit of a stiff stick next to you. And here I am, having to mentor him. The irony isn't lost on me."

A knock sounded at her door, and she swiped a sleeve across her damp eyes. "Come in."

Merrow entered with a small bowl of cooked thistleberry mush and milkweed juice. "Good morning, Princess. I pray you've rested well and are ready for your mission."

She smiled wanly at him. "I rested well, thank you. This looks delicious."

"Rowan made it for you. He wanted to be sure we welcomed you properly." He placed his limb arms behind him and stood tall against the light coming from the window behind him.

Horra struggled to smile convincingly back at him. The memory of Woodsly's seed popped into her mind and then the seedkeeper's comment of Rowan's brain still being sapwood.

After the debacle with the worqs the last eve, guilt doubled in her gut. "I mucked it up a bit, didn't I? Bringing the seed here so late? If I hadn't hesitated after the poisoned forest, you could've reversed some of the damage. I'm to blame for his slow development, aren't I?"

Merrow placed the items on a table. "Although I admit to wondering the same thing, none of us can predict what would've happened. Perhaps you would've chosen a different path and another such calamity would've kept you from making it to the Weald completely. What-ifs are the worse kind of torment."

He held her gaze with one so knowing, it made the hair on her arms lift. "If you'd known your mother's wish wouldn't have healed her, would you not have tried? If you'd have known the worqs were waiting in that forest for Murda, would you have taken her place and been abducted instead? The ifs are unceasing in life and would be the undoing of many a wonderful creature. One can only take what they're given and make the most of the circumstances."

Horra picked up the spoon. "Has anyone told you that you're creepy in a mind-reading sort of way?" She dipped it into the bowl as he silently grinned at her. "But thank you. Sometimes I need to remember that I don't have all the answers."

The woodgoblin sat on a chair beside her bed. "Now that we've cleared that up, I want to remind you that Rowan will not be like Woodsly. I say this because I know you cared deeply for him and may wish he were still around to guide you." He spread his leafy hand wide. "The roods have sensed your sadness, and we all grieve the passing of a most beloved member."

The tasty paste in her mouth turned into glue.

"Though there are times I see a glimmer of your old

instructor in our new druid friend, Rowan is emotionally stagnant, as you might have noticed. He's intelligent, yes. But he'll need a firm hand to guide him in compassion and matters of the heart." Merrow hesitated. "Sometimes I sense thoughts in his head that are odd. As you know, druids can communicate via root systems, hearing each other without speaking. And since no druid has released their lifesource as Woodsly has for hundreds of years, we have little documentation on how this all works." He shrugged his knobby shoulders. "Rowan knows things I haven't taught him."

"What kinds of things?" Horra flicked a glance at him, noticing the pinched bark around his eyes and his lips.

Merrow clacked, clearing his throat. "Ancient things. Things I don't comprehend."

Horra swallowed another thistleberry-flavored glob. "Have you inquired of the roods?"

He sighed. "They have been uncommonly silent. Do you still have the woodencloak?"

Horra reached for the knapsack, which she slept with, and pulled out the cloak.

"Good. I want to carve more protection blessings into it, and then I'll carve them into Rowan's bark along with the other fortification sigils before you leave." He took the woodencloak from her. "Finish eating. I fear it will be an arduous journey ahead for you both."

Though the seedkeeper was too polite to say it outright, she understood the 'you're going to need all the luck you can get' meaning in the tone of his rickety voice.

The cereal congealed into a brick in her stomach.

CHAPTER 20

~ ROWAN ~

S moke wafted in the air as Merrow drew protection blessings and sigils on Rowan's bark. Merrow assured him that the carvings wouldn't hurt, but his bark was still thin, more fragile than it ought to be, so it scratched uncomfortably.

"You look like a poody bird with your face all scrunched up like that." Horra grinned.

It wasn't that Rowan didn't know what humor was. He understood the concept. But how one found amusement in another's distress was beyond his grasp. "It is impossible not to show discomfort with a wand burning into my flesh."

Torren leaned forward and assessed Rowan's arm. "At least it works on you. It wouldn't work on us. Troll hide is impossible to tattoo because of its thickness." There was a note of something in his voice. Rowan couldn't put a name on the emotion.

He'd go with the facts instead. "It's true that troll's hides are the thickest in the Wilden Lands. Most magic doesn't penetrate its density, especially the female gender, because of their contrary nature. Females have uncompromising personalities, making them difficult to deal with."

Torren snickered and pointed a finger at the princess. "Called out."

Horra glared back at him. "At least I wasn't mesmerized."

Torren's smile vanished immediately, and he looked in the other direction.

The communication between them was confusing, so Rowan decided it was not something he was supposed to understand. Like the whispers of the roods he deciphered, but which Merrow didn't, it must be some inner secret between the two.

"Enough banter, young royals. We've more important things than pointing out each other's faults." Merrow lifted the ironwood wand and blew on the last symbol. "Rowan, you can relax now. I've finished." He glanced at Torren. "I do apologize, Sir Rindthorn. I have nothing to offer you as protection."

"Sir?" Horra snickered. "Since when is he a 'sir'?"

"Since he was born into a royal household," Merrow stated as he packed up his tools. "I believe Woodsly taught you both this in Oddar's Royal Lineage courses."

Unperturbed by his instructor's words and tone, Horra sniffed the air. "Smells like a campfire. Wish I had some blood sausages." Horra took the woodencloak from Merrow and stood to put it on.

"Woodgoblins do not have a sense of smell. They ingest carbon and expel oxygen from their roots and leaves." Rowan stated as Merrow left to collect his supply pack from the stone hut.

"Can you taste, then?" Torren asked.

"My tongue has no taste buds, no. My roots can sense nutrients in the soil, which I can then process as needed. I have read in *Beasties: An Instruction Guide* that trolls have a diverse set of taste buds, allowing them to enjoy a wide range of foods."

Rowan couldn't imagine what it would be like since he had nothing to compare it to. All he had was the information he'd read. The only reason he favored sap water was because it didn't saturate his fibrous stem as quickly as water did.

The trolls discussed food and how different creatures preferred different sustenance, which he tuned out. In the background, he caught whispers of warning and panic murmuring along the ground. The roods were agitated, but he couldn't tell why.

One word came through the commotion clearly. "Fire?" he questioned out loud.

Horra snapped her mouth shut and inhaled deeply. "That's not smoke from your carvings." She jumped up and pulled out her dagger. "Fire! We need water."

Torren followed the princess's alert stance, looking around. "Where is it coming from?"

Rowan ran to the well and grabbed a bucketful of water, unsure what else to do. He rushed back to Horra with it. "Here."

Horra's eyes were wide as she stared at the canopy of Yew trees above them. "We're going to need way more than that. Look!" Her voice wavered as she pointed to the far edge of the forest. Flames lit the sky like the sun. Unlike the sun, a dark haze of smoke outlined the inferno.

Rowan's thin bark tightened, and his senses heightened.

A crash resounded, and a huge burning limb fell to the ground. Rowan knew that fire was dangerous. Merrow had warned him many times not to go near it. Pain echoed across the rhizosphere, the forest's root communication system. It tingled along his tap roots and burrowed into his core.

The troll princess stood tall, taking charge. "Rowan, find Merrow. Torren, get your horse and Nimble. I'll try to put the fire out on the ground over there."

Overwhelmed by signals of alarm and dealing with the onslaught of pain, Rowan stood transfixed. The wards had failed. Something had invaded the Weald. That couldn't be possible. All his textbooks talked about how secure and safe the Weald was. Merrow had also assured him of the Weald's untouchable status. He couldn't process what was happening.

Horra shoved Rowan. "Go. Find Merrow!"

He shook his head, clearing the conflicting messages in his mind. "Yes, yes. Of course." He took off at a run toward their living quarters.

Torren, he noticed, was already at the stables. Nimble, having sensed danger, had turned into a boulder. The troll untied the steed and smacked its hind. It took off running. Horra dashed off to the well with a bucket.

Sap quickened through his limbs, spurring him into action. He hurried to the stone barracks, but it was across the center of the Weald. Fire spread like spilled water across the treetops. The land was always dry inside the Weald thanks to the spells keeping it hidden. It didn't reflect the weather on the outside, always holding steady in temperature and humidity. When Rowan asked, Merrow told him they drew from wells deep in the magical garden area, so they never needed rain or snow. Before Rowan could make it to the stone hut, flames engulfed it. "Merrow?" he yelled.

No answer.

"Merrow, call out to me so I can find you." Rowan circled around the clear end of the stone building. "Merrow?" The fire was spreading from the ground where piles of limbs had fallen, and up the great Yew trees. Heat surrounded him.

Something tugged at his trunk.

"Rowan. This way. We have to get out of here." Horra screamed over the growing roar of the flames. She held her arm over her mouth and nose.

"But, Merrow—" he reached an arm toward the building and an ember landed on it. Pain, real and torturous, exploded. He squealed in agony and thrashed at the wound to make it stop.

In a swift motion, Horra swept him off his rooted feet and ran. Orange, angry flames were everywhere—all around them. Crackling, devouring. Roods shrieked, begging him to stop the fire. They called out the words 'petrification' and 'unable to move' in terrible screams.

Rowan fought to get free, but the princess was stronger than he gave her credit. She held him in a firm grip as they jostled through shrubbery. Some trees that could move about lifted their roots and shifted. Dirt and dry detritus clouded the ground as they did so. All of them moved the same direction he and the princess were going.

However, the old trees were slow. They'd been planted for decades, and their lateral and heart roots were too deeply set to do anything more than clear a path on any other day. Many hardened roots broke in their haste, causing more confusion and injury. It all filled his mind with a whirl of pressure and noise. Those who weren't succumbing to the flames were killing themselves to get away from the fire. It was horrific.

Smoke thickened the air, making it hard to see. They ducked a falling branch, Torren yelling when the flames caught his tunic.

"We need to save the trees." Rowan choked out, fighting the sensations overwhelming his woodstem.

They were dying. All of them. It was a massacre.

Flames leaped up in front of them, and Horra jerked, fell, and dropped him.

Torren grabbed him, tossing Rowan over his shoulder as he outpaced the fire. Stronger than the princess, Rowan could not even move in the male troll's grip.

"We're going the wrong way. The trees need our help," Rowan yelled over the loud blaze. He glanced over his shoulder to see where they were going. "You can't get out this way."

Horra was breathless as she tumbled over obstacles behind Torren. "I don't care about getting out. I just want to stay alive."

"But the Yews—" His sap sang hotly through his fibers. It pounded in his head, drowning out some of the tortured screeches coming from the spirits as the trees turned into piles of soot and ash. This wasn't an ordinary fire. It burned far too quickly for that.

The Weald was impenetrable. Merrow had taught him the protections and safeguards. Over a dozen spells went into keeping the Weald hidden. How could this be happening?

And how could the roods survive?

CHAPTER 21

~ *ROWAN* ~

Torren jostled Rowan as he outran the fiery danger. "We can't save the trees. It's spreading too fast. It must be dark magic. I've never seen fire move so quickly in all my life," the male troll gasped and shouted above the crackling and intense rush of the flames.

The trees stretched and moved, scattering at odd angles as if unsure where to go. They were perturbed, befuddled, and running into other trunks in their haste. This was unlike their ordered movements when they guided guests through the forest. It was chaotic, violent—unnerving to watch. Each direction Torren navigated, another tree would unbury itself. Trunk-like roots unrooted and fled everywhere.

Torren skidded and changed direction enough times that Rowan became lost in where they were located.

Dirt flew. Yews moved, leaving gaping holes behind. The heat grew so hot, the new sigils Merrow had carved in Rowan's soft wood melted together.

Smoke thickened, covering the ground to roll across the Weald like a river, covering the forest in a dense haze.

Torren coughed and stumbled, dropping Rowan to the ground and landing on top of him.

Luckily, his wood was flexible. Rowan pushed at the troll's massive shoulder with no effect. "The forest is trying to save itself. The trees will keep moving, trying to outdistance the fire until it's gone. They'll trample us." Rowan beat his branch hands against the massive troll, who gasped and paid no attention to him.

"I think—we're safe here," Horra panted out. "Is there anything—we can do—to help them?" She'd landed near Torren. Both trolls were struggling to breathe. Black covered their noses and mouths.

"How—" Torren choked and gagged, coughing.

"The trees can't cross the border. They're trapped within the magical force that hides the Weald. There's nowhere for them to go."

Torren finally rolled off of Rowan and he glanced around, trying to figure out a solution. "There's a small pool on the southern tip of the Weald. We may be safer there."

Embers dropped from above, searing his bark and landing on the trolls. They all screamed in pain.

"Then let's go." Torren struggled to stand. Horra caught his claw and helped him.

Rowan took a moment to orient himself, stood, and pointed. "This way." He moved his roots as fast as he could manage, but he hadn't had any rigorous training. However, with as many tendrils as his feet had, he made better progress than the hunched-over trolls.

The air grew less polluted the farther south they traveled. The troll's breaths rattled as they hustled. They were finally quicker, keeping up with Rowan.

In the distance, trees creaked as they spread to get away from the fire. The earth groaned with the motion of the roots. These trees made their way toward the pool as well. Rowan hoped they made it in time or no trees would remain. The Weald—his home—would all be gone.

He couldn't fathom it.

They reached the more open meadow area that he'd rarely visited. Merrow, with his limp and cane, couldn't come to this area. Flowers waved in the ashy wind. Several trees had arrived just in time, creaking past them as they headed to the bigger pool. They settled around it in a timber mass. Lush branches that were once tall and firm were bare and hung low.

Horra coughed, heaving into the grass. She scooted to the trickling stream which ran off the pool. She scooped up water in her claws and washed her eyes, nose, and mouth, then dampened her singed hair. A blister formed on one of her burned ears along the pointed tip.

Torren did much the same thing. He immersed his burned arm in the cool depths and groaned, his voice raspy.

Rowan glanced back toward where they'd come. "I don't understand how this happened."

Horra cleared her throat. "I was so stupid!" She smacked her claw down and splashed water. "The worqs must've followed us." Her eyes glowed orange, reflecting the fire she stared at. "It's all my fault. All of it."

"There has never been a fire in the Weald," Rowan said.

"Not making her feel any better stick-boy." Torren scowled at him.

"My apologies. I meant to say this, no one has ever attacked the Weald before. How could you have known they would do such a thing? Fire should not be conceivable."

Horra's shoulders slumped. Tears streamed down her sooty face, and she coughed vigorously. When she recovered, she glared at him. "*Gah*, what is it that's choking me so badly? And how are you not coughing?"

Rowan steepled his twig fingers like he'd seen Merrow do while instructing him. "Yews, you may or may not know, are poisonous. Breathing in the smoke from them is quite hazardous."

The princess's mouth opened wide. "And you didn't think to mention this to us before?"

"It never occurred to me. Woodgoblins such as I don't breathe as other creatures do, so it is not noxious to us."

"But I've seen other woodgoblins breathing." The princess's voice was scratchy and raw.

He rocked back and forth, glad for the opportunity to explain his physiology. "Ah, but I said woodgoblins such as I. My body structure differs a great extent from other woodgoblins not born from druid's unique seed. For example, I have no actual feet but feeder roots which take in nutrients. Not to be mistaken for permanent root caps, which are what keep trees strong and stationary." He raised one of his trunk-like legs. The multiple roots which he'd just described fanned out from the outer edge. He wiggled them.

Torren chuckled. "Did you swallow an informapedia?"

"Swallowing an informapedia would be impossible to accomplish unless one digested it page by page." Rowan sniffed. "And I don't eat paper. That's cannibalism."

"That was sarcasm, Rowan." Horra, who had finished her coughing fit, spoke clearer now. She stood and stared at the distant blaze. "That means—"

"I recognize the definition of sarcasm, Princess. I don't understand the necessity of it." His voice squeaked on the end of his sentence—a sign that he was entering his adolescent development stage. He'd read about it in *An Introduction to Druid Growth and Maturity.*

Horra scrunched her dirty face. "I miss Woodsly."

Torren uttered an agreement.

Rowan ignored them both. He focused instead on the Weald.

Orange flames flickered, and all Rowan could see were the shadows of charred trees. The fire was dying down and, try as he might, he couldn't connect with any of the trees now.

Any of the Yews that had made it safely to the pond were in a state of shock. Their roots being bared for the first time in hundreds of years—possibly thousands. Yews lived long past a millennium if the conditions were right. And the Weald was a perfect environment. Or at least it was. It would take these trees years to reroot, regrow their epidermal cells, and regain their ability to communicate.

"We need to go find out if Merrow is safe." Rowan hoped, but the odds were not good. His instructor had had no protection except the stone building, which wasn't saying much against a magical fire. Even if protected, the heat would've been too intense to survive. He'd likely be a chunk of charcoal by now.

"We also need to check and make sure that Nimble survived, and then we need to find Torren's steed." The princess patted ashes from her grimy clothes.

They walked back, stumbling over the charred hunks of forest, keeping to the edge where no glowing embers remained, and back to the center of the Weald. Every few yards, Torren would whistle for his horse.

As Rowan figured it, the male troll wasted his wheezing breath. "Most likely, the steed found its way out of the Weald. The forest itself wouldn't have barred it's exit since the fire had taken up much of the spirit's attention. If I were to guess, your steed is safe on the outside, awaiting to be beckoned back into service."

Both trolls glanced at him.

He held their gazes with a steady one of his own.

"It was much better when I thought you didn't speak." Horra mumbled low, but not low enough for him to miss.

Rowan wasn't sure if it was a statement of fact or if she was using the tiresome application of sarcasm once again. Either way, his sentiment was the same about her.

CHAPTER 22

~ HORRA ~

Horra's footsteps sent puffs of ashy fragments into the already contaminated air. She'd torn off a scrap of her inner shirt and wrapped it around her nose and mouth to keep the poisoned air from doing any more damage. Torren followed her example.

The destruction to the center of the Weald was catastrophic. She recalled the vast array of rare and exotic plants she'd noticed on her first visit to the Weald. Now, everything was gone—possibly for good.

Rowan stood stock still as he took in the devastation, an unreadable look on his wooden face. Though he nattered on like a know-it-all, she knew it must distress him.

"I need to check on Nimble," she said to him before turning to Torren. "Stay with him, will you?"

Torren nodded, and she made her way through the blackened, fallen debris to where the stables were. She placed her claw on the boulder that was her pet but pulled it away imme-diately. It was as hot as a forge. She shook her claw, mentally adding another burn to the many scorch marks she already received.

Frustration gnawed at her gut, but she held it back. She'd need her pet to get out of the Weald—to where she wasn't sure. But there was no staying here now. "Hey, Nimble, there's a good boy. The fire's gone. It's safe to come out now."

The boulder remained unmoved. A moment of dread entered her mind with the thought that maybe the gulgoyle hadn't survived. Though it was a fire-creature, this was magical in origin with poisonous air. It was possible her pet was gone. Tears welled in her eyes, making them sting as more of the grime around the lids dissolved with them.

They needed another animal, Torren's steed, if they could find it, to be sure.

Torren crunched his way over to her. Rowan dawdled behind him, looking dazed. "Any luck?" he asked.

Horra wanted to stamp her booted feet and scream. She inhaled slowly, careful not to set herself up for another coughing fit. "No. I adore him, but he can be so stubborn." She turned to glance at where they'd come from. Rowan had his hand on the stone wall of the barracks. Piles of ash and debris vomited out of the building. "What's Rowan doing?"

Torren's skin had a grayish pallor to it. "He's checking to see if he can locate Merrow, or any of the other roods. Do you think any survived?"

"I'm unsure. We can't stay in here forever with this poiso-nous air. How could I forget how dangerous the Yew trees were during a fire?" Her throat was still raw, and her stomach roiled like she'd swallowed something that was now kicking around to find its way out.

He ran a claw through his green, singed hair. "If we can't

get Nimble or find my steed, we'll be on foot. I don't really like the idea of camping now that we've seen what happened to Murda."

"What choice do we have?" The boulder next to her cracked and she stopped.

A final, loud snap, and Nimble freed his wings and shook off his rubble-like barrier. When the gulgoyle lifted his head, it revealed Merrow's prone, unburned body.

"Rowan!" she screamed, then succumbed to choking coughs.

"What is it?" he soundlessly made his way across the blackened rubble. He stopped a few steps short of Nimble. "Is he alive?"

Horra, still clearing her throat, put two fingers at the hollow on the seedkeeper's neck. "His heartbeat is thready."

Rowan dropped to his knees and placed his thin hands across Merrow's face. He glanced around as if searching for something. "I need lifesap. I could save him if I had any."

"Where would it be?" Torren asked.

"In the housing quarters. It would be a white, filmy liquid in clear jars. Look in my bedroom, the last room on the left.

Torren rushed off.

Horra could hear his raspy breathing as he left. It wasn't a good sign. "Is there anything else we can do?"

Rowan bent over Merrow and shook his head. "When one becomes a seedkeeper, their spirit becomes intertwined with the roods. When they suffer, he suffers. It's part of the seed-keeper's burden."

"So, if they die—" She couldn't say the rest.

"He dies, yes."

Horra glanced back at the stone building. What was taking Torren so long?

When Torren finally reemerged, soot coated him in a thick

layer. Only his eyes shone white against his specter-like body. Strapped over his shoulder was a lump. As he grew closer, she realized it was her knapsack. He didn't hurry back.

She put her claw on Rowan's arm. "I don't think there was any left."

Rowan was silent, his eyes closed as he hunched over Merrow.

Torren rejoined them as they waited for the seedkeeper to take his last breath.

They didn't have to wait long.

Magic rose and then quickly abated. The body before them glowed and then changed to a pile of sticks and bark, much like Woodsly's had done. Only this time, there was no seed. Horra choked back a heartfelt sob. She lowered her head, let her tears fall to the ground, and prayed silently for the Creature God to welcome Merrow's spirit into the great unknown.

The Weald became silent in the aftermath of its longtime keeper's death.

CHAPTER 23

~ ROWAN ~

Burned branches littered the path where Rowan and Merrow used to walk. No glimmerbugs flitted in the air. Not even a breeze dared to move across the Weald.

Rowan placed a sprig of a flower on the area where they buried his friend and mentor. They'd hidden the grave in case anyone invaded the Weald in their absence. Magic could remain in the cells of wood for some time. Elves, he somehow knew, though he couldn't say why, had ways of using the dead for nefarious purposes. That would not happen to Merrow. Not while Rowan was still alive.

He didn't know the benedictions or the rites he needed to observe. They were in a hurry, and he still had to consecrate the land and try to reseal the protections before they left. He only knew eight out of the twelve. Rowan hoped they would be enough.

He placed his hand against the biggest surviving stump

and communicated his grief and loss into a great void. Though there were no roods to hear him, he did it anyway to show his respect.

"Every tree in the Weald holds a spirit of a woodgoblin or a druid. Some come here to root before they die and fossilize. Rooting before death allows one to regenerate into a new tree, which passes one's knowledge through their roots to the rest of the Weald. Today is a significant loss for not only us, but to all the creatures everywhere. Goodbye, Merrow, my trusted instructor. Goodbye, Kryk, Master General Rood. And goodbye Woodsly, our last great warrior rood. We will miss you all. May your journey to the Ever After be blessed."

Rowan dug into the sensory details coming to him through his leaves and his roots. The soil held a poisonous tang, worse than the ash of the dead Yew trees around him. It was like the magic of the mildew and rot he fought on his lower limbs. It had the same resonance. "I sense the residuals of something dark and dangerous. Insidious. No doubt, this was the Erlking's work."

"Is there something we can do to get rid of it?" Horra asked him, the first she'd spoken since they buried Merrow. The red rings around her eyes were as bright as her hair.

"I need to say some blessings before we try to reset the spells that protect the Weald from outside forces." He stood and brushed off his bark. "Torren, find the largest chunk of yew bark you can. Horra, I need clean water. If you can't dig out the well, get it from the stream."

The two trolls hurried to do as he asked. He said silent prayers to the Creature God as he awaited their return. He hummed as he prayed, his eyes closed to form a deep meditational link.

Torren cleared his throat. "I found this. It's the biggest one in the center. I could look further if you need."

It was as long as the troll was tall and almost as wide around. "It will do fine." Rowan took the bark and uttered blessings over it, all that he could remember from his training, anyway. He then drew symbols on it with shards of burned sticks, similar to the ones Merrow had carved into his trunk. It wasn't as permanent as the ironwood's would be. But it was better than leaving the Weald open and vulnerable.

His twig fingers didn't have the practiced stroke Merrow's had, but the symbols weren't shaky or misshaped. His arms, however, zinged with the magic of the land, and his fervent intentions behind the protections. He covered the wood with markings, knowing it might not be enough if the Erlking attacked with fire again. Next, he took some of the ash, and, crushing it in his hands, sprinkled it over the bark.

Horra arrived, wheezing, the thin fabric over her mouth moving with her labored breath. She handed him a small bucket filled from the stream.

"Thank you, Princess."

He prayed over the water, his crickety voice rising in the deathly quiet. When he finished his ministrations, he poured the water over the ash on the bark. Gray mist rose as the water poured over the toxic filth. It rose and spread, encasing the whole of the destruction. Strength poured out of him inch by grueling inch until the mist cleansed the land and set the protections in place once more. They were weak, but set, nonetheless.

With his energy depleted, he panted, his brow sweating. He sat crumpled next to the worn-out princess, his bark too tight and his eyes bleary.

After a few moments of recovering, he searched one last time for any spark, any hint of communication, but found none. A great vacuum existed where there was once an endless din of information passing along the roots and whispered among the leaves. Merrow hadn't prepared him for this.

He took comfort in how the essence of the holy water, together with the blessings and hastily erected barrier, spurned the invading evil. Greater druids than he had placed them long ago, creating a superior barrier than any he could imagine generating. But his boundary would hold, and that was as good as he could do.

Rowan sat back and allowed the comfort of his home to give him energy enough to leave.

"Follow Horra," something whispered in the wind.

Startled, Rowan glanced up to find the troll princess gathering herbs from Merrow's garden. She hunted in a section that somehow remained untouched by the fire. "What're you doing, Princess?" he asked.

"These herbs are rare. We'll take them back to Oddar and put them in our Conservatory to save them. Then we'll replant them when we rebuild the Weald." Her eyes glistened when she glanced his way, possibly a trick of the light.

The prospect of rebuilding the Weald zinged through his wood. Would it be possible? Looking around now, it didn't seem so. A quote from one of the holy books came back to him, "All things are possible if you trust in the Almighty Creature God."

"What did you say?" Torren asked.

Rowan brushed his hands off and made his way to the princess to help. "Trust not on your own understanding, but in the Creator of life itself."

Horra turned toward them. "My mother used to quote that to me before she passed." She picked up the plants carefully and placed them in the bucket. She then placed them inside her bag. "You have to believe in something, right? Where there's no hope, you must find the light and follow it."

"I guess," murmured Torren. He didn't sound convinced.

"Now, let's get out of here before Torren and I croak, and I don't mean our voices."

CHAPTER 24

~ HORRA ~

Minutes later, they exited the Weald past the pool on the southern side. Not only did it allow Horra to water Nimble, but she noticed some useful plants.

Torren left them to go search for Murda's horse. His whistles echoed, assuring Horra he was still close by.

"What are you making?" she asked Rowan as she slathered the burns on her arms with an ointment she'd concocted from slippery elm bark. She would treat Torren's wounds as well, when he returned.

"A pack for supplies." Rowan didn't glance up at her. He stitched some flax-string into straight and even seams. He used a needle from a porcuvine bush, which slipped through the tanned bark easily enough.

Horra held the casting bowl out to him. "Want me to rub some on your burns?"

"I have tingleroot I found in my room to heal my bark."

Though the fire destroyed the barracks, Horra was heartened to learn he'd found several items hidden beneath a chunk of stone that fell, protecting them. Rowan used several strands of flax and braided them for the tie opening.

Maybe the wood boy wasn't so bad after all.

Horra tore a spare tunic she'd taken from her knapsack into strips and wrapped them around her coated burns. She only had one inner shirt, and she'd already torn that beyond repair. It wasn't any good using the tunic she wore with the Yew smoke tainting it. Her clothes were a total loss.

"Tingleroot?" she asked. "What is that made from?"

Rowan fed the braided string through the seam. "I don't know. I never asked Merrow."

There was, no doubt, many things lost forever in the fire. It hurt her heart to think of such knowledge obliterated so quickly. Anger toward the Erlking replaced her sadness.

"Do you know where this side of the Weald will take us when we leave?" Rowan asked.

Horra dug into her knapsack and pulled out a parchment. She unfurled the map of the Wilden Lands onto a stone.

Rowan set his pack down and studied it. "It's missing something." He ran a limb across the map.

"What do you mean? This is an official map from Oddar's library, drafted just last season. There's nothing missing." She worked at keeping her voice neutral, but the woodgoblin's stiff assurance rubbed against her the wrong way.

He ran a twig finger from the Light Kingdom of the fairies along the Shining Sea to the Half-Lands and the Great Sea. From there, he traced the Goblin Lands in the south to the Giant Lands in the north. "What's beyond the Dunder Lands?" he asked.

Horra studied the parchment, recalling her cartography class. "The Elf Lands start beyond the Iron Mountain range where the dwarfs live. Like the Weald, the elves ward their lands. Only elves go in. And they rarely come out."

Rowan waited several moments before frowning. He glanced around them and then at Horra. "Did you say something?"

Horra frowned back at him. "The Elf Lands. They're warded—"

"Yes, yes. I heard that." His roots dug into the soil. "I thought I heard something else."

Horra wondered what the woodgoblin was talking about. Had the fire and then Merrow's death affected his sanity in some way? "Are you okay? I mean, I get it. I was a little thrown when I lost Woodsly."

"It's nothing." He focused back on the map, a grim twist to his mouth. "Merrow talked about the Riven. We're unable to contact anything beyond its borders. Something has contaminated the ground there with a pervasive evil, much like I expelled to cleanse the Weald."

"Balk, a mercenary I know, talked about the Riven. He traveled there last I knew. It's not on a map anywhere, and no one seems to know where its borders lie. He spoke of it being near the bridge of Hobgoblin Pass. I assume the edge is near there somewhere."

Rowan measured the distance on the map. He used the end of a charred stick to circle the blank area on the parchment where Horra knew the Elf Lands should be. Their scribes, however, refused to draw something they had no sure measurements for, and so it remained blank on all of their maps.

Rowan clacked, a mini mimic of the noise Woodsly always made that had driven her crazy. Funny how it comforted her now.

"That's a day's travel from where the Wilden Lands' end,

on the other side of the dwarf realm. There ought to be a way to measure it for safety's sake." Bark above Rowan's eyes furrowed.

"Well, we don't have it now, and we have to work with what we've got. We're wasting daylight debating what should and shouldn't be on a map. We need a plan to start somewhere." She rolled the parchment up.

Rowan glanced at her. "We start where the worqs ambushed you and see if we can follow any signs of which direction they went. That is, if you want to find your companion."

Horra froze, a claw holding the map halfway inside her knapsack. A ripple of fear and guilt flowed across her thick hide. "I thought we'd go back to the castle first." Her voice wavered.

"Are you unwell?" Rowan asked.

She pulled the woodencloak out and put it on. "I'm fine."

"Horra?" Torren joined them, without the horse. His hair was wet and slicked back from the stream. His clothes were damp and stained, but looked as if he'd scrubbed them out.

"Yes?" she answered him after she stood, stupidly glancing around.

He jerked around at the sound of her voice. "Where are you? I can hear you but I can't see you."

Realization dawned on her. "Here." She pulled the hood off of the woodencloak. "I forget no one can see me."

"I could see you just fine." Rowan said, as Torren visibly relaxed. "I told the princess that I think we should go back to where the worqs attacked you to see if we can find your companion."

Torren blanched, expressing the same emotions she held. Neither of them were eager to go back to that forest. "I thought you said it was dumb to take on more than our share of worqs at one time. I realize getting Murda back is essential. But we should return home now and let the king know what happened. Maybe get some reinforcements to help us in our search for Murda?"

Rowan stilled, as if considering it. "You make sense. We'll head to Oddar first."

Annoyance prickled Horra's scalp. She'd already mentioned that. Wasn't she supposed to be the one guiding the young druid? But did he listen to her? No. He listened to the same thing she said after Torren mentioned it. The only difference was, she hadn't thrown the woodgoblin's own words back at him. She flattened her lips, not wanting to get an argument that would delay their leaving. "Do you have everything you need? We should leave as soon as possible."

Rowan held up a twig finger. "Just let me gather—"

Horra flipped the hood back over her thick hair and walked away before he could finish. If he wasn't going to listen to her, then she wasn't going to listen to him. Let him see how it felt.

CHAPTER 25

~ ROWAN ~

Rowan shoved the items he'd saved from the stone building into his newly sewn bag and followed the princess. He wasn't sure what her haste was. But once she was outside of the Weald, he wouldn't be able to sense her and, unfortunately, he needed her now.

Though Merrow had taught him about trolls, he'd not instructed him on the finer nuances of dealing with their contrary personalities. Rowan rushed to follow, sure the girl might leave without him if her attitude were to be an adequate scale of her intent.

He decided the information about female trolls being contrary was underestimated. He rushed out of the Weald, the magic buzzing his bark as he strode through, and made it to her side. Torren trailed him.

As soon as they stepped over the border, icy wind nipped at his glossy leaves. They shriveled against the bitter onslaught. His bark tightened to keep him warm from the unfamiliar temperature. "What season is this?" His voice was uneven, matching the shivers that wracked his bark.

"Winterlude. It snowed on us before we made it to the Weald." Horra bent over and picked up a clawful of the white precipitation. "This is snow."

"I know what snow is." He quivered, his leaves shaking. "I've just never experienced it before. Is it always this cold?"

Snow blanketed the ground up to the princess's booted ankles. It glittered like glimmerbugs. The sun was high, but on its midday descent, so darkness was only a couple of hours away.

"Yes, and no. It's always cold, but not always this cold. Unlike Wintertide, Winterlude is the season change before Springtide. It's usually warmer than this, but winter is not over yet, hence the storm." She glanced around. "Do you know where we are?"

He knew the basic layout of the Wilden Lands. "I've never been outside of the Weald, Princess. Technically, we should either be in the Gnome domain or near the Half-Lands. Both areas flank the Weald to the south. But which one we are nearby is as much your guess as it is mine." Liquid ran down his nose and he sniffed. He put a twig hand up to his face, surprised. "I am leaking."

"Oh, yeah. Noses run in the cold. You're fine." Horra's words whipped away with the wind as she turned from him to study the landscape.

Perhaps they should've camped one more night by the pond. However, the princess insisted they make their way back to the castle immediately.

Rowan couldn't fault that line of reasoning, but possibly it wasn't the best choice, considering the ordeal the trolls had just been through. Rushed decisions, Merrow had instilled in him, were where mistakes were made.

"What do we know of the Gnomes?" Torren glanced around, his eyes darting back and forth.

He answered Torren's question. "Gnomes are earth-dwelling gardeners with an affinity for precious stones and magical bones. They live in dirt huts or in tree houses, always having a garden wherever they live. Thought to be jealous of the trolls for their mining techniques, they are neither friend nor foe to your kind," Rowan recited.

Horra glanced at him, then back at Torren, an emotion he couldn't read on her face. "That's textbook, yes. But I ran into some gnomes in the Deep Barrows on my way home from the Weald. The ones I met were smallish creatures. The man was grumpy, and the woman very welcoming. They don't get along with spriggans, who are trying to bully them out of the Barrows completely. Overall, they seem harmless unless you come upon them after something cuts down their tree."

Rowan eyed her questioningly.

Horra ignored him.

Torren whistled for his horse.

Horra spun around to face him. "*Shhh*! We don't know who's around yet. There could be worqs near here."

Rowan straightened his shoulders and gathered his twig hands in front of him. "Worqs do not have advanced hearing. Though they descended from a long-extinct race of witches, their thick skulls and stunted amygdala do not make them overly sensitive to sound stimuli."

Nimble's head whipped up, and he shied backward away from her.

Horra glanced around, her nostrils flaring. She stiffened. "We should go." She grabbed the lead to her animal and jerked it.

Rowan sensed nothing to be afraid of. This troll princess

was too impulsive and bossy for his liking. "Whatever is the matter—"

"Now, wood boy!" Horra grabbed him around his trunk and lifted him into the air before he could plant his feet in the ground to stop her.

Several items fell out of his bag. "Wait—"

"Hurry, Torren. Get on Nimble," she yelled over her shoulder at the confused male troll.

"Put me down," Rowan insisted, adding a crack to his voice for effect. He needed what had dropped from his sack.

"Not asking you. I'm telling you. We're in danger." She kept running, and he clumsily gathered the remaining items in his bag and fastened it shut. He couldn't see if Torren followed. "Princess, we should stop to assess the best course of action before we act rashly." A few of his cold-shriveled leaves dropped to the ground as she sprinted with him. He bumped up and down on her shoulder in a most rattling way.

Horra swung Rowan up on Nimble's back and jumped on in front of him. The saddle was a tight fit. "Hold on, stick boy."

Torren jumped on behind him, crushing him face first into the back of the princess's head. "*Mmphthl.*"

And they were off and running. Nimble was swift, even though there were three of them on his back. Rowan twisted his head to the side so he could see where they were going, but the wind whipped the burned, red strands of Horra's hair in his face, blocking a clear view.

He reached out to the trees around him, but he was being jostled too much to be successful. They jumped over a log, and just as he made a link and was about to exchange information, the surrounding air stilled. Magic held him suspended.

Horra screamed over her shoulder. Her words, however, came out sluggish and muted, as if spoken through resin. Rowan worked to speak, ask her what she was saying, but nothing came out of his mouth. Not even a wooden click or clack. The air was thick, almost warm, without the wind blowing at him. It would be a relief had he not known it was a bad sign.

The instant Nimble's front hooves touched ground, time sped up, spitting him out of the pause. Cold bit at his bark again. Nimble wobbled but righted quickly. Torren's heavy form left Rowan in a sandwiched death hold. The male troll's claws clutched Horra's clothes tightly, leaving him very little room to move.

"Rowan? Can you hear me?" Horra's voice was higher-pitched than normal. "Torren, can you check on him?"

"*Ynth.*" His tongue had become overlarge in his mouth, as if swollen by water. Nimble darted right, and Torren shifted against him as they turned, jolting him. He swallowed a bit of sap and cleared his throat to try again. "*Ybrth.*"

"What?" Nimble cut Horra's next words off as the animal raised back and jumped over a large ravine. Up they went, floating, and then they landed down hard on the ground.

Behind him, Torren groaned. His grip loosened.

Something had to have injured the male troll. "*Asplenth dwath abrethia.*" Why weren't his words making any sense? He grunted, which sounded normal, so he tried again. "*Undobreva argot naha.*"

Horra sat up and turned slightly. They passed beneath trees, a wild-eyed Nimble still running and dodging back and forth. Smoke wisped from the animal's nostrils. The shadow of the surrounding forest made it harder for Rowan to see Horra's face clearly. "I understand five different languages. But I don't understand a word you're saying."

"*Blashormit prellimia tra.*" Rowan shook his head. The log. It had to be a magical trap. A powerful one. He searched for the information Merrow had taught him. *Kerfudity?* No, that only makes the speaker confused. He was not confused, he just couldn't speak clearly. *Confoundation?* Possible. *Plexity?* Maybe.

"You're not helping me here, wood boy."

Torren leaned heavier and heavier against him. Nimble passed through the forest up onto a road, causing Torren to slump completely against him. Rowan grunted.

"Okay, good. I understand grunts. One grunt for no and two grunts for yes."

He shook his head, but the princess continued on.

"Did something happen to you?"

He sighed and then grunted twice.

"Is it something I can do anything about? I mean, did you break a chunk out of your tongue or something?"

One grunt.

Horra sighed. "Okay. I'm going to get Nimble settled down to a trot and we can figure out what happened. Sit tight, Nimble's pretty shaken up."

There was nothing else he could do, especially with an unconscious Torren leaning heavily against him.

CHAPTER 26

~ ROWAN ~

Rowan was glad for his flexibility, otherwise the troll's weight would've snapped him in two. Horra hadn't helped when she leaned over Nimble's neck as they pounded across a hilly landscape.

They'd already galloped past one small village of earthen homes, trampling through a winter garden. No doubt they'd left behind an angry gnome or two. Another set of mounds showed another village was on the horizon. He witnessed it all while squished against the princess's back.

The gulgoyle darted left, and Torren's weight shifted.

"*Bargulah da ferflin,*" he bellowed, trying to warn Horra, but it was too late. The male troll fell off. His claw caught in Rowan's roots, and they both tumbled to the ground. Rowan's bag dropped as well, falling at his side. Torren rolled on top of him, the weight cracking his trunk. "*Ngahk,*" he cried out.

"Hey!" Horra yelled as the beast thundered away from

them. Her screaming entreaties to stop the animal echoed until there was silence.

Rowan pushed at Torren, to no avail. He slapped at his cheeks without response. The troll was entirely too large a creature to move. Rowan dug his roots into the ground, past the layer of snow and top frost, hoping for some help from the land's magic. This land was well tended, rich in nutrients, and he used what he could reach. If only he had some lifesap, but there wasn't any. His only real hope was Horra regaining control of her gulgoyle and coming back to get them.

The sun slipped ever lower as he used all his strength to consume the resources in the rich ground. With a last grunt, he could reach no more. It swirled in his epidermis. He willed it to absorb and strengthen him. Eyes closed, he concentrated. Nothing of merit happened. The air grew chillier, biting at his bark that wasn't covered by Torren. He was thankful, however, that the male troll was warm enough to compensate.

"Glory be! Are you'n all right?" a deep voice spoke, startling him.

Beneath Torren's prone figure, Rowan couldn't see who spoke. "*Na doprolgs,*" he said, but broke off when he remembered something was wrong with his tongue.

"What'ya think?" one voice whispered.

"I'nt sure. Looks funny t' me," another whispered back.

Rowan took a deep breath, rallying his patience. All at once, the weight was gone as they lifted Torren off and flipped him onto his back. "*Whoosp trunfle da,*" he thanked them.

Two gnomes leaned over him, one a thick-limbed male and the other a hefty female, wearing a thick coat over a dress. The dress was the only way he deduced one was a female, as they were both muscular and wore hats.

"Take'n hand. We'll help you up."

Rowan accepted their extended hands and withdrew his

roots from the snowy ground so he could stand. Hand on his chest, he bowed instead of trying to say thank you.

"Did the bigger'n one break you? Can you talk?" The female asked.

He shook his head. How did one express gratitude outside of the Weald? He considered. There were no flowers, since it was winter. He had no food or drink to offer them. He reached for his bag to see what he had left of what he'd packed.

Inside, he found a small package of seeds that hadn't burned from the fire. He offered them to the couple and bowed his head again.

"Thanks, but you'n need to," the male smiled. "We gnomes practice good cheer. You all right now?"

Rowan noticed the wagon and a small pony, a trit-trot breed by the looks of it, nearby. The gnomes were obviously on their way somewhere when they'd come across him. He motioned with the seeds once more, wishing they'd accept his gratitude.

The woman smiled and gently took the packet. "Thank you kindly."

"Is your other'n okay?" the male asked, his eyebrow raised.

The smoke and fire had made Torren look unkempt, like a swamp troll. Luckily, there was no blood. Torren's chest rattled a bit, creating a sort of snore when he breathed in, now that he lay on his back. Rowan smiled and nodded at the duo. Trolls were the heartiest species in the Wilden Lands. And from what he'd seen of the princess so far, she was a determined creature. She would return. It was a question of when—not if.

The couple waved and got back on their wagon before their pony plodded away, breaking through the unmarked snow. Theirs were the only tracks he saw, revealing this area wasn't well-traveled.

Rowan sunk to the ground, the pretense of strength in his

limbs gone. The sun shone brilliantly as it set and the wind swirled off the coat of white around them, carrying a distinct chill. It was going to be a cold wait.

It was dark when Horra returned.

"I'm sorry. For such a large animal, Nimble gets spooked easily." She dropped to the ground beside Rowan.

Torren was still asleep, or possibly unconscious. Rowan wasn't sure. He'd had basic medical training, and this was beyond what he knew.

"Are you okay?"

"*Pfarblglat*," he frowned at the princess.

"Right. You're a bit tongue-tied, it seems. I've heard of it, but I've never treated it." She nudged Torren's shoulder with her boot. "Torren?"

Rowan shook his head.

"Is he injured?" She knelt down next to the male troll's head.

He shrugged.

"Well, we can't leave you here in the middle of nowhere while the Erlking and the worqs are loose." She glanced around. "Are you okay for the moment while I scan the area?"

He nodded, frustrated he couldn't speak.

"I'll go look for somewhere to hole up in. I don't think my tent is big enough for all of us."

Rowan counted the stars as they came to sparkling life in the sky. He knew all of them in case he was ever sea-bound and needed to navigate. The Star of the West, the biggest star in the sky, winked and glittered like a jewel. Goblin's Toe was just off to the south of that star, and the Will-o'-wisp constellation hung in the east.

Nimble's footfalls rumbled before he could get to all the formations. Horra had tied ropes around the creature's neck and attached a small wheelbarrow to his back. "I found something we can haul Torren in, at least for short distances. And thank the Creature God, I found an abandoned gnome home. It's bigger than the others I've seen."

She led the gulgoyle around until the cart was next to Torren. "Help me roll him in."

Together they heaved and pushed until finally, the male troll lay flat on his stomach on the wooden contraption. Out of breath, Horra took another rope and tied it around him, securing him to the conveyance. She then helped Rowan into the saddle once more.

It wasn't far from the abandoned mound house she'd found. Nimble trailed after the princess as she steered the gulgoyle. The home was enormous, as far as mound houses go. He assumed it must've been for a large family of gnomes.

Snow covered everything, and there was a bald spot with a patch of dead grass showing where the princess must've found the cart.

She tied up Nimble. Rowan helped her dig out a path to the mound house. They then located the door, which wasn't on the front as he thought it might be, but hidden behind the broken trunk of an old tree along the back.

"I don't understand why it's abandoned." Horra unpacked the saddlebags, her green cheeks ruddy from the cold. "I don't think the spriggans bother the gnomes here. I hope they don't come home and find us here. That would be awkward."

Rowan nodded, though she didn't look at him. She was too busy unloading the supplies from the gulgoyle. He sunk his roots in to see what he could find about the house. He caught the essence of violence and danger. The roots cried out about rats who had come and dug into the land, defiling it. Sorrow echoed about the gnomes, the land's faithful caregivers, being driven from their homes.

An owl hooted in the distance. It had spotted a rat, but instead of preying on it, the owl was warning others of its presence.

Horra came back out. "Well, let's just get settled then."

"*Rogarith ardul blat.*" Sap flew from Rowan's lips as he communicated the danger to the princess. He shook his head and waved his hands at her.

"I know it's not as nice as the Weald, but it's all we have. It's not safe to go any farther with Torren out like he is. We'll just stay the night and then reassess in the morning."

The warnings from the roots made his sap flow faster. He tried once again to get the troll princess to stop and listen to him.

But she ignored his befuddled rambling words.

Bushes only feet from him rattled. Loud snuffling sounded. Two golden eyes gleamed in the shadows.

The rat.

Rowan's sap turned to ice in his stem.

CHAPTER 27

~ *HORRA* ~

The wood boy was acting funny, waving at her and drooling. She couldn't understand a word he uttered, thanks to whatever happened to him during their ride.

She shook her head as she searched the gnome's house. Perhaps a good night's rest would ease whatever magic was going on and they could rally in the morning. It would be a tight fit, even if it were a larger than normal gnome mound.

Rowan's unintelligible words reached her ears. Something was agitating him. She needed to get them all settled. Stepping outside, she tripped over a critter the size of a bog badger. She landed on the ground with an "*Oof.*"

"What?" she murmured as her backside hit the ground hard. Though she knew badgers didn't exactly hibernate, it shouldn't be out on such a frosty night. Unless it was rabid.

The creature squeaked as Rowan swung his bag and hit it —a rat, not a badger. Beady eyes glinted gold in the darkness.

It was too large to be natural, and it reminded Horra of the giantized catterwump and the torentula she'd encountered in the giant girl's bedroom.

Horra scrambled to get up, the snow soaking into her clothes and making her already cold claws clumsier. She picked up a stick that leaned against the house. It was someone's walking stick with a metal tip. Taking a wide swing, she caught the rat as it was getting ready to attack Rowan. The stick crunched against the side of the rat's head, knocking it sideways and into a pile of snow she'd scooped. Rushing toward it, she smacked it over and over, her fear and frustration combining in a frenzy of emotion inside her.

A touch on her shoulder startled her. She readied to hit her next target—and stopped. It was a wide-eyed Rowan. "Sorry, Rowan. I panicked." All the heated anger she'd had disappeared like steam in the air. She lowered her arms and let go of the stick. It landed on the ground next to the rat, which lay unmoving on the ground.

Rowan shook her arm. His stubbly eyebrows wrinkled in concern.

"It's okay. I'm fine now." Her heartbeat slowed, and her thoughts cleared. She rubbed her arm, which burned from the assault. "We need to move this thing or we'll never be able to get Torren inside."

Rowan wasn't much help once again. He wasn't very strong yet, with his whip-like arms. Weakness wasn't something she was used to. Trolls were quite stout and capable. But she bit back any snippy remark that came to mind. "I've got it, thanks," she told Rowan, to get him to stop trying to help.

She dragged the critter by its feet, away from the mounded house and over to a woodpile. It was well and truly dead. Horra had no guilt. The critter wouldn't have thought twice about eating them. Too bad Pidge wasn't around to make quick work of it. Horra huffed out a breath and wiped her claws in the snow in case the rat had been sick. An owl fluttered into the tree beside the covered woodpile and hooted at her.

"It attacked us first," she said defensively. However, not all animals were like Pidge and could understand her. "Never mind."

She rolled the cart closer to the doorway and flipped it so Torren was sitting. "Hold the handles for me," she told Rowan. Torren's shoulders were wide, so she had to roll him to the side to get him through the gnome's door. Rowan held his feet and pushed, and together, they slowly got him inside.

"What has he been eating lately? Stones?" She gasped and bent over to catch her breath. As she huffed and puffed, she realized an easier method of moving her classmate beneath her clawed feet.

Taking the kitchen rug, she rolled Torren on it, and then pulled him and the rug across the stone floor and into the next room. She tucked him against the far wall, leaving them some room to move around. The house was cold, though not as cold as the wind had been, and the scent of the dirt walls reminded her of her favorite place: the Conservatory.

"Rowan, can you grab some of the cut wood outside so we can get a fire going?" she asked.

Rowan was already snooping through the shelves and had made a pile of several jars of dried ingredients. Startled, he glanced up at her. "*Dbrtha?*" His shoulders sagged.

She raised a claw dismissively. "I'll get it."

He looked relieved when she trudged back out the round door. The hair on her nape rose uncomfortably, but nothing came out to attack her. Snow fell again, making her hurry.

She took care of Nimble's needs, tying him to a lean-to style barn, then brought wood to the mound house, stacking it outside the door for easy access. She turned from the pile she'd made and glanced back at her pet. He was too large for the mound house and it seemed harsh to leave him outside.

His golden gaze blinked and smoke curled from his nostrils. "I trust you to take care of yourself out here. Turn to stone if the spookies come out to play. Let your fire keep you warm. I'll check with you in the morning."

He twisted in a circle before finding a comfortable spot. She took a small blanket from a hook inside the lean-to and laid it over him.

Snow flurries turned to an all-out storm, pouring from the night sky. She sniffed the air. Her intuition told her the storm would take a while to pass. Thankful they'd found adequate shelter, she closed and bolted the door behind her.

Snow stuck to her booted feet and dampened her smoke-smudged clothes. Her claws were stiff, and she was shivering. Rowan rummaged through jars on the counter in a determined fashion.

First things first, though. She started a fire in the ironstone oven. When finished, and after checking on Torren, she went into the kitchen to see what the woodgoblin was up to.

He'd laid out jars and all kinds of herbs on the counter. The fire lit the room with enough light for her to see clearly with her night sight. Rowan concentrated on the items and hadn't noticed her approaching him.

"What're you doing? Trying to cure your tongue-tied-ness?"

He nodded vigorously, his shriveling leaves rattling.

She gave him a wide smile. This, at least, she was good at. "Well, you're in luck. I'm very good at potions."

CHAPTER 28

~ *HORRA* ~

Rowan frowned at Horra.

She frowned back.

"If you were Woodsly, you'd know how good I am." Her voice held more of a whine to it than she'd meant to let out. "He said I was his top student in several generations."

He still looked unconvinced.

"Whatever. Our woodgoblin maids use different things to loosen their knots and gnarls." She picked through the items. "Snake oil," she said. "It's a great conductor for most potions. And let's see," she murmured as she dug around.

Rowan poked her with a stick finger. He held out the *Physical Physick, a Guide to Magical Ailments* book.

"We can try it, but I wish I'd have brought my Medicinal Curse Book with me. It would have more in-depth cures for hexes and curses, which this seems to be. The Physical Physick only helps common magical maladies."

His expression was one of eagerness, so she flipped

through the contents section. Wind howled outside the door. Snow leaked in at the bottom of the frame, chilling the warmth she'd managed with the fire. "Find something to put across the door while I take a peek at this, please."

He bustled behind her as she studied a few potions.

"*Gnumph.*" The noise came from the inner room where Torren lay. He must finally be waking up.

Horra flipped the book over and went to check on him.

Torren was sitting up and rubbing his head. "What happened? Where are we? Why does my head hurt so much?"

She briefly explained to him what happened after leaving the Weald.

Rowan leaned past Horra with a pouch of powder in his hand. In his other, he carried a small glass of water. She recognized it as a headache powder. Her father used it once in a while. Rowan nodded at Torren, encouraging him.

"What's he doing?"

Horra took them from the woodgoblin, hoping Torren might trust it more if she gave it to him. "It's for your pain. We've been searching for a cure for him. He must've found this medicine in the gnome's supplies."

Torren took the powder and dumped it into the water. He swirled it and drank it in one gulp. He gasped. "That's awful."

"Good. Then I was right about what it was." She patted Rowan on the arm before turning back to Torren. "Can you stand? I could use your help."

"What? Miss Top-of-the-class needs my help?" Torren snorted, laughing.

Horra spun around. "See, Rowan. I told you I'm good at potions." She strode past him and back into the kitchen.

Once there, she studied the ingredients, trying to recall some of the more basic hex reducers and antidotes. None of them came to her tired mind. After knocking over a third jar, she declared, "I'm going to rest for a while. Torren, you're in charge."

———

~ *ROWAN* ~

It turned out the gnomes had a small library with several instruction guides that would be helpful in possibly finding a cure for his condition. Rowan searched their *Guide to Magical Ailments* book for turgidity curses. After an exhaustive search, he'd found nothing.

Then Horra woke up, and he had to wonder at the troll princess's exceptional ability to talk endlessly about anything and everything. He pulled another book out and flipped through the table of contents. Then another. And another.

Though the gnomes were better stocked than he might've otherwise imagined, the cure was still elusive.

It was incomprehensible that he couldn't figure this out. He'd sailed through all of Merrow's instructions. He'd even mastered complicated courses his instructor said had stumped well-seasoned druids. His roots dug into a small section of loose dirt to connect with the roods, but again, only silence. The fire had severed whatever link he'd had. All the knowledge passed down from generation upon generation was gone. And with it, the ability to consult with the roods and possibly have a simple, quick cure.

"Have you heard a thing I've said?" Horra asked him. The wind outside of the door and windows had disappeared, the ceaseless whistling through small gaps silenced as the storm finally died down.

He blinked at her and then shook his head.

A loud sigh followed her frown. "I'm going to get more firewood." She donned the woodencloak once more and opened the door. Sunlight spilled into the dark mound house. A snow barrier came up to her waist, so she had to dig to get out. Cold air replaced the warm atmosphere, and his bark tightened once more.

The door shut, and the light dimmed.

Relief at being left alone was short-lived when Torren woke up. He and Horra had been taking turns resting. Rowan needed little sleep, especially if his roots had access to soil rich in nutrients, which, luckily, the mound floor had.

"Why so glum?" Torren asked as he rubbed a claw through his bedraggled green hair.

"*Spramallo ardeanoth blachrot.*" It was therapy to speak, even if it didn't come out as it was supposed to.

Torren turned his head, curiosity plain on his green face. "I almost understood that. Can you say it again?"

Was that sarcasm? The princess was sarcastic. Perhaps all trolls were. He repeated what he'd just said.

"I understood the word curse, but that's it." Torren leaned back against the far wood counter. "It sounds similar to the worq's dialect, but not quite the same."

That was the first helpful piece of knowledge so far. Rowan nodded his head and gestured for him to go on.

"When the Erlking mesmerized me, I could see but not control some things I was doing and what was happening around me. But there were things I realized afterward that were impossible, or not quite as they seemed in my head. Like, for instance, when the music was playing, it sounded like a song that was familiar. It was one my mother sang to me as a child. I was quite fond of it and it was—" He waved his hands as if trying to grab hold of something. "Comforting. It made me feel safe."

Rowan nodded.

"Anyway, the impossible thing was that I could communicate with the worqs, but it was normal, like I was talking with another troll in my head. I didn't understand that what I was saying was in an unfamiliar language. The Erlking did that somehow with his magic. So, maybe this curse thing isn't what it seems. It's just a trick. Maybe you are making sense, like in a different language such as Worqen."

The silence stretched as Rowan considered his words. They made sense, but what could that mean? What type of dark magic had befallen him?

He shook his head. He hadn't realized being out in the real Wilden Lands was going to be so difficult.

CHAPTER 29

~ ROWAN ~

After a lengthy pause where Rowan stood deep in consideration, Torren glanced around. "Where'd Horra go?"

Rowan pointed to the door where snow melted into the dirt ground, leaving it a muddy mess.

"I think I'll go help her and check on Nimble."

Rowan didn't pay attention as Torren strode outside. His mind was on the possibilities of what he'd told him. Could he just be speaking another language? It all sounded right in his head when he went to speak. The magic had broken something between his thoughts and his words.

He focused on considering the possibilities and trying to figure out which curse it could be if it weren't *purfidity*. Numerous curses and hexes filed through his mind as he discounted them one by one. As a whole, his knowledge was complete. However, Woodsly's rood had assured him that there were far more hidden elven magics than any of them knew or understood.

"I sensed it, you know."

Rowan started at the sudden sound of the princess's voice. He became aware of the sound of Torren's grunts while he started a fire in the next room.

Horra had changed from her drab, smoke-stained tunic and pants to a clean sheet, possibly a gnome's bedsheet. A large pot of water simmered on the stove behind him. "That magic that caused you to talk funny. It was like the moment I met Kryk after I stumbled out of the poisoned forest. Like we were in a bubble and time stopped around us. But this energy was focused on you, maybe Torren too. It didn't do anything to me."

Rowan wouldn't have described it exactly that way, but he nodded.

"What kind of magic is that—the ability to stop every-thing? It can't be black magic if a rood did it, right?"

"No." He'd meant to grunt once, but the word came out. The sap in his bark rushed from his crown to his rootling feet. Had he broken the curse?

A wide-eyed Horra stood up. "What'd you just say?"

"*Mrflbg.*" Rowan shook his leaves in frustration. "*Mrflbg.*"

She walked up to him and opened his mouth. Her claws pinched at his bark. He pulled away from her, but he had unconsciously rooted himself in the dirt floor while he'd been deep in thought. He jerked backward, but she poked at his tongue, then scratched around his cheeks with her clawnails. "Say *ah.*"

He gurgled out a sound that turned to a choke at the end as her clawed nail invaded his throat.

Horra let him go. "Are those viny things in the back of your throat supposed to be tied like a knot?"

He grunted three times because he was unsure. Though he knew many things, this was not one of them. Merrow slanted his instruction more toward the scholarly side. Not medical. He really only had a basic understanding of his own body.

She *tsked*. "I don't know how you talk with all that tangled stickage in your throat. No wonder Woodsly was always so clackety sounding and he cleared his throat hundreds of times."

Merrow never seemed to have an issue with that, and neither had he until now, so Rowan didn't respond.

It convinced him whatever happened wasn't *purfidity*, however. Which left Torren's hypothesis. He was speaking another language.

Which language could it be, then? And why would the Erlking leave a trap like that out in the middle of the Wilden Lands? What could he possibly gain by setting a curse that made it impossible for individuals to communicate?

On the surface, it made little sense other than to confuse people. He had to wonder how many others would fall into one of the Erlking's traps. There was much to consider.

"The rat is gone." Horra mentioned as she dug through the supplies once more, looking for her and Torren's next meal.

Her glance toward him held a meaning that didn't translate. He arched his shoulders at her.

"It means that something bigger ate it or it wasn't actually dead like I thought. Rats can burrow easily into mound houses, especially a rat as big as that one. And rats run in mischiefs, they're not solitary animals." At his confused furrow, she explained. "A group of rats is called a mischief. I don't think we're safe here any longer. As soon as my clothes are dry, we're leaving."

CHAPTER 30

~ HORRA ~

Horra left some coins on the counter to compensate for the food and supplies they used while they holed up in the gnome mound house. She shut the door tight and left some wood inside for the gnomes whenever they returned.

"So, I believe we need to go this direction through the Halflands." She held her trusty compass in her claw. It pointed north, behind the mound house and off to their left. They were farther south than she realized, causing her a rush of panic. It would take a couple of days to return to Oddar and her castle. If she'd learned anything on her last expedition, it was that there were many things that could go wrong if one wasn't careful.

"Then let's get going. The days haven't grown long enough to dawdle." Torren stuffed the last of their belongings in the gulgoyle's saddlebags, cinching them tightly. He patted his side, where his dagger and sheath hooked to his belt. "Though the worqs are out during the day now, it's still better to camp at night. Did you pack your tent?"

Horra's heart sank, remembering how she'd used it during the first snowstorm of the Wintertide—a much worse storm than the previous eve's was. "I packed a new tent, yes. I pretty much destroyed my last ten on my first trip through the Wilden Lands." She donned the woodencloak and climbed upon her pet. "You next, Rowan."

The druid woodgoblin had been quiet since she announced they were leaving. She supposed his first ride had been eventful enough to make him nervous.

Torren helped him up before climbing on himself. With a flick of the reins, they were off.

Nimble was a warm comfort against the bitter wind. Though the storm had left, and snow was usually a good insulator, the air held an unsettling bite to it. "Is it me or does something feel off?" she asked the other two.

Rowan muttered something unintelligible, his hands clutching her jacket tighter.

"I sense it, too," came Torren's reply.

"Keep your eyes open. Yell if something catches your instincts wrong." Several thoughts zipped through her mind. Getting back to the castle. Telling her father what happened. Figuring out how they would go about finding Murda. Her eyes were wide, though her mind spun.

They traveled the countryside, having no real gauge for roads or pathways except for fences. She checked her compass several times, something she wished she'd done when they first left the Weald, to keep them on track.

Several hours passed by without speaking, and she was sure they were getting to the edge of the Halflands by the time the sun lowered in the sky. She skirted the small villages so no one would see or recognize them.

Nimble trembled beneath them.

"What is it, boy?" she whispered. Though the woodencloak hid her, she wasn't sure what she looked like riding on back of a gulgoyle. Rowan was recognizable as a woodgoblin, not something that was unusual here. But Torren, being a troll, and a large one at that, would catch anyone's attention.

Smoke curled from her pet's nostrils.

A shadow caught the edge of her sight. But when she turned her head, there was nothing but a pristine landscape. However, she knew when to trust her gut. "Hold on, guys. I'm changing course."

Nimble followed her nudge to the left and down into a gully. She'd gotten a bit too comfortable traveling in the open. Perhaps she would evade whoever or whatever might be hiding.

Horra could make out the chitters and squeaks of rats. Distinct sliding sounds of the critters following them into the ravine sent her pulse racing.

"C'mon, boy. You are part gully dragon. Let's lose these pests." She encouraged Nimble. Rats, though, were intelligent enough to sniff them out and quite able to follow them.

"Torren? Can you take over leading Nimble? I'm going to cause a distraction. Race for another mile or two and hide. I'll come find you." She took one of Rowan's clinging hands and placed the leather reins in them. "Pass these back."

Before anyone could disagree with her, she jumped down and into the snow.

After the warmth of the gulgoyle, the snow was shocking against her body. She fell and then slid with her claws over her head until she stopped next to an evergreen tree. Grabbing the woodencloak, she quickly arranged it so it covered all of her, including her thick curls. Spotting an evergreen, she climbed up the tree and dug out her survival knife with a ridged blade.

Her claws were already stiff as she sawed quickly, the chittering noises of the rats getting closer. Her arms burned as she chopped until finally a big limb fell, obscuring the path. She scooted around to the other side and started on another limb.

The first rat, a dark one the size of a swamp piglet, ran headlong into the first limb. Her second limb dropped just as it climbed over the first limb. That one toppled on its head, stopping it and two others which followed it into the first limb.

Rat one sniffed the air.

Horra sat still as she could, holding tight to the evergreen trunk and praying silently for the woodencloak to work. A gust of wind rushed across them, bowing her tree. It was the break she needed. The wind blew her scent away from the critters.

Two more of the rats joined the three already blocked by the evergreen branch. With a few squeaks, they rallied and darted around the limb, but they headed in the wrong direction once they got around her barrier.

She waited for a few more minutes, watching as the group disappeared deeper into the small forest before she climbed down.

Once on the ground, she headed the correct direction.

Her footsteps halted as a snarl came from behind her.

CHAPTER 31

~ *HORRA* ~

Horra turned and faced the largest rat yet. It was the size of a sewer trog and came up to her knees. The critter was a dark brown against the snow and the green limbs. She grabbed her knife and held it in front of her in a ready position.

The rat hissed, the gold of its eyes reflecting in the dim light. It rose on its back feet, the paws on it speckled pink and black. Instead of attacking, it sniffed the air.

Horra took a step backward into the evergreen bough, ready for an attack. However, it dropped and snuffled against the snow. And then it hit her—she was wearing the wooden-cloak. She relaxed but kept an alert watch on the rat.

After nosing around the stamped down area, the rat gave up and headed around the limb. Horra waited for it to leave, which it did slowly. Once it was out of earshot and lost in the deep snow, she made her way in the direction she'd seen Nimble steer her two companions.

It took several minutes to find them. The wind covered their tracks with loose snow as it blew. Nimble's rumbling, smoke-filled greeting alerted the other two to her approach. Torren's head swiveled around, trying to locate her. She waited until she was a few feet away before lowering the hood, just in case.

"There you are. How'd it go? Are you all right?" Worry lines creased Torren's green forehead. Frost coated his thick eyebrows.

"I'm fine. It was close, though. Good thing I still have the woodencloak or I'd be rat bait." She shook the snow out of her cloak and climbed up the rope to get on the gulgoyle.

Torren, who had been sitting in her spot at the front of the saddle, shifted back to his spot behind Rowan. The woodgoblin's leaves had all turned brown and rattled against his bark. She wasn't sure what that meant, but she knew his stem was thin and his bark thinner still. He needed to get somewhere where he could warm up.

"Sorry it took so long. There was a spotter rat at the end of the pack. He was pretty big, and he lingered to sniff around a bit."

"I always knew rats were intelligent, but doesn't it seem strange that they're out in packs hunting like that?" Torren scanned the horizon. Gray shadows of mountains in the distance blended into the darkening landscape.

"I recall the shopkeepers complaining about infestations the day the fairies came to Oddar. I'm thinking it wasn't a coincidence." What she didn't say, and what she now believed as more suspicious, were the rats she'd run into in the passageway that day. However, she couldn't admit to the hidden space, or she'd break the royal blessing on it.

She dug around in her pants pocket and took out the compass. "We're farther west than we ought to be. If you look that way, you can see the dwarf mountains. We should probably head there to set up camp."

"But that's so far off course. And dwarfs are not friendly. How long would it take to get back to the castle if—and that's a big if—we get to the mountains? Then we don't get caught by the dwarfs and can find a place to camp. And then finally we leave first thing in the morning?" Torren asked in a rush, frustration clear in his tone.

"It's going to take a couple of days, regardless. And that's if we don't have any other run-ins with worqs or rats." Horra grasped the leather straps and snapped them. Nimble belched and moved, jerking them as he did so. "At least we have a chance at survival. What I'm worried about is what's happening to Murda. Will we find her in time, or has she become the worq's next meal?"

Their brisk pace allowed them to reach the foot of the mountains in good time. The trees grew sporadically, as she remembered from her last jaunt through them. Horra stopped Nimble and slid off. "I think these will be safe. They're too small for the dwarfs to occupy. We just need to find a cave or someplace sheltered along the edge. Rowan stay here on Nimble. He'll keep you warmer than coming with us. Torren, come with me and help find a solid spot to camp."

Rowan muttered some gibberish, his branch arm raised in protest.

"We won't go far, I promise." Horra untied her knapsack from the gulgoyle's belt and shrugged it on.

Torren jumped down, landing in the snow and sending some of it flying with the breeze. He untied his pack and fell into step beside her.

They walked for a short distance, following the outline of

the rock base. "What do you think of Rowan?" he asked quietly when they were out of range for the druid to hear.

"Like you said, he's an informapedia. Which isn't a terrible thing. We've both had loads of schooling on many subjects. But the tongue-tied thing and his inexperience will present the biggest challenges we've ever had to deal with. It's beyond anything Woodsly taught us." She stopped and let out a deep breath that fogged in the air. "It seems like the Wilden Lands have turned upside down, and I'm not prepared for it."

Torren's face was grim. "I get it. Without Da—" he shook his head. "Nothing will ever be the same for me again."

Horra walked on. There wasn't anything she could say that would make it easier for him. Her world had changed when her mother died three years ago, and it had never been the same. Nothing anyone said would change that.

"Horra." Torren pointed to a cleft in the rock. It was beneath a flat rock ceiling and though there was snow, it wasn't piled deep.

"Go back and get Rowan and Nimble. We can tie the gulgoyle to one of these trees for the night. I'll clear us a space."

By the time Torren returned with Nimble and Rowan, she had the ground cleared of debris, had paced and measured the space, and had dug her tent out of her pack.

Rowan was visibly shaking, ice forming on the crown of branches on his head. His bark was no longer a grayish-brown, but a pale gray.

She didn't want to admit it, but Torren was faster at setting up tents than she ever was. "Torren, can you set up the tents, face to face, so we can open them into each other? It should help conceal us and protect us from anything that might come across us in the night. I'll go get some rocks and sticks to start a fire. And get wood boy there out of the wind."

It was harder than she liked to find what she needed. The snow was deep, and she sank to her knees in the stuff. She walked a semi-circle around their campsite so she didn't get lost. The moon was bright in the sky, however, making it at least easy to see.

Noises broke the stillness, halting Horra's search. She stood waiting, stock still.

Several figures appeared, cresting a small incline far enough away. She couldn't tell who or what they were.

As Horra waited, notes of music tinkled and tickled her hide. Without thinking, she slapped her claws over her ears. Her movements went unnoticed, however, as a band of several creatures holding lanterns walked in a strange formation, their faces up, not down, to watch for obstacles in their way. They wore no expression, just walked straight-forward through the frigid night. Their footsteps kept time to the notes of the music that emanated from nowhere—no one held any instruments that she could see.

She glanced back at their campsite and then back at the group. They all appeared to be young, albeit different creatures. There were a few goblin children, some hobgoblin youngsters, a dwarf boy, and was that an ogre girl? There was a dozen in all.

"Oh, vinegar and beans!" she whispered into the cloak as she turned to follow the last child, claws over her ears, to see where in the Wilden Lands they were going.

CHAPTER 32

~ HORRA ~

Horra didn't want to go far, but the group followed the mountain along its base. Her arms grew weary from holding them to her ears, but she didn't dare put them down. Just when she was about ready to give up and head back to their campsite, the group deviated from their path.

Lined two by two, they turn and walked toward the stone wall.

They're going to walk straight into the mountain! Hidden behind a large boulder, some trees and part of the mountain's side blocked her view.

Horra held back a gasp when the first two stepped and then disappeared. The others followed without flinching, each gone the moment they stepped up to the mountainside.

What in the name of dragon's fire was going on?

Horra slowly moved around the trees and past a portion of

the rock wall to the spot they vanished. She kept the hood on the cloak clasped tightly and glanced right and then left. With a racing heart, she made to follow them and ran headlong into the hard rock.

She jerked backward, her nose throbbing. Her sniff sent a spear of pain through her nasal cavity. Tears stung her eyes. Great! She broke her nose.

The rock was solid as she ran a claw across the mirror-type surface. For a moment, she'd thought the side might be like her tent, a type of magical camouflage. However, running her claw across the stone assured her that wasn't the case.

"How?" she whispered.

She stepped away and then returned to search the stone. Was there some kind of release, like in the passages? She ran her claws over every inch of the mountainside along a great swath of the base. Nothing happened.

Horra walked around the area and tried several things with no success. The mountain was a mountain, not some illusion or trap door. By the time she gave up, she wondered if she had truly seen the children at all. Shoulders hunched against the cold, she traced her way back to the cleft, picking up some sticks and stones as she went.

"Not that way," Torren's grumbles echoed in the still night air. "Hold it like this."

She hurried to get to them so she could shush them. For as long as she was gone, they had only put up one tent.

"What're you guys doing?" she quietly admonished them while dumping her wood and stones. She yanked her hood down.

"Finally, you return. Where have you been?" Anger coated Torren's words. The heated glance he sent Rowan's way showed the source of his annoyance.

Rowan held the tent pole at the exact wrong angle that it needed to be, a stubborn tilt to his wooden head.

"Be quiet, you dunkle-heads!" She hissed at both of them and rushed over to help with the second tent, knocking Rowan out of the way. She pulled it taut so Torren could set his side.

"Why? There aren't any rats in sight." Torren hammered the peg into the hard rock, the ping of the metal on metal piercing her ears.

"No, but something else is out there. There were strange children who walked straight into the mountain. We're not alone."

That got Torren's attention. "What do you mean, they walked *into* the mountain?" He stared at her, his hammer up in the air, stilled mid-strike.

"Just that. They walked right into the stone side." She pointed to her nose. "Something I couldn't do no matter what I tried."

A grin flickered across his lips. His arm dropped to his side. He coughed and the teasing look vanished, but not before she got a glimpse of his laughter.

"It's not funny." She tugged on the tent pole, wanting to forget the whole thing. "I might've broken my nose."

"It's a little funny. What'd you do? Try to follow them and walk into the rock wall?" He worked to fit the other pole, hammering less loudly than before.

"It doesn't matter. What matters is there was strange music accompanying them. It was like they were in a trance or something. I followed them up the side of the mountain until they just disappeared."

Finished setting that pole, he came around to her side. The tent spanned the space of the cleft with only a narrow path on each side to walk by. Nothing big would get around them.

Torren barely had room to get his broad shoulders between the walls and the sides of the tent.

Torren stood over her, a serious expression on his face. "You think it has something to do with the Erlking?"

"I know it does. And their presence here doesn't make it safe. I'm also curious about how they did it and where they went. Why are they here? You know how many people have gone missing. Maybe this is part of what's happening to everyone."

Torren cleared his throat. "Then we need to rescue them. We can't let what happened to Da happen to anyone else." His voice was raw, filled with emotion.

She moved so he could set the last two poles. "That's why I'm so late getting back. I had to see if I could figure it out."

Torren hammered the third peg into the ground and moved to the last one. "But you couldn't?"

She shook her head, which was aching now. Her nose was tender as she tested the spot she'd injured. "Maybe we'll see something I missed in the sunlight. For now, I'm exhausted. We need to get some rest."

"I don't know if I'll be able to sleep much after what you've just told me." Torren finished setting the final peg and stood to face her. "If you would've told me a year ago that the Wilden Lands were a dangerous place, I would've laughed at you."

Horra didn't say so, but she agreed with him.

It was getting more dangerous by the day.

CHAPTER 33

~ ROWAN ~

L oud snoring reverberated inside the tent, impeding Rowan's meditative state. Once the troll duo had settled for the night, and despite the male's insistence he wouldn't sleep, they'd both dozed off quickly. Thus began their symphony of rattling noise-making.

Because the male was so much bigger than the female, they put Rowan inside the princess's tent to rest. Except he didn't need to rest. The nutrients from the gnome's mound were enough to suffice him for another day or so. Unless something else befell him.

Rowan stretched his roots across the rocky ground, extracting the few nutrients it provided. He'd need to transfer the sugars he had stored to maintain his energy, which he was finding wasn't easy in the cold weather. And so far, trouble plagued the trolls, and it served him well to be prepared.

Horra moaned and turned in her sleep, her arm flopping

over his legs uncomfortably. Her bush of red hair fanned out like a patch of vines.

He extracted his limbs slowly and quietly unzipped the tent. There would be no respite inside the tent, even if it were warmer than the outdoors. The woodencloak hung by the opening, so he grabbed it, shrugging it on as he made a quiet departure, zipping the tent up behind him.

A silvery moon glittered atop the white drifts and the tufts on the trees. It wasn't hard to find a spot clear enough for him to recline. He stayed beneath the stony ceiling at the end of the outer tent so that the wind wouldn't make him shiver.

Again, he extended his roots in search of communication or information. The trees around him, except for the evergreens and firs, were dormant. It was to be expected, but it made him long for his home. The flora had always been so alive, the constant hum of messages sent back and forth, a rush in his mind. Here it was mostly soundless. He was unused to the silence, and it put him on edge.

Especially since he couldn't even communicate with the two living beings he should be able to speak with.

He flicked a shard of rock. It bounced off the cleft wall and landed dully in the snow. Nimble rumbled from his spot beneath a tree. He opened one golden eye and sent out an annoyed puff of smoke. The gulgoyle wrapped his tail around his massive body and closed his eye.

A crystalline note drifted on the breeze. One single, beautiful tone that tingled the veins on his few remaining leaves. The sensation spread past his sapwood and into his heartwood. The nutrients he'd ingested flushed up his trunk to his crown in a dizzying rush.

What was this incredible sound?

Rowan crawled to the edge of the cleft and poked his head outside the shelter. Something in the distance glowed ethereally. As he grew closer, the shape became clearer. His eyes widened.

It was a dove tree, an extinct elven tree which used to grow among the frozen northlands. Round, white flowers ending in a crisp tip covered its canopy. The longer he gazed upon it, the more distinct the note became, changing into a symphony of delightful sound.

It was magnificent and welcoming. A voice like chimes on the wind beckoned him to come to it. That thought crowded everything else in his mind until there was nothing else. Rowan stepped out from the shelter of the cleft, the wooden-cloak falling to the ground behind him.

Nimble let out a guttural groan. Rowan's head swung toward the animal.

The note hit a crescendo, and he turned from the beast to look back at the incredible, dazzling ghost tree. Nothing else needed his attention. With a surety his branches hadn't had since he'd unrooted, he walked toward the exquisite tree, his arms outstretched and a wide smile on his face.

~ HORRA ~

Horra awoke with a start, her heart racing and sweat soaking her tunic. She looked around groggily, trying to recall where she was. Her sleep had been deep and troubled. Visions of worqs and rats teaming up to take her down filled her mind with nightmarish images.

"It was just a dream." She panted, clutching a claw to her chest. The blanket was suffocating, so she tossed it aside and then remembered she wasn't the only one in the tent. "Rowan?"

No answer.

Air inside the tent was frigid, freezing off the heat from her damp clothes immediately. Everything inside her wanted to return to the warmth of the sleeping bag, but some instinct made her uneasy. Why wasn't Rowan answering her? If he were merely outside the tent, he should still hear her.

"Blast you, stick boy," she muttered as she rolled over to get her boots and coat.

Her boots were there, but the woodencloak was not.

"What—" She hurried to unzip the tent and stuck her head out of the opening. Despite it being cold inside the tent, the chill didn't compare to the icy temperature outside. Shivering, she scanned the area to her right and then the left. There, a couple of feet beyond the end of her tent lay her woodencloak.

But Rowan was nowhere to be seen.

She tucked herself back inside the tent and jammed her clawed feet inside the boots. Without a jacket, she unzipped the other tent, startling Torren. He jerked upright, screaming.

A quick glance verified the woodgoblin druid wasn't there. "Sorry, I was looking for Rowan. I thought maybe he decided to switch tents."

Torren scratched his head. "What do you mean, switched tents? He's not in your tent?" He yawned wide enough for a piskie to get swallowed whole. Even though they'd just set up their shelters, the inside of Torren's reeked of male stinky feet.

Horra scrunched her nose. "If he was, I wouldn't have rudely invaded your space." She yanked his tent opening over her head and re-zipped it. With a heavy sigh, she got out of hers and slipped along the sides to pick up the woodencloak. It had a bit of snow covering it, either from the wind or from being dropped in the snow. But thankfully, it was much warmer than having no coat at all.

"Rowan?" she called out, quietly at first. But when she got no answer, she yelled.

"What're you doing?" Torren arrived at her side, his coat and boots now on.

"I'm trying to find our friend. You know, the only one who can save the Wilden Lands from the Erlking? He's missing, and I found my woodencloak outside of my tent."

Torren's eyes narrowed as he scanned the area. "Where would he have gone? It's not like he has to go to the bathroom like other creatures."

"Yeah, I know. It's one of the few things about him I like."

Nimble rumbled from beneath the tree she'd tied him to. He was alert, and his golden gaze stuck to a spot in the distance.

"What is it boy?" she spoke to him gently.

Nimble pulled at the rope holding him captive to the tree.

"I think he knows where Rowan went." She hoped her guess was true. However, it wasn't like her pet to act like a hound.

"Is that possible?" Torren rubbed his face. He still looked exhausted, and the sun was barely lightening the night sky on the horizon.

"I don't know, but we have to at least try. We can't lose Wilden Land's only hope of survival. And I won't lose another creature that I care about to the Erlking."

CHAPTER 34

~ HORRA ~

Horra and Torren left the tents as they were, grabbing whatever supplies they'd taken from Nimble the night before—which weren't many since they had all been tired. Horra climbed up onto the gulgoyle, reaching down and realizing Torren needed no help getting up onto the animal.

"Sorry, habit," she bit out, adrenaline and fear mixing in an odd rush of emotions.

"It's okay. Let's just get going so I can get some breakfast." Torren settled behind her. Nimble needed little encouragement. As soon as she untied the rope, his rigid stance took off in the direction he had been staring.

Horra had to grab hold of the pommel while Torren jerked, caught her, and then righted himself.

"I take it back. Nimble must know where Rowan went." Torren's voice was lost in their rush and the wind.

She let Nimble have the lead, letting him go where his instincts told him. They pounded along the mountainside, almost in the same pattern she'd had the night before, while following the mesmerized children.

The sun lightened the sky, night giving way to morning. It was cold enough for the moisture to glitter on the branches and snowbanks—like diamonds and pale aquamarines when the sun finally filled the sky.

No footsteps marred the pristine land, no paths, or any signs of creatures moving through the thick cover of snow. She recalled, however, when she'd worn the woodencloak in the early winter that she'd left no trail. Obviously, it meant some kind of magic was in play to keep any traces of their movement from showing.

"What do you think happened to him?" Torren asked.

Horra shrugged. Her initial thought was that he couldn't sleep—if woodgoblin druids slept at all—and got lost. However, there'd been no sign of him.

"You don't think the Erlking has anything to do with it, do you?"

Horra wondered if Torren realized he now had her in a death clutch. Luckily, it was only the woodencloak he held on to. However, she worried he was reliving his father's disappearance. "It could be anything. Maybe wood boy saw something interesting and simply chased after it. He'll tell us all about it when we find him. Or, well. He can't talk right now. When we find the cure for him, he can tell us all about it."

She was fumbling, trying not to overstep or upset her classmate. He'd gone through too much with his father's disappearance and then with them finding him like they had. The ordeal had been dreadful for her. It must be a hundred times worse for him.

Suddenly, Nimble stopped, throwing Torren into her and

jamming the pommel into her gut. "Buckets, Nimble! A little warning next time."

Torren slid off, and Horra followed him. Nimble sat alert, his smoking nose pointed at the mountain.

Torren glanced around. "Is this the place from last night?"

"Maybe? I don't know. It all looks the same now in the sunlight. And it took me longer to get here than it did Nimble, so I can't be sure." She moved around, noting that once again her movements seem to slide right through the snow while Torren tore it up as he moved.

"Let's check the side of the mountain." She went over and ran her claw across the frosted rock. Torren fell into step beside her and took her left side, traveling away from her.

They each tested the gray stone from the ground to where they could reach on their clawtips. Nimble stayed in the same spot, unmoving. She and Torren had gone way past where the gulgoyle sat on guard.

They must be missing something. "If I were a secret latch, where would I be?"

"Have a lot of experience with them?" Torren snorted his laughter.

She wanted to throw the fact she'd used hidden latches since she was a young troll in his face, but she stopped herself. Her mother had been insistent that only royal women trolls should know about their secret passage. So, she kept her lips pinched tightly and said nothing.

However, she went back to where she started and searched the foliage along the edge of the mountain. Torren joined her, and they made quick work of shuffling around the base.

Horra punched her claws to her hips. "There's got to be something. Those children walked right into the mountainside. There must be some way for them to do that."

Nimble yawned, and fire flew out of his mouth, igniting a small bush growing from a ridge on the mountain.

"You're doing it, Nimble! You're making fire." Horra stepped over to pat her pet's head.

"Horra! Look." Torren's words halted her.

There, where smoke wafted from the singed bush, was a metal rod stuck into the stone.

"What is that?" She squinted to get a better look.

It was too far up for her to reach. "Torren, see if you can move it."

He strode past her to check. However, even stretched on his clawtips, he couldn't reach it.

"Come, Nimble. Right here, boy," she crooned to the gulgoyle.

Nimble came closer, and she guided the animal to where the saddle would be right next to the handle, then she climbed upon his back.

Once there, she stepped onto the saddle to get a little closer.

"Be careful." Torren called out, startling her.

"I was being careful," she grumbled and re-situated herself. "Hold steady, boy." The rod was within reach now, and she leaned over and pulled on the lever.

The mountainside opened silently.

Tinkling music trickled out of the mountainous depths. A path ran from where the wall opened into the mountain, the sides chiseled as if done on purpose. On the trail, there were traces of footfalls in the dust. Several footfalls.

Chills raced across Horra's hide.

Horra patted Nimble's side. "You did it! Good boy." She slid off him and landed beside Torren.

"Wow," he said, his eyes wide as goblets. "I believed you, really, I did. But this is—"

"Impossible. Yeah, I know." Horra thanked the Creature God for putting the levers in the castle to the secret passageway. Even though Torren spotted it, she had known to look for them. "Let's find Rowan."

She made to move, but Torren stopped her with a claw on her shoulder. It held her tight. "What happens after we go in? I mean, does the wall shut and lock us in?"

Horra faced him. "I don't know. It seems likely since the wall was in place after they all walked in. I wasn't far behind them."

Eyes wide with panic, he turned to look down at her. "Maybe one of us should stay out here in case it does." His breathing grew heavier, a sure sign of a panic attack.

"I'll go. You sit here and wait for me to return." She pulled the hood over her head. "I have the woodencloak. I'll be safe."

"But you're the princess. If something happens to you, your father will flog me." Torren's voice edged higher.

She put a reassuring claw on his arm. "Torren. I am the princess. It is my responsibility to keep you and Rowan safe. Sit tight. You've always wanted to rescue me just to prove you're better at something than I am. Maybe this will be your chance."

Her humor made the pinched look on his face relax somewhat. But he didn't laugh as she intended. "Just sit tight. I'll be back as soon as I find Rowan, okay? Keep Nimble safe. Maybe take him somewhere close by so you can keep watch on the doorway but at a safe distance."

Torren shook his head at that.

She didn't wait to see if he followed her instructions. Fisting her claws, she strode purposefully into the mountain.

The door closed without a sound behind her.

CHAPTER 35

~ ROWAN ~

Rowan awoke in a dark, dank place. Water dripped from somewhere as he strove to gather his thoughts, but his mind was hazy. Despite the muggy air, his roots were tight with dryness and his tongue seemed waterlogged along where he would swallow.

It was too dark to see well, so when he got up, he bumped his crown on something—a ceiling, perhaps? *"Brfhof."* He wondered aloud at what time it was, but for some reason, his words came out wrong.

"Gerspicha." He called out for Merrow just as incoherently, and received no answer. No animals startled or shifted around. All was silent.

Bent over, Rowan let his stiff roots search out possible obstructions, finding rocks and debris everywhere. He couldn't dig into the ground. Was it rock? It had to be. There was no soil here for him to gather energy and clear his mind.

Rowan shook his head, willing the blurriness away. He sat

back down to wait for the grogginess to ease. Woodgoblin druids didn't usually sleep for they gathered whatever nutrients from their surroundings. Why was it that he seemed to have just woken up? Why wasn't there any kind of soil or nutrient source here? The questions came and then wisped away like smoke in the wind.

Sleep wouldn't make his mind as clouded as it currently was. There were many things that could have put him in this state. He considered the more obvious reasons first: poison, injury, or—

The rest of his thoughts wouldn't come together. This place was the opposite of the Weald. It gave him no reassurance or comfort. There was no hint of flora around him, so it must be somewhere plants didn't normally grow. Several places fit that description, but the words were frustratingly evasive.

He closed his eyes to seek any kind of metaphysical link to any living thing near him. It wasn't something he'd ever done before. His roots always garnered information and knowledge. They'd never failed him until now. Noises in the distance— something hitting the rock or subtle shuffling sounds—echoed against the hard surface, reached his ears.

But nothing gave him any idea of where he was, what day it was, or why he was here.

Faint notes of music drifted to him, making him tired. He yawned, almost choking on the lump in the back of his throat. He curled up on the hard ground, closed his eyes again, and fell into the darkness as sleep overcame him.

The next time he awoke, he was shivering. He wished his bark provided better protection against the unwanted temperature. The Weald had spoiled him with its unchanging atmosphere. Sitting up, he considered where he could be.

His voice was rickety when he called out for Merrow. His

instructor didn't respond. Had Rowan fallen into some sort of hole? He shifted his roots to get a grasp of where he was. He found only rock, dust, and musty air.

Nothing he did answered his questions, and his mind had grown uncharacteristically dim. It took much of his energy to stay warm enough not to knock his limbs together and create friction enough for a fire.

Fire, he knew, was dangerous. Very dangerous. It burned and destroyed.

Images of a forest aflame flickered in his mind and then was gone. "*Despargo ami nobreth.*" What was happening?

Despite his slim build, his limbs were heavy, weighted down. It was too much effort to try to rise and move. He closed his eyes and fell back into the blissful nothingness of sleep.

~ *HORRA* ~

The mountain was much like any other she had been in. Dust and rocks littered the ground, water dripped somewhere, and the air was stale, if not a bit on the musty side. Horra pulled the hood of her woodencloak over her head. "Mustn't run into any dwarfs," she whispered, recalling her last traipse through the lower Iron Mountains when she'd left the castle and had gotten lost.

She'd had Pidge to keep her company then. Though she wouldn't want to put her pet pudge wudgie in any danger, it would be nice to have Pidge here to keep her company. Sighing, she charged on ahead. She dared not call out, so she kept a keen ear out for any noises.

Luckily, her vision wasn't bad, even though it was dark inside the mountain fortress. She moved around boulders sticking out along her path or large rocks that littered the floor. She was grateful there were no shards of kobold metal, stalagmites, or stalactites to dodge.

Methodically, she moved from the doorway left along the carved-out wall. When she came to a dead-end, she backed farther out. How far could the wood boy get? He'd been slow moving before. Even running for his life had been a monumentally slug-like slow that had brought out the worse impatience in her.

A rock rattled in the distance, and Horra froze in place. When nothing else happened after a long time—probably a minute—she continued on. Her boot connected with a rise in the floor, almost tripping her.

This would take forever! Being more careful, she made her way to the other side of the inside wall and worked back to the right of the doorway. She worked silently for several minutes, focusing on the ground and for any sounds.

Muted rattling caught her attention—somewhere to the right and far away. She worked toward the sound, finding the area rockier and rougher.

Squeaking, followed closely by the thwapping of wings, startled her. Bats. Dodging them, she knocked her knee against the rocky floor. Her leg throbbed with the rapid beat of her heart. "Vinegar and beans!" she exclaimed and then slammed her lips shut. Her movements must've disturbed them. She'd need to be more careful.

Hora stood monument still until she decided she hadn't given herself away, resuming her movement toward the faint vibration.

After what seemed like ages, she worked around a bend to a section that sloped down. Small rocks and debris rolled with each footstep she made, putting her on edge. Even with the woodencloak hiding her, that kind of noise could betray her position. Her surroundings grew darker, if that were possible. She clung to one wall, unsure if the path would become steeper.

Her foot caught something, and she stopped.

The soft rattling changed to something akin to a snort. "*Fenaw.*"

The voice didn't sound gravelly like a dwarf. She didn't want to move backward and risk loosening more pebbles.

A *click-clack*, followed by a hacking rang out, breaking the quiet. "*Mmmnah.*"

"Rowan?" Horra whispered, her shoulders tense. Her instincts told her this wasn't a safe space, though she couldn't say why.

"*Ktahk,*" Rowan's clackity voice responded.

Horra reached out and found a pile of sticks that must be the wood boy. "Rowan, it's Horra. Come this way. I'm here to rescue you," she spoke as quietly as possible. Her hide crawled with an awareness, like the feeling of being watched from a distance. She tugged the woodencloak tighter.

Rubble and stones ticked and rolled as the creature she assumed was Rowan moved to get up. She guessed, because despite her nightvision, it was too dark to see anything.

A light broke through the darkness. Tinkling music quickly followed.

Stupid Piskies!

Horra jumped to cover Rowan with her body, praying the woodencloak would protect them both.

CHAPTER 36

~ *HORRA* ~

Horra tackled Rowan, and they fell in a heap against the uneven, rocky floor. She swung her arm up to his face, missing his mouth but then finding it and muffling him.

Several piskies darted overhead, their wings buzzing as they moved, shifting their radiance.

A dark figure stepped out of the shadows, revealing a hooded man—the Erlking. Two worqs flanked the evil elf. Horra recognized the one off to his right as one of the worqs who had beaten her before throwing her into her castle's prison.

"*Sshhh*," she breathed out next to Rowan's head. He stilled beneath her. Unfortunately, one piece of his body was poking her ribs, making breathing difficult. But she didn't dare move.

"You imbeciles. Where is he? Where'd you put the druid?"

Anger, or was it panic, made the Erlking's voice tight. He glanced around, searching for Rowan.

The worq made a series of strange words in answer to his master's inquisition. For the first time, Horra wished she understood Worqen.

Meanwhile, a piskie buzzed by and sat on her back. Horra's heart pounded in her ears as she stayed as still as possible. Taking slow breaths, Horra waited for the piskie to leave. Her lungs and body protested, but she held out. A moment later, the piskie flitted off. She gulped air as silently as possible to ease her discomfort.

Thank the Creature God for the woodencloak, she thought to herself. It took all her concentration to remain silent while returning her breathing to normal. She realized then that the Erling and his minion were in the middle of a heated discussion.

"Thinking is not a requirement for your kind. I am in charge here," the Erlking snarled, swinging his long cloak around and facing the worq speaker. If possible, he was more emaciated than before. Possibly it was the harsh lights of the piskies swinging around his caped figure. "Your job is to bring the children to me so I can change them. Is that too hard of a job for you?" He theatrically swung back around, glancing about the area but not finding her and Rowan. He hissed, spittle flying out of his too-pale lips. "The door troll was better suited for your job."

The door troll? Though she realized he'd been on the Erlking's side, she couldn't believe he would lead innocent children to the Erlking's feet. She'd inform the king when she returned.

The worq answered with twisted words, the consonants hard and thick sounding. Piskie light made his round face mottled. The grayish pallor to his skin was distinct against the

178

dirt-colored gray of the other worqs. She wasn't sure what that meant, just that it stood out distinctively.

"Good. There's too much at stake to lose track of my newest adversary. With him under my command, I will take control of the Wilden Lands and then destroy Endwylde. I will obliterate all my enemies with one grand crescendo." He raised his bony fist into the air in triumph. He dropped it quickly. "But I can't do it without him. Do you understand me? Spread out and find him."

Horra waited for them to leave and then waited a few moments more. Darkness descended once the detestable group disappeared deeper into the mountain. Finally, it was safe enough to get up, so she did, inhaling a lungful of oxygen once the stick was no longer poking her side.

She rubbed her eyes against the dimness left behind after the piskies left. She wished she had a torch or lantern. That convenience, however, might get her caught by the Erlking. Darkness was a better option. "You okay?" she asked.

"*Krucken ada bendo.*"

"Yeah, sure." He was obviously still tongue-tied. His inability to communicate was getting to be a problem, but they had no time to waste figuring it out at that moment. "Let's get a move on before they come back and find us." She reached down and lifted him to his feet, an effortless task since he was so thin. She took his arm and gently pulled in the direction she had come. At least she hoped so. She was going by instinct and smell alone to find the secret doorway. Every distinct part of the mountain so far had held a different scent, allowing her to map it in her mind's eye despite the darkness.

Slowly, using her free arm along a wall, they made their

way toward the mountain's opening. Rowan only lost his footing twice, but Horra kept him from falling. Her boots kept her clawed feet safe, even if she hated wearing them.

Eventually, as they neared the doorway, the musty atmosphere changed to a drier dusty odor. The area lightened up enough for her to make out the outlines of protrusions and obstacles. After what seemed like hours later, she spotted the clearer area where she'd entered. She wondered for a second if Torren and Nimble were safe and waiting for them. Hopefully, her troll classmate was using his survival knowledge.

They approached the wall, the only wall that was smooth. Relief was sweet. "We made it." She rushed, half-carrying Rowan to the stone panel just as it opened.

With a swallowed squeal, she tossed herself sideways, taking Rowan with her. They landed together behind a smallish boulder resting against the mountain wall. Horra wrestled against Rowan to pull her hood over her bright red hair, stuffing the waves inside as best she could.

Sunlight poured in, almost blinding her. She had been in the dark for too long, and her eyes were having difficulty adjusting. Fortunately, she wasn't facing the door, which would've been brighter. She couldn't see what was going on. The music, however, was a giveaway to what was happening. More children were being brought in. A big group of them, by the sound of the footfalls against the gritty rock ground. Fear and anger swirled around her chest in a choking grip.

Stealthily, she turned her head, keeping one claw on her hood to remain disguised and limit her exposure to the music. A dozen children walked in, all staring straight ahead, no expressions on their faces. They ranged from hobgoblins, goblins, small gnomes, and—

Horra stifled a gasp.

Torren was the last to enter. He towered over the other

children, shadowing them against the brilliance of the sunlight. She couldn't see his face, but he walked as regimented as the others did, his footsteps in time with theirs. Her heart crashed against her ribs. He'd been mesmerized again.

———

SILENTLY, the door thunked closed.

Horra blinked to adjust to the dimmer atmosphere. Unaware of the danger ahead of them, the children continued their staccato pace, driven by the errant notes.

She rolled away from Rowan, who then stirred. He shoved at her and made guttural moans. She shifted to let him out in case she was squishing him. Instead of moving to sit up, he pushed her off him and drove past her. His strength surprised her. He kicked her, and she fell sideways against the boulder they'd hidden behind.

Pain exploded in her shoulder. She'd landed on a sharp edge. Tears immediately formed in her eyes, blurring her vision of Rowan racing after Torren and the children.

Twisting, she stared at them, her mouth hanging open.

"Stupid Erlking with his dumb music!" she grumbled. Holding a claw to her shoulder, she got to her knees and stood.

Gathering her senses, Horra raced after her two companions, wanting to catch them before they got too far in the mountain. She reached Rowan first. With a grunt, she pulled him off the path and to the side. Once there, Rowan fought against her with surprising strength. He was determined to follow the others. She lugged some large rocks and piled them against his trunk. "Hope this doesn't break you." Her wild pulse rushed through veins, making her body hum. "Stay there," she ordered him.

Rowan didn't so much as blink in awareness. He struggled

against the rocks, ignoring her. She had little time to get to Torren and snap them both out of it so they could escape.

She scrambled to the path where the group of children still marched. Instead of the path she had taken earlier, they moved in a different direction on a trail she hadn't noticed. Torren wouldn't be as easy to subdue as Rowan, so she braced for him to attack when she caught his arm.

He jerked against her touch, pivoting and grabbing her. It was a new move she hadn't seen him do, and it caught her off-guard.

She swung her arms up to protect her head. "Torren, stop."

At first, he didn't stop hitting her. She took his swipe to her chest, countering it with a fist to his gut.

He doubled over, coughing and sputtering, knocking her sideways and allowing her hood to drop away from her head. When he finally opened his eyes, he smiled. "Horra?" Surprise rang in his voice. He tugged her close and hugged her, making her stumble. "Where have you been? I've been waiting hours for you to come back out. I'd given up hope when this group came by." He jerked his head at the disappearing troop.

She pushed away from him, dusted herself off, and rearranged her hood. "It took forever to find Rowan, and then we ran into the Erlking. Where's Nimble?"

"Turned into a boulder right after the music started. Hey, isn't that Rowan." Torren pointed.

Horra swiveled around to see. Sure enough, Rowan limped his way down the path the children had taken and around a bend. The children and Rowan were gone from their sight within a heartbeat.

She groaned. "He's mesmerized. I can't keep him from following the music." She stumbled after him, but he had somehow vanished completely. There was no sign of him. She stood in the middle of the narrow walkway, searching for where he would've gone.

"Where—" Torren exclaimed and then shut his mouth. "Another secret passage?"

Horra stamped her feet. She'd had him! "I don't know. Feel along the walls and see if you can find anything."

She took the opposite wall that Torren chose. Together they searched with no luck. "We have to get him. I overheard the Erlking telling the worqs his plans. He wants to take over the Wilden Lands and then Endwylde. He's going to destroy everything."

"Can he do that?" Torren crawled along the ground.

She flung her arms out. "He took over Oddar. Now he's taking children every time we turn around. And Rowan's under his spell too. What do you think?"

Torren stopped and then glanced at her. "I guess you're right. Keep looking."

Horra did just that. The rock wasn't as sharp here as it had been in the dwarf mountain she'd gotten lost in. However, that didn't mean it didn't cut her claws. "I'm going back to where he ran from us and try again." Distracted, she stepped on something that crunched loudly and the ground fell out from beneath her.

She screamed.

CHAPTER 37

~ HORRA ~

Horra flailed as she fell, wondering how the children didn't scream like she did when they dropped. It would've made finding Rowan easier. However, unlike her wild ride down the volcanic slide in the dwarf's mountain, there was nothing but air this time. She floundered, her arms and legs swinging wildly in her panic.

It was not a simple drop.

She hit the ground hard on the side of her left hip. "*Agh!*" she yelled in pain.

Torren's cry warned her he was coming, and she rolled over and away. He hit with equal effect, squealing in agony. "Are you okay?" he asked, panting.

"Peachy." Horra rolled to her right side so she could stand. Her injured side throbbed, and she gently rubbed the spot she'd hit, knowing it would soon be one large bruise. A glance around didn't indicate where the children were. There was nothing but a cavernous room. And there was no music. "Could we have fallen through a different trap door? I don't see or hear anyone here."

"Hello?" a thready voice echoed. It sounded familiar.

"Hello?" Horra called out. "Who are you?"

Whoever they were cleared their throat. "I'm Murda, a troll. Can you help me?"

Torren gasped.

Horra's heart skipped a beat. "Murda! It's Horra. Where are you?"

"I don't know. My claws are tied and they put something over my eyes. I can't see anything."

Horra didn't want to tell Murda they couldn't much see either. With her nightvision, she could see a few feet in front of her, but the rest was blackness. "Hold on. Torren's with me. We'll find you." She helped Torren stand. "Can you walk?" she asked him.

"It's just bruised. Nothing broken."

That was a relief. "Good. I can't tell where Murda is. You go that way." She shoved him the direction she meant for him to go. "I'll go this way. Yell if you find her."

"Okay." Torren took off, following her instructions. After few steps, she could no longer see him. The only sign of his movements were the heavy footsteps against the gritty ground.

A thunk sounded, followed quickly by Torren's grumbles about stubbing his foot against something. Luckily, he couldn't see her roll her eyes.

"Murda, keep talking to us so we can find you. Are you okay?" She worked her way across an uneven, sloping area. It was a miracle neither she nor Torren had broken any bones when they'd landed. Nothing here was even, and rock formations popped up at regular intervals. How had Murda gotten here?

They kept Murda talking, though she could tell the girl was weary. Finally, Torren called out that he'd found her. Horra worked her way around a maze of shelves, mounds sticking out of the floor, and rock pillars to get to them.

She found Torren studying the shackles the worqs had placed on Murda. He'd already taken the cloth from her eyes. It was too dark to see what shape Murda was in, but a quick touch at Murda's wrist let her know she'd lost weight. That was not a good sign. Murda could be dehydrated, which Horra wouldn't be able to help with.

"Are you all right? Did they hurt you? Have you been here since they took you?" she asked, trying to assess the situation.

Torren snorted. "Give the girl a chance to answer, why don't you?"

Murda gave a half-sigh-half-hiccup. "Yes, I've been here for what seems like forever. They brought me straight to this mountain, but because the music didn't work on me, instead of sticking me in a dark room with some others, they beat me and left me behind." She took a breath. "Probably to die. So, I crawled around. I couldn't get the cloth off because they tied it around my stupid pointy ears." She rubbed them, the hand-cuffs clanking as she did so.

"Anyway, but because of that stupid cloth, I fell down a steep incline of some kind. That's how I ended up here. I'm not sure how long I've been here. I've fallen asleep a couple of times. Whenever I try to find my way around, I run into some-thing. It's been maddening. You two are the first ones I've come across." She slumped against the rock, her voice raspy and dry. "How did you find me?"

Horra didn't want to admit she hadn't exactly been looking

for her. "We got lucky, I guess. We're going to get you free somehow."

Torren raised her shackled arms and placed them on top of a nearby flat stone shelf. It was low enough not to strain Murda's arms. "I'm going to try and break these with a stone."

"I think they're magicked." Murda muttered. Her voice was weaker.

"Here's one." Horra handed Torren a stone. She worried Murda had been injured and might not realize it. They needed to hurry and get her out of here. If they could find the way out now.

The sound of stone hitting metal echoed, bouncing loudly around the inner room. Torren struck the chains over and over again. He broke the first stone and tried another one. And then another when the next one crumbled to pieces.

He stopped, his breathing coming out in gasps.

Horra grabbed a different, smaller stone and pounded on the chain until she grew tired. "This is. Never going. To work," she puffed, exhausted. Her stomach was rumbling, and she wanted nothing more than a drink of water.

Murda had fallen silent in the meantime.

"Murda?" She shook the girl's shoulder.

"*Hmm.*" She snorted and then fell back into soft snores.

"We may have to escape with these still intact." Torren examined them one last time. "They must have a spell on them. Nothing could withstand us pounding on them otherwise."

"Too bad Balk isn't here. He could manipulate metal and get her out of them." She sighed. The responsibility she had for Murda, Torren, and Rowan's safety weighed her down. "We have to get Rowan before we can escape. And we can't leave her. I don't want to take the chance of the Erlking or the worqs finding any of us before we can get out of here."

Horra shifted. The hard rock floor made her backside sore, especially her tender left bruised side. "Besides, I don't even know how to get out of here. Is there another path out besides the trapdoor?" Exhaustion and desperation churned in her gut like a bad stew.

"I'll search the room and see if I can find a way out. You stay here with Murda." He rose before she could protest, and strode off, rocks shuffling as he walked. The dim surroundings seemed to swallow him.

Horra's shoulders bowed. Tears stung her eyes. There was nothing in any of Woodsly's survival books about being lost in a mountain while some mad-elf collected mesmerized children. Like when she was in the castle prison, helplessness settled in her heart, making everything seem bleak. She let the tears flow.

She must've dozed because a sound woke her. Her tears now crusted her eyes, and she rubbed at them. Murda snored softly close by. How long had they been sleeping? Horra raked her claws through her gnarled hair. Exhaustion set deep inside her bones. She shifted, her sore limbs protesting with the movement. One leg had fallen asleep, and she slapped at it to wake it back up.

A clacking noise stopped her halfway between sitting and standing. When nothing else sounded, she turned in a circle but couldn't see anything. She tugged the hood back in place. Carefully, she moved closer to Murda, extending the woodencloak to cover her classmate as best she could.

Several silent minutes passed before another rattling echoed. The hair on her arm raised when grinding footsteps sounded. Horra leaned further into Murda, dismayed that it didn't awaken her friend, but glad for it.

"Horra?" Torren's whisper reached her. He sounded like he had a mouth full of cotton. Was he hurt?

"Over here."

More shuffling and then he drew closer. "Take off your cloak. I can't see you."

Horra moved to pull her hood down when Murda's claw stopped her. "He could be mesmerized." Her raspy voice was less than a whisper.

Horra's heart pounded hard against her ribs. "How can we tell without seeing his eyes?" she barely mouthed the words back.

"Wait," was Murda's only reply.

Several moments passed and then came the tinkling notes.

Horra lowered her head. This was so not good.

Murda slumped away from Horra, and she feared her friend would be visible if the piskies had followed Torren.

"Lean into me," she barely made a sound as she spoke close to Murda's head. Thankfully, Murda did as asked and together they huddled as the music grew.

"Horra?" Torren's voice echoed against the stone walls, masking the direction it came from. His words were thick, slurred. Murda was right. He must be mesmerized.

It would be so much easier if everyone were deaf, like Sageel had been when the Erlking had taken over her castle.

That thought had Horra's mind racing. What if she could block Torren from hearing the music? Was there something she could use to make that happen? She didn't have her pack with the cotton bandages she'd tucked inside it. The only thing she had were her clothes. But she couldn't rip them right now to stealthily stick them in his ears because Torren would hear her.

What could she do?

Scuffling sounds set her nerves on end and made her blood rush. She attempted to keep her breathing steady, but it was difficult with her heart pounding so hard.

She'd have to knock Torren unconscious to block off his

hearing. It was the only way. Horra wasn't sure she could do it. He was too big and strong. But she had to try. They were never getting out of the chamber otherwise.

"Don't move," she breathed at Murda. Slowly, she took her cloak off and placed it around her friend. "Use this. I'm going to try something."

Murda tightly clutched Horra's arm in distress. She squeezed it and extracted her arm from the girl's gripping claw.

Searching, she reached around for something big enough to clonk Torren on the head with that wouldn't accidentally injure him too much. From experience in simulated battles, she knew he had a thick skull. Still, he might not thank her too much if she gave him a concussion. That is, if she could get a good shot off.

After a few seconds, she found what she was looking for. The stone was slightly bigger than her palm, rounded and heavy. Sounds of Torren searching for them were unmistakable over the heavy silence. To keep Murda safe, she moved several paces away in a different direction. She crawled up onto a knee-high rock shelf and tested her weight, finding it balanced her well enough for a surprise attack. It was also open on one side. If she could lure Torren there, she might have the chance she needed.

"Torren?" she called in a low voice, wanting to lure him but allow her to track him. It wouldn't do to get him running at her like a mad swamp swine.

"I still can't see you. Lower your hood." It came from her left, closer to Murda than she liked. The music followed the crunching sounds of his steps.

CHAPTER 38

~ *HORRA* ~

A small measure of relief flushed through Horra's veins that there were no piskies or worqs popping out to surprise them. That was, unless they were lying in wait for her to reveal herself. However, she didn't think the worqs, or the Erlking were that patient. Any or all of them wouldn't hesitate to face off with her.

Unsure what had happened to Torren, she couldn't take many chances, though. Woodsly's training zipped through her mind. The most obvious being to redirect and confuse her enemy. In this case, that was Torren.

She kicked at a shard of rock, sending it clattering. Using all her senses beside sight, she listened to be sure Torren was on his way toward her and not Murda. No lights came on, and the music didn't grow any louder, which she found odd. With the maze-like layout of the room, though, there was no proper way to tell which way he was going.

To hurry it along, she tapped the stone once against a pillar and waited, hunched for the attack. Torren's less than silent footsteps came closer.

There, in front of her, she could sense his presence, though she couldn't tell why. It wasn't the music, or the sound, but a warmth or fullness to the space. She waited, crouched, so he wouldn't distinguish her from the rock for a few more moments. Then he was near enough she could hear him breathing.

She sprang. Rock in her claw, she aimed for where she thought his head might be. With a thunk, the rock landed, and Torren groaned. Though it was a solid hit, it could've been his shoulder. Whatever she hit, it hadn't knocked him out. He grabbed her, but she got out of his grip. She swung around, holding the rock up for another opportunity.

Curiously, the tinkling notes came from where she thought his pocket was. Horra wrestled with him. They both rolled on the rock-strewn ground, shards digging into Horra's hide as they each struggled to get the better of the other. She pinched him, and he squealed and rolled away. A crunch sounded, and the notes ended.

However, whatever the music had done to Torren, he remained affected by it. He didn't stop but kept fighting back.

"Torren, stop!" She shuffled to get an open shot at his head.

He didn't pause. He yanked at her hair and punched blindly, like a rabid jerk. Was he mad *and* mesmerized? All she could do was try to defend herself, which she wasn't doing a stellar job of. He got a solid hit to her chest, almost knocking the breath from her. She didn't stop to nurse herself. She didn't have time. Torren had always been a better fighter simply because of his size and brawn, and he was proving it right now.

At a clear disadvantage, she did what any girl would do while fighting a bigger aggressor off. She kneed him. She hit her target.

Torren cried out then. And he let go of her.

With a hasty swing, she smacked him on the back of the head, praying she didn't do any real damage.

With an *oof*, Torren crumpled and stopped moving.

Claws shaking, she searched his neck for a pulse. She gasped when she found a strong beat, assured he was only knocked out, not dead. "I'm sorry, Torren."

"Horra?" Murda called.

"Here. Everything's okay," she yelled back. To herself, she muttered, "At least I think so." She rubbed at a tender spot on her arm that Torren had clipped with his claws.

Horra searched Torren and found the shattered chunks of what once was a musical instrument—probably a pan flute like she'd seen the Erlking use before. Besides the wood pieces, were some slivers of thin metal wire which must've held it together. She unwound it from the wood and tucked them in her pocket.

Bolstering her courage, she hefted Torren over onto his back. After taking a deep breath, she swung and slapped him hard on the cheek.

"*Wha—ow!*" Torren kicked at her.

She scooted away from the assault and grabbed the stone again.

"Horra?" His words slurred as if he'd just awoken. She'd always wanted to knock some sense into him, but she prayed right now she hadn't permanently injured him. "What happened?" he asked in a much clearer voice.

She dropped the rock. "You tell me." Horra stood and dusted herself off. "You went to look for a way out and then came back mesmerized.

"I did what?" He groaned. "I thought I was dreaming about Combat Training class where you were on the opposite team."

"Yeah, well, it wasn't a dream, and this isn't training class.

Not only were you mesmerized, you brought the music with you." Horra knew she should be more empathetic to his weakness for music. He wasn't a female troll, after all. But the fact she couldn't completely trust him against the Erlking made her tense. "Stick this in your ears." She tore off a strip of her ripped pant leg. Using her teeth, she then tore that strip into smaller pieces and handed them to him. "See if you can hear me when you stick them in your ears."

"Okay." He grabbed the strips from her claws, though a bit reluctantly, and did as she requested.

When he finished, she snapped her claws in front of his face. "Yo, Torren!" she yelled.

He shook his head and removed one bunch from his right ear. "I can barely hear you."

"Good. Let's go get Murda free and get out of here."

Back at their friend's side, Horra used the metal pieces from the musical instrument to dig at the lock on Murda's cuffs.

"What's taking you so long?" Torren whined. He'd been in a bad mood since she'd knocked him out. Not that she blamed him, but his grumpiness didn't help her mood.

"I'm not a locksmith or a lock picker." Her claws were getting sore from twisting the metal back and forth, up and down, in every direction she could finagle them into going. A twist and her clawnail gave way, breaking to the quick. "*Ow.*"

"Let me try." He took the two slivers of metal from her. "I've done this a few times before."

"Oh, yeah? When?" she asked, wanting to think of anything except for the situation they were in.

"Not telling you. You'll only use it against me somehow."

Horra moved out of the way. "After you just attacked me? Yeah, I probably would."

Torren worked the pieces more purposefully than she had,

and within a couple of seconds, something clicked. The shackle loosened and opened.

"Oh, my lands, thank you, Torren!" Murda's exclamation was muted, but genuine. "Where's the exit?" she asked, her voice holding a glimmer of hope for the first time since they'd found her.

Torren let out a deep sigh. "I'll see if I can find the way again. I don't remember much other than looking around in the dark. So, we'll have to be careful if we find the way out. Something is out there waiting for us."

"Something? Or someone?" Horra couldn't help but say.

"Maybe both."

"Is your head okay?" she finally asked him. He'd been so surly since coming to. She hadn't wanted to make things more tense. But if she were truly responsible for him, she needed to know. "I hit you pretty hard a couple of times."

He rubbed a claw on the back of his head. "It's fine. Are we ready?"

Horra couldn't let it go. "Are you mad at me for clobbering you or at the fact you got mesmerized again?"

"Let it go, okay? I don't want to talk about it." Torren flung the metal cuffs. They clanged off the rocks, landing some distance away with a splash.

She stared at him. "Did you hear that?"

"What?" Torren asked, frustration in his tone.

Sometimes he was so exasperating. How he'd gotten as good of grades as he had when he clearly didn't pay attention was beyond her. "Stay here with Murda. I'm going to go get the cuffs. We might use them."

She shuffled her feet along the floor, searching for them. He hadn't thrown them very hard, so they couldn't be far. And she wanted to check out the water. Blast this darkness! It was difficult to see anything.

Splash. Her foot found the edge of some sort of pool. She got down on her knees and bent over the water. Nothing poisonous or contaminated tinged at her senses. In fact, the scent nagged at her mind. It was familiar, like a vague memory or a dream.

Horra dipped a claw in to taste it and gagged. Salty. How did water get this salty in the middle of a mountain? She spat it out. She rolled her sleeve up and stuck her arm in to see how deep it went. Back on her feet, she inched farther in, but it got deep fast. She tried again, but she couldn't touch the bottom.

They'd all been lucky not to fall into it. She gave up searching for the cuffs. Most likely, they'd already sunk to the bottom of the pool. Frustrated, she stomped her foot, splashing water. She wished she were more fearsome and able, like her warrior foremothers. Every time she turned around, she was in another infuriating situation she had no clue how to get out of.

She lowered her head and tugged at her hair. Woodsly had constantly admonished her that royals should express their frustration in private, away from the public eye. Usually, his reminders came when she was throwing a fit over something. Her hide tingled as she struggled to wrangle in her emotions.

Horra slogged back to where she'd left Torren and Murda. "Let's go. You lead, Torren. Plug your ears and try not to lead us into a trap." She worked to soften the bite in her voice.

"Okay." His hesitant reply let her know she hadn't succeeded.

"Sorry. This whole situation is frustrating."

Murda handed Horra her cloak. Instead of putting it on, she held it out to Torren. "Take the hood. I'll hold the middle. Murda, you get the hem. Let's stay close. Ready?"

Torren stuffed the cloth in his ears and took hold of the

hood. "Let's go." Together in a line, they made their way out of the maze of rock in the dark chamber.

Several steps away, her boots crunched on the broken pieces of instrument. She ground them extra hard, allowing a small satisfaction to lift her spirits. However, she had to wonder how many of these instruments there were. Enough to equip every worq? Grinding one into pulp wasn't enough. She needed to destroy them all.

They stumbled around, Torren leading them faster than she would've liked through a maze filled with protrusions and tripping hazards. Horra could tell when they left the open area and entered a smaller, confined space. The air changed, and the ground was smoother, like a walkway.

Horra reached out a claw to find the wall, and Torren stopped. She ran face-first into his wide back. Behind her, Murda did the same thing to her. She tapped Torren twice on his shoulder, hoping he understood she was questioning his hesitation. Whether he did or not, he jerked on the cloak and steered them left.

Nobody spoke. They shuffled along, though the path was clearer. Horra didn't trust it—not after falling through the floor. Poor Murda was too drained of energy to do more than drag her feet. The walk was endless, and since Horra couldn't see well, her ears picked up on every echoing noise. The scents changed from time to time. She dragged her claw along the walls when she could to take in as much information as possible. However, more often than not, the rock was sharply uneven, scratching at her palms. Eventually, she stopped trying.

They marched on, though it was as if they were outside of time in their dark little mountain bubble. Inclines came and went. They made their way either left or right, with no clear sign of whether they were heading deeper inside or toward the outside.

Torren tugged on the cloak, slowing Horra. She pulled on Murda's section to slow her down. A few steps and then they stopped once again.

Murda's breathing rattled. Horra's legs ached, especially the side she fell on, and her claw clutching the cloak was stiff. Torren moved, and then he pushed the hood into her chest.

"I think we're getting near something." Torren whispered. "Can you smell that?"

Horra had been too caught up in her thoughts of what they would do if they couldn't find a way out to notice. Smoke and the scent of food were faint. Like an old fire that lingered in the air. Her heart stuttered. She doubted the children were being fed well or at all. So, that meant it must be the worqs or the Erlking himself—maybe their sleeping quarters. "Yes. It's like a camp."

"Do we head back?" His breath tickled the hair on the top of her head.

She wanted to groan. It had seemed an age since they started walking. Her clawed toes in the boots had blisters. Exhaustion weighed her down. There was no going back for her. "Let's keep going. Just don't let your guard down and put the stuffing back in your ears."

Torren grunted, moving around. After a couple of moments, he grasped for the hood, so she shoved it back at him. In a blink, they were moving again.

It wasn't far, just around a couple of bends, when flickering lamp light glowed in the distance.

Shadows swallowed small carved doorways along the walls, creating the essence of a hallway with rooms off to the sides. Could this be where the worqs were staying? The smoky scent wasn't any stronger as they crept closer to the light.

198

Murda was the first to stop this time. Horra glanced back, noting the girl's widened, fearful eyes. Torren pointed at them to go back. They slipped around the last bend.

Torren yanked the cloth from his ears. "What do we do now?"

Muted noises of someone moving around came from the direction of the light. "There's no music. I don't smell the worqs—only a distant smoke scent from a fire. Let's creep up and see what's going on. If we're quiet, we won't give ourselves away."

Murda shook her head, her bottom lip trembling.

Horra placed a gentle claw on her arm. "You stay here in the shadows and whistle if anything happens to warn us. Okay?"

Her broken nod wasn't like the once self-assured girl who'd started this journey with her. Whatever had been done to her was enough to make her skittish now. Horra smiled, hoping to boost her confidence. She squeezed her arm and joined Torren at the corner. Together, they made their way toward the lighted room.

Horra didn't like leaving Murda behind, but she focused on the task ahead. They tiptoed as stealthily as they could, minimizing the crunching of their boots against the gritty path. The carved-out spaces were too dark to see clearly enough to know what they were. And the air held a weight to it, as if magic was in use. Everything in her gut told her to investigate them, but reason kept her trained on the light-filled room.

Finally, they made it to the edge of the doorway. Marks against the hard stone revealed it to be chiseled, similar to what the dwarfs would do in their mines. In fact, these hall-ways looked exactly like dwarfs had made them. Horra ran her claw over the smooth lines. Was this an abandoned dwarf mine? If so, where were the dwarfs who once mined it? She shook her head. That was a worry for another day.

Horra tugged at Torren's shirt and slipped on her wooden-cloak, tucking her hair into the hood. He nodded at her and stepped back.

Horra eased herself around the threshold. A half-dozen lit lamps hung from iron hooks hammered into the stone haphazardly. Cracks webbed out from the crooked pins, making her wonder when the weight of the heavy metal lanterns would fail. It was obviously an old carve-out. Soot from fires covered the back wall.

Along the other walls were books, papers with strange symbols all over them, and instruments. Hundreds of instruments. Pan flutes, lyres, ornate horns with big brass ends, and many others she had never seen before.

She knew immediately that she'd entered the Erlking's sanctuary. Before she could do much more than gawk, a shrill whistle broke the silence.

Horra scrambled back to Torren, who was no longer in the corridor outside the lit room. Footsteps crunched.

Panic sent Horra running for the first shadowed room. Magic buzzed over her body as she dodged inside the door. The magic caught her and then let her go, just like when Nimble jumped over the trap. Zings tingled along her hide as the magic washed off her like water. She stumbled, landing on her claws and knees.

Before her, huddled along the walls of a tiny chamber, were dozens of scared children. Some were weeping. A few stared off into space. Others glanced around, confused.

"Who's there?" a young goblin boy asked. His eyes glanced toward her, but he looked right through her.

Horra didn't answer right away, unsure what the situation was.

A worq growled, its footsteps mashing against the gritty pathway. He grumbled something in Worqen, his voice deep and gravelly. Another answered him back, that voice not as low sounding.

Horra limped to a free space against the wall, glad her woodencloak kept her hidden. Light from the Erlking's inner sanctum allowed her to see the worqs when they walked up to the door she'd just entered.

The first one growled an order to the second one, who moved to toss something inside. A pile of sticks?

Only if those sticks were alive.

Horra's eyes widened to see Rowan get tossed just inside, right next to her feet.

CHAPTER 39

~ HORRA ~

S he'd never been happier to see the stick-boy than she
was at that moment. At least until the first worq
stepped inside and kicked Rowan, who resembled a pile
of moss-covered brambles, into the room.

The brute snorted and growled menacingly at the children
in the room. In a swift twist, he moved through the doorway
with no hindrance and was gone.

How was he able to move through the doorway unimpeded? She'd gotten caught in the magic, and she was immune
to most magics. She raised her claw just above the barrier. It
hummed. Horra wished she knew more about magic, but that
wasn't her concern now.

She glanced at Rowan, who groaned on the floor. His
crown dangled, broken. They'd obviously roughed him around.
As if they needed to. He weighed less than a piece of firewood.
Her teeth ground together.

A woodgoblin girl peeked out from behind a bigger goblin.

Her crown was knotted in a strange arrangement. Worry creased her bark, and her eyes glistened. She stepped out to go to Rowan, but the goblin boy in front reached out and stopped her.

"If they catch you, they'll do more than just give you elflock. They'll punish all of us." He pushed her back as everyone else nodded in agreement with him.

Elflock.

Horra searched her brain for the term. She'd come along it somewhere in her studies, but there was little information about the elves given to them in their elementary training.

Rowan lifted his head up. "*Bgornam de maglamet.*"

The children gasped at his nonsensical words. Some moved farther away, scared.

"Oh, for piggle's sake." Horra jerked her hood down. "He's not contagious."

Cries of alarm broke out. One or two of the children started crying.

"It's just a cloak. See." She opened the front so they could see she was more than a floating head. Then she crawled over to Rowan. However, she was afraid to touch him since he'd obviously been injured already. "Are you okay? Blink once for yes and twice for no."

He gazed at her with wide, amber eyes. "*Dflongo.*"

She was ready to admonish him for not blinking when he blinked three times. "What's that supposed to mean? Maybe?"

"*Crumuga.*"

"*Crumuga* is right," she muttered as she scanned his wooden body for more wounds. Scrapes covered his bark, and the moss and lichen covered him to his chest now. But otherwise, he seemed to be intact. "We need to get out of here."

"We can't go out there. It stings." The goblin boy motioned his sausage hand toward the doorway.

203

Horra glared at him. Goblins were known for being difficult when they set their minds on something. Her father had remarked in the past about how stubborn and oppositional goblins could be.

In Woodsly's Modern Day Mediation classes, he'd listed a couple of ways of dealing with goblins. The first being to let them have several choices, the best of which would be the choice you wanted them to make. The other choice was to not deal with them at all—which is what Oddar had done. There were no treatises or agreements made between the two nations.

So be it. She had too many other things to worry about than goblins, such as getting Rowan out of here and finding Torren and Murda. "You can stay here. Anyone who wants to come with Rowan and me is welcome to it."

"How?" came the meek reply from the woodgoblin girl. She tried once more to get around the goblin boy, but he shifted, preventing her from moving.

Horra glared at him. "I don't have a problem when I go through. Maybe if I take you all through one by one, we can get out without the magic affecting you." Horra lifted Rowan up. It wasn't hard. He was as light as kindling. "I'll go through with him first."

She stood and walked through the door. Rowan jerked and gagged, so she stepped back inside the carved-out room. "Vinegar and beans!"

"Told you." The goblin boy sounded pleased she'd failed.

Rowan hadn't done that when the worq threw him in. Why was that?

Horra studied the doorway, looking for symbols or spells marks. Merrow used some helpful symbols on the wooden-cloak. It only made sense there would be something here the Erlking used to keep the magic in place. She stood the wood boy up on his rooty feet. "Rowan, do you see anything here that shouldn't be?"

He limped over to the wall and examined it. He rubbed his hands along the walls and his roots along the floor. "*Nmblud.*" He stretched on his roottips for the top of the door. The light on his trunk revealed the melted marks Merrow had placed on him.

"Rowan. Your sigils were ruined in the fire. Could it be that without them you're not immune to the Erlking like you're supposed to be?"

Rowan spun around, his mouth open, giving her a clear view of his knotted-up tongue. It pulsed and moved as if on its own. He spoke quickly, everything he said congealing into one solid string of unintelligible sounds. However, he was energized, pulling at her cloak.

Her cloak.

She took it off and draped it over him, hoping as weak as he was that he could still stand beneath its weight. "Try now," she encouraged him.

He walked through, and though the magic held him for a moment, he came out on the other side unscathed. She whooped in delight.

Was it just the cloak, though? Horra had to know. She stepped from the room to the hallway. Besides the magic suspending her for a moment, there wasn't any problem. Real hope bloomed in her chest. "Okay. We now have a plan."

It took far longer than she wanted to get all the children out of the room, though in reality it was only a few minutes. Some children hesitated before coming, fear clear in their expressions. Surprisingly, the goblin boy was one of the first to go through, courageous bully that he was. But it was only after she'd proven they wouldn't get hurt by using the cloak.

"Where'd you get that thing?" he'd asked her when he came out safely.

"Nowhere you'd find it," was all she replied. As a troll, she might be contrary. But she was braver than he was any day. This wasn't a secret the roods would give to a coward that shoved other children around.

After the last child made it out, she put the woodencloak back on and went in search of her other two companions. She moved through the fifteen children to go back to where she'd last left Murda. Hopefully, she and Torren would be together.

"What about that room?" It was the goblin boy again. He pointed to the room with the Erlking's musical stash.

"What about it?" she tried, but not completely succeeded in, keeping the annoyed frustration from her tone. Though she wanted to destroy the instruments, she wanted to find her friends first.

"What's in there? I know the Erlking went in there once." He stepped toward it, halting outside of the threshold.

"Knock yourself out. I'm going this way." She turned and didn't glance back to see if he went in or not. Maybe he'd destroy the instruments for her. "Murda? Torren?"

"*Gablogofant. Degranto.*" Rowan called out along with her.

They searched two of the rooms without success. Though crudely carved like the others, there weren't any children in them. It looked like bedrooms the dwarfs would've used when they mined here. They were smallish, without decoration or carvings. Though dwarfs loved their mountain treasures, they lived simply, without ornamentation. Usually, without baths too.

She called out to her friends as she and Rowan moved down the hallway.

Something rustled in one of the other doorways. Horra rushed over to it. "Torren? Murda?"

"Here," came Murda's voice from the opposite direction.

She rushed toward it and entered the rough doorway, pausing once again mid-step before the magic let her go again. Inside were another twenty other children, along with Torren and Murda.

"There you are," Torren stated far too loudly.

Murda elbowed him and then motioned for him to remove the cloth from his ears.

"What?" He yelled before realization dawned on him. "Sorry. I can't hear anything with them in my ears."

"Yeah, we all know," Murda returned, a frown on her green face. "Are you okay? They didn't find you, did they?" she asked Horra.

"Not with my cloak on, no. But I found Rowan. C'mon, let's get you guys out of here." She held a claw up to another goblin in the back who was about to protest. "I've already helped fifteen other hostages escape. But if we don't hurry, the worqs could come back."

One by one, Horra got the new group out of the second room. Once outside, Murda glanced at everyone. "We need to keep them from getting mesmerized again in case we run into one any of the worqs."

Horra put her claws to her lips and whistled just loud enough to carry above the din. Immediately, everyone stilled and turned toward her. "You need to stuff something in your ears so you won't hear the music and fall prey to the Erlking again. Just tear off some cloth and stick it in your ears." She showed them by tearing another small strip from her shirt and sticking it in Rowan's ears. "See, it's easy to do and effective. Then, as we move, take hold of the person in front of you so no one gets lost. There are traps set up throughout the mountain."

She wasn't completely sure of that, but the trapdoor they'd fallen through was enough proof for her.

Before everyone could get finished, high-pitched, off-key music drifted over their heads. Several notes in a bruising, discordant racket assaulted her ears.

"Oh, piggle's feet." Horra exclaimed, frustration mixing with anger.

Luckily, everyone hurried to get their stuffing in place. Horra stood in the middle of the group, the hallway being too narrow to allow more than one or two creatures to stand beside each other. Where she stood, it was dim, but bright enough to see clearly. And because most of the creatures were smaller than her, Horra could see above them.

Another note drifted to her, and she turned her head toward the lighted room. How'd the Erlking or worqs get behind them? They'd just been there.

"Hey, guys. Look." It was the goblin boy with one of the pan flutes in his hands. He dashed through the door and into the hallway, a broad smile on his face. "I'm the Erlking." He put it to his lips and blew out some squeaky notes.

As more creatures caught sight of him, others turned to glance his way. None of them were happy about seeing him and the instrument.

"Knock it off, Drungle." A goblin girl stepped around several others and slapped the boy on the head. "You're being stupid and careless. What would your mother say?"

The goblin boy's face fell. "I was just having a bit of fun, trying one of them."

"Can't hear ya." The girl tugged at one ear, pulling a hunk of her shirt out. "Now, stuff something in your ears so we can finally get out of here."

He glanced around at everyone.

Impatience stretched in Horra's gut at his foolishness. "It's just pieces of shirt or pants. Whatever you can tear apart. It keeps you from getting mesmerized by the music."

Drungle stood there as if in a daze.

Horra huffed at his slow reaction. "Unless you want to be mesmerized again? In that case, you can stay here." She considered whether they should go into the room and break all the instruments. However, her instincts were telling her she needed to get the children out as soon as possible. They were her biggest concern, not the instruments. "Now if you'll just put that back, we can get going. It's going to take a while to find our way out."

Everyone shifted restlessly, waiting for Drungle to return. One hobgoblin girl pushed another woodgoblin boy when he got too close. Others around them stepped in to keep the two from fighting. It seemed as if everyone was anxious as she was to get out of the mountain.

Drungle finally returned.

"Ready?" she asked him.

"Yeah."

"Then stuff those ears." Murda yelled.

Horra glanced at her friend, her eyebrows raised.

"What? He's keeping all of us from getting out safely."

Horra nodded. She glanced to the back of the hall to see the boy sticking something in his ears.

Finally.

Horra made sure Rowan was beside her before she pushed her way to the front. "Murda, can you take the back, please? We should have someone who can hear on each end. And stick Torren in the middle."

"Going." Murda moved to do what Horra asked.

At the front, she held her cloak's hem out to two hobgoblin girls to grasp. Clasping Rowan's stick hand, Horra gave a nod and started moving into the darkness.

CHAPTER 40

Horra's feet burned. Her injured side ached, as did her back and shoulders. She also grew to detest the dark. It was forever slow, retracing her steps, and because of the darkness, she was never sure if they were going in any kind of circle. She didn't know where they were going at all. She stopped periodically when someone tugged on her cloak. It had become the signal for a break, and they took more than Horra wanted, but she couldn't be a great warrior and walk off without them. Her patience was ready to snap.

"*Bluffarto*." Rowan announced in the silence. It was the first time he'd spoken since they started back.

Horra tugged on the cloak, signaling that she planned on stopping. She let Rowan's twig arm go. "What is it?"

Rowan took her claw and placed it against the ground. Then he stood and twisted her in a different direction. He repeated his actions again.

"You're saying we need to go that direction?"

He shook her arm excitedly.

"Okay. Change of direction it is." She yanked on her cloak once, and they were heading the direction the woodgoblin druid indicated. The ground inclined, a real challenge since she couldn't see. Several times she tripped on something, falling on her claws and scraping them. The children behind her fell on top of her legs and then it took minutes to get them all back up again.

Going upward was a good sign, though. At least, that's what she told herself.

Around the curve of another incline, the air changed. It was no longer completely stale and nose-stuffingly musty. A slight change, but Horra's heart jumped. She'd been going by instinct by this time, her sense of sight having allowed her other ones to stretch beyond what they normally did. Exhaustion had gone some time ago—now she'd entered a weariness that went to her bones. Her only fear now was that they wouldn't be able to defend themselves should the need arise.

Rowan grabbed her arm and squeezed it tightly. "*Abremore. Abremore.*"

"What is it?" Was he excited or afraid? It was hard to tell. "Do we need to go another direction again?"

Rowan hurried ahead of her, and she had to grab to keep her hold on him.

Faint light made her blink. Rowan tugged her onward.

Amid one step to another, they entered an open space.

Not just any open space. It was the doorway.

Happiness bubbled inside of her, making her giddy.

"*Abermore.*" Rowan jumped up and down like an excited child. She stood transfixed. "You did it. Rowan, you found the way to the opening." Lightheaded, Horra almost fell to her knees.

They stood in a tunnel-like hallway, along a wall opposite of where she'd entered. The ceiling rose only inches above her head and was shadowed by large columns on one side. It's no wonder she hadn't seen it before, not that she'd been looking.

She turned and took the two girls' hands that had been clasping her cloak, and pulled them farther into the space, moving them toward the smooth wall where the doorway opened. Children filed into the open area, murmuring and making relieved noises.

Her heartbeat slowed as the wave of elation died down. Now she had to figure out how to get out. She rubbed her eyes and took in the room once more, just to be sure she wasn't imagining it. She wasn't.

"Horra?" Murda called out.

"Up here. We found the doorway, but I don't know how to open it." She traced her claws over the smooth, chiseled door-way, searching for a trigger.

"That's easy." Horra recognized the voice from the goblin boy. "Just use one of the flutes."

"Why don't you have your ears stuffed like you're supposed to?" Murda's rebuke echoed off of the walls.

"I don't like the scratch of it in my ears." He practically growled the words.

Horra could almost see his shadow at the back of the group. None of the others responded to it, they still had the stuffing in their ears. They were all merrily climbing over the boulders and other debris.

"If you jeopardize us getting out of here, I'm going to box those ears, and we'll see how you like that." Murda's voice shook with anger.

Horra didn't blame the girl. She wanted to smack him as well.

He showed no signs of acknowledging Murda's anger. "All I have to do is play a couple of notes. Watch."

"No!" Horra and Murda yelled at the same time as Drungle played the same flute he was supposed to put back, but hadn't.

Sharp notes came out of the instrument, ringing in Horra's ears.

The floor shifted as the doorway lifted. Though it moved everything around them, it was silent as soft rain. Dwarven magic. They had dozens of secret doorways and openings in their mountains. No wonder it had been almost impossible to figure out. Moonlight filled the space where the rock wall rose. Glittering white-blue, the light made Horra blink against its brightness.

All the children ran, screaming at their newfound freedom like a flock of scared swamp swine. They crashed into the newly fallen snow, which glittered like diamonds across the mountain's base. Trees glistened with a layer of ice and mounds of the white powder. It was breathtaking.

However, there was no stopping the rowdy children. After being jostled around, Horra grabbed Rowan and rushed out and off to the side of the mountain, praying they would all get out and not draw the Erlking's attention. The children were unmindful of the danger. They laughed as if they had no cares in the world.

Murda skirted the throng, following Horra. For the first time since they found her, Horra could look over her friend. She had cuts and bruises on her face, her green hair was a tangled mess around her head, and her clothes were torn and dirty. But other than looking weary and bedraggled, Murda seemed to be all right.

Torren exited next. However, he had to dodge the smaller creatures who danced around him in joy. They twirled around in delight at their freedom. Where they got their newly found energy, Horra couldn't say. Even though she was overjoyed at having left the prison of a mountain, she didn't think she could so much as shake a leg without falling over.

The last to leave the mountain was the goblin boy, looking quite pleased with himself. He held the flute out like a prize.

Anger stirred in Horra's stomach like angry bungbees. She stalked over to him and ripped the flute from his hand. "Who do you think you are? You could've summoned the Erlking with that thing."

"Hey! It's not a pan flute like those guys use. It's just a regular one. Give it back," he yelled at her. He took a swipe to get the instrument back, but Torren tackled him. Three times the goblin's size, Torren subdued him quickly.

Bending the goblin's arms behind his back, Torren jerked him to stand and face Horra. "Tell Princess Horra how sorry you are for not listening and doing as you're told and then attacking her."

Horra was stunned at his vehemence. She'd never seen him act so official before.

Drungle whined. "But she took my toy. It was mine. I stole it. She didn't." His lip quivered and tears glistened in his dark eyes.

Horra stepped toward him. "Doesn't matter if it's a pan flute or not. It's not a toy. If it's the Erlking's, then it has dark magic. It would be enough to mesmerize everyone here except for Murda and me. You can't play with something as dangerous as that."

"But it's mine," he wailed.

Horra ignored his sobbing and tucked the instrument into her pocket. She whistled again to get everyone's attention. They needed to get away from the mountain as fast as possible. As it was, the children were as rambunctious as swamp gators. Another whistle gained their attention.

She motioned for them to remove the stuffing. "We can't stay here, and you have to be quiet again. I'm sorry, but we aren't safe yet. I have a camp with some food and water. It's not much, but it's something. I have to find Nimble, my pet, and then we need to head to my camp."

"What if we don't want to go with you?" The goblin girl spoke, her eyes on Drungle, not Horra.

"It's not a good idea to split up. But I can't stop you from going out on your own. If you do, you are no longer under my protection. I can't help you if you get captured again."

The two started furiously whispering back and forth. Drungle pointed at her several times. He clearly didn't want to stay with her or their group.

Horra turned and whistled softly for Nimble, hoping he would still be nearby. There was no reply.

The children played happily, except for the two goblins. Horra left them under Murda's care to look for her gulgoyle.

Torren came near. "You looking for Nimble?"

"Where do you remember leaving him?" She searched the trees for any sign of a boulder or the gulgoyle. She detected nothing to indicate his presence.

He pointed. "That tree."

She hurried to the tree, and though she found an area the gulgoyle had mussed while they waited, there was no sign of him. A glance around showed no boulders or anything else that might be him. With her shoulders slumped, she headed back to the group.

"Let's go." Horra waved an arm at them. Rowan came first, reaching her before anyone else reacted. Most of the children followed shortly after, smiles on their faces and laughter on their lips.

The two goblins stood off to the side, no longer murmuring

to each other. They had their hands behind their backs as if hiding something.

Horra narrowed her eyes at him, but they moved off away from her assembly.

"Never mind them." Murda fell into step beside Horra, next to Rowan. "They're nothing but troublemakers, anyway."

"I know, but they're still children." Guilt over Horra not being able to protect them sat like a rock in her gut.

Rowan stopped her with his arm. He shook a stick finger in her face. He waved as if dismissing the two.

"You want me to leave them? Why?" Horra recalled how he expressed that he would've left Murda when the worqs took her. Surely this wasn't the same thing to him.

Pointing at the two, Rowan lifted each finger on both hands and then started once more on his first hand.

Torren broke in. "I think he's trying to say they're older than the others? Is that right?"

Rowan nodded again.

Horra thought about what her father would say. "That doesn't absolve me from being responsible for them."

Rowan took her claw in his. It was such an odd thing for him to do. It caught her off guard. "*Brgunda dala omado.*"

"I don't understand you." Horra frowned at him.

"I think he's trying to say something about goblin traditions or something." Torren scratched his head.

Understanding dawned on Horra. "Oh, right. Goblins are adults when they turn sixteen, just like trolls. They can vote and marry at that age." She glanced back at where they had stood. "And though they act like children, those two are probably goblin adults. Why would they be among the children the Erlking kidnapped, then?"

"Who knows why the Erlking does anything?" Anger and

some other dark emotion made Torren's voice deeper. "He mesmerizes adults too."

"Yes, but I didn't see any adults in that mountain." Horra struggled to understand the reasoning behind why the children were being taken and then held prisoner. "What evil plan does he have for them?"

Murda stepped away. "I don't know, but I don't want to stick around here talking about it."

Horra trailed her friend. "Me either." Her gut, however, didn't completely agree. Her stomach churned with regret at letting them walk away. She knew it was useless, but she couldn't will the emotion away.

"It's not worth risking all of us for the two of them." Torren walked ahead, his longer legs moving him effortlessly into the lead despite the deep snow. "Keep the cloth-stuffing close at hand, guys. You never know when we might run into the Erlking or a worq."

Horra stared at him, noting he didn't look back. Sorrow for the state of her friend's heart pierced hers. Fear that Torren would turn bitter entered her mind. And bitterness, Kryk had warned her, could lead to one's downfall.

CHAPTER 41

~ ROWAN ~

Rowan's limbs were weak. The moon was too bright for his eyes. And the troll princess was too reluctant to leave the straggler goblins behind. Merrow had taught him to give goblins a wide berth, stating they were as obstinate as trolls were. The difference being, one could work with trolls, but not goblins.

Possibly, it was just goblin contrariness clashing with the trolls that made it unbearable to be around them both at the same time. However, he was more than exhausted and overwhelmed. He longed to sink his roots into the ground and suck in the nutrients that would heal him and re-energize his fibers.

Walking through the mountain had splintered his roots. After walking for so long, the short distance to the campsite was reassuring. One rope tie on the outside tent had come loose and was whipping in the wind. Would an animal have found their way inside? He hoped not. His pack was still there, along with everything he'd saved after the fire in the Weald. He longed to have it back in his possession once more.

His legs grew heavier the closer to the campsite he got. Luckily, the moss growing on his bark gave him some insulation against the icy air. However, he recalled that the space wasn't huge. It had been big enough for two of the troll's tents with space to walk around them. It would be a tight fit for the over thirty creatures to rest.

"Torren, we'll need to reset the tents up across the mouth of the crevice so we can all fit inside. We'll use the tents as a windbreak. I'll find some more wood to start a fire. Murda, you and Rowan help Torren and direct the children to help."

Horra's orders broke Rowan from his thoughts. He happily followed the rest of the group.

Everywhere he went, though, a child rushed to do the job. After several tries, he gave up and sat out along the back wall, waiting for them all to get finished.

Watching them work together, Rowan wondered at the genetic makeup of the hobgoblins. Though the woodgoblins and gnomes were eager, they were less able to follow instructions. It surprised him somewhat, for he was a woodgoblin, albeit a druid one at that. He certainly didn't have trouble following instructions.

Impressed with the troll's ability to take control and adapt to the situation, he noted both Murda and Torren eagerly doled out the workload. It was a trait he hadn't expected from the more primitive-acting trolls. He admitted silently that he might have to change his mind about them.

Murda came over and sat next to him. She looked rather peaky, though it was hard to tell with the green cast of troll's skin. "*Comhamido?*" He hoped she'd understand he was asking about how she was feeling.

She glanced at him before turning back to the group finishing the second tent. "I'm tired. And hungry. And I could use a gallon or two of water to drink. How're you? You look a little green around the gills." She fluffed some of the moss on his arm.

He shrugged. "*Hampilor.*" The moss was at least soft and kept him warmer than he was without it, though that wasn't saying much. The air was freezing, and he still shivered. He just hoped the moss coverage wouldn't continue on to his face. Looking through it would not be desirable.

Horra returned with three woodgoblins in tow. They'd gathered armfuls of sticks and logs. Snow stuck to them like sap on bark. It took them two trips to get all the kindling back to the camp. While they did so, Rowan reached out with his sensors to communicate with the trees. As before, they were all in a hibernation state, and he received no response.

Before the fire, he'd never considered not being able to speak with the roods. Woodsly had been most helpful, with careful anecdotes and slips of information here and there. They had been too busy as they traveled from the Weald out into the wild for him to truly notice how isolated it was to not be in constant contact with the trees.

He gazed up at the treetops, which bowed and rustled with wind gusts. Realizing he was not immune to the Erlking's music magic put him into unfamiliar territory. He was used to knowing the correct answer to everything Merrow had tested him on. To be so fallible was ... disturbing. He was the next druid. He was not supposed to be so imperfect. It made him question everything he knew about himself. He hadn't expected his mission to be so trouble-laden.

Longing for his home hit him first in his chest. The sensation then raced through his stem. It left an ache in his fibers that he couldn't rub out, though he tried. It settled into the cells of his being. What was this feeling he'd never experienced before? More longing for Merrow's wise counsel prodded him. He didn't like this sensation at all. How could he get rid of it?

"We're ready to set the final stake. Let's get this tied up. I'm ready for a nap." Torren's voice rang out over the din of voices, breaking Rowan's dark musings.

Rowan sniffed back moisture caused by the frigid cold. Though the tent's wyvern skin sealed them in admirably and would camouflage them well, the cold remained. Despite the shelter, his shivers grew worse.

Sealed in now, the trolls made quick work of getting a fire built and started. He remained against the wall and well away from the fire. They were all desperate for warmth, he knew. But the crackle of flames brought back a wave of memories. He turned away and watched the troll princess drag several stones from the edge to the center. He cringed when sparks flew as she rolled the stones into the fire.

Rowan wished he could be like Nimble and change into stone. He'd never have to fear fire again. It was useless to muse such nonsense. But he couldn't stop himself.

Horra passed him again to gather the last two rocks. She caught him watching her. Her eyebrows crashed together above her large brown eyes. "It's safe, I promise. Heated rocks can keep you warm while you sleep. Woodsly taught me that in my first Wandering Wilderness class. It came in handy when I escaped the castle with your seed."

He nodded, glad he couldn't converse with her at this moment. Though she guessed his fear of the flames, he wasn't ready to discuss it with her. Maybe someday he could ask about Woodsly. It would be beneficial to learn about him. A shiver racked his body.

Horra hesitated, as if wanting to say something else, but she snapped her mouth shut. "Rowan, sit here closer to the fire." She piled up two flat stones halfway between where he sat and the fire. "The fire will thaw the ground soon, and this is far enough away that you won't get burned. You should be able to dig your roots in shortly and I'll find the bag you sewed and bring it to you in case you need anything in it."

"*Bruffold*," he thanked her.

She seemed to understand, though she also watched him more carefully as he took his place on the stones she'd sat out for him. He sniffed and sneezed. Ice was settling into his stem. The warmth was quite appealing, even though it scared him. He faced it as another fit of sneezing had a fresh fear coming to his mind. Fire was one thing. The Crud was another. And from what he knew of it, there was no returning from that fate.

Rowan took the tin cup when Murda came by with warm, melted snow water. She placed a blanket around him, but he paid her little mind. His focus was on sucking down the water she offered, letting his fibers soak in the glorious, life-supporting liquid. "*Bruffold*," he murmured to her when he handed the empty cup back.

He automatically clutched the slick banket around his frail frame. Horra was right. The heat thawed the ground, and instead of snow, it turned to muddy puddles. Rowan sighed into the silky fabric.

Minutes passed. Several of the other children drifted off to sleep right away. He thawed before the ground did, but when it happened, he sleepily dug his roots in. For the first time in days, he relaxed.

He closed his eyes and relished his link to nature and the sustenance it gave him.

~ HORRA ~

Rowan fell asleep almost as soon as he dug his roots into the soil. His bark was looking a little too pale, and his sniffles were concerning. Horra was glad Murda thought to give him one of their sleeping bags.

Torren, true to his impeccable tent skills, had created a tent tower. The stretched fabric was taller and kept them warmer than they would've otherwise been. Wind only penetrated around the tops of the tents, which helpfully circulated the warm air around their camp and sucked out the smoke from the fire.

"I'm not sure how you do it, Torren, but you fixed it better than I imagined. It would've taken me hours to figure this out." Horra waved at the tents. "If I figured it out."

"Yes, good job, Torren." Murda agreed with Horra, as she grabbed some berries from his claws. It was the last of the food they had left in the knapsacks.

He straightened his wide shoulders, a half-smile tugging across his tusks. "So, what you're saying is that I am the best at camping?"

"Fine. Yes, you're better than I am at some Wandering Wilderness skills." Horra hated to admit it, but it was true. "I'm still better than you at potions, though."

Torren didn't argue with her on that point.

With the young ones now settled, she took a stick and rolled the stones she'd heated close to all the children. One or two per child, depending on how big they were. There were dozens of stones, so she didn't worry about running out of them. Her only problem was that she was so incredibly weary. It took everything she had left to get them all in place. She flopped down by the tent next to Torren.

"Here." He handed her a handful of dried berries and a couple of crackers.

She took them gratefully, wishing she'd have known they'd need more food. They could've borrowed more from the gnome's house. However, it was a blessing to have what they did, and she wouldn't complain. She drank from the canteen someone had filled with melted snow, washing the food down her dry throat.

"What do we do tomorrow?" He took the canteen back, then stretched out his shoulders and his neck.

"Sore?" she asked as she crunched on the last bit of cracker.

"Only where someone bashed me on the head." He rubbed the spot for emphasis.

Horra was glad he still had some humor left after everything he'd gone through lately. She preferred it over his surliness. "Point taken. It will be difficult with this many children. If we knew where they all lived, we could deliver them to their homes." She let out a deep breath. "But that would take too long. I think our best course of action is to head back to Oddar. We can care for the children at the castle and work on reuniting them with their families later."

Torren yawned widely.

"I can see your tonsils." She bumped his arm.

He closed his mouth and chuckled. "Thanks for saving my hide. Whatever happened." He stopped, a serious look crossing his face. "I don't remember a thing after leaving you to find a way out of that room."

Murda settled on the ground against the tent's opening near to where they sat. They were the last three awake.

Horra squeezed Torren's wrist. "I believe you. From here on out, we have to be smarter about dealing with the Erlking. We need to remain vigilant. Now stick that stuff in your ears and get some sleep."

"Don't have to tell me twice."

He was snoring before Horra could even close her eyes. She and Murda exchanged disgusted looks.

"Men." Horra rolled her eyes. Murda nodded as she lay on her side, her arm beneath her head.

The wind picked up and whistled above the tops of the tents. It pierced the silence, dissipating the drowsy warmth Horra had fallen into.

Murda jerked upright.

Horra frowned.

It wasn't the wind. It was one of those infernal instruments. The air grew heavy as the notes became less a whistle and a more of a shrill note. Horra slapped her claws over her ears against the onslaught.

Even though the sound could have woken the dead, no one in their camp beside Horra and Murda moved.

Thank the Creature God for small favors. However, both she and Murda could hear it.

Had the Erlking figured out they had escaped and was now searching for them? Horra motioned for Murda to go to sleep. "I'll take first watch," she mouthed to her friend. The tent's ability to camouflage had kept her safe so far. She was confident it would continue to do so.

With a frown, Murda curled back into a ball and closed her eyes.

A hint of giggles leaked through to Horra's ears. If she wasn't mistaken, it sounded like the two goblins. Had Drungle snuck another instrument she hadn't seen? A frown tugged at her lips. She wasn't fool enough to tear the tents down now to get to them. Besides, they'd chosen to go their separate ways. Her empathy for them dried up. They were foolish to stick around in the open anywhere near the Erlking's mountain.

Though she doubted they would cause any real trouble, they could draw the Erlking near, and that wasn't ideal.

"Idiots," Horra whispered quietly enough to not wake Murda. They were going to make an already long night even longer with their hijinks. She clunked her head back against the stone wall next to the tent.

CHAPTER 42

~ ROWAN ~

Rowan woke up to silence. Everyone was sitting as still as one of Merrow's garden statues, their faces turned to the sky. He glanced up, but there was only a dull gray expanse. The sun was out, therefore it was daytime, but little light shone through clouds. He moved to get up, but Murda caught his shoulder, stopping him. Claw to her lips, she pointed upward.

Before he could form a word, she slapped the same claw over his mouth. Everyone turned to look at him. All the children were wide-eyed, silent. It differed from their boisterous play outside of the mountain the last eve.

What was happening? Why couldn't he hear anything? Had he been hit with another of the Erlking's spells? That was more than dismaying. At least with his tongue being tied up, he could still hear.

Horra was asleep on the ground at the side of the tents, a blanket wrapped around her head. At least he hoped she was asleep. He couldn't tell from this angle. An itch pricked his ear, and he realized he still had torn fabric in it when he scratched at his lobe.

Rowan relaxed with relief. With a yank, he pulled one hunk of stuffing from his right ear.

High-pitched music had him slapping the stuffing back in quickly. His ear rang even after he shoved it back in as far as he could get it.

Murda's lips twisted as she stared at him. Was she mad or did she simply have something in her teeth? It was hard to tell with troll females. He couldn't read them, and emotions weren't something he understood well yet. So, he sat back and waited.

Murda held a clawed fist up. Slowly, she unfurled her sharp-nailed fingers. With a wave, everyone moved at once, pulling at their ears and removing the stuffing.

He followed their example. The music was thankfully gone, though his one ear still rang.

"Good morning slug-a-mug," Murda greeted him. "Sorry about that. The music has been going on and off all night. You never know when it will start or finish. But I'm getting the hang of this tune, so I can tell when it's about to end."

"*Grothmuk.*" His shoulders drooped.

"Hang in there." Torren handed him a tin cup full of melted snow. "The princess was up most of the night, what with all the musical racket going on. I didn't get much sleep either." A grin tugged at the male troll's green lips.

Murda smacked him on the arm. "You're a slug-a-mug too. You only just now woke up. I took the second shift to give Horra a chance to rest. I'm the one who's tired."

They laughed together. Rowan noted how much friendlier this troll female was to the male troll. Torren took the empty cup from his hands before he could assess why that would be.

Murda got pulled away to help a hobgoblin child, and Torren walked over to the tent to examine it. He opened his mouth to ask a question, then snapped it shut. A slight movement from his tongue assured him it was in the same condition as before. There was no use trying to communicate until he could figure out how to loosen it.

He spotted his bag clutched in Horra's claw. She twitched in her sleep, her face hidden by the blanket atop her frizzy red curls. Her torn clothes were stained and rumpled. The hiking boots on her feet were damp and scuffed. Nothing about her shouted royalty.

Rowan considered whether to pull his bag free from her hold.

"Can you help me?" A gnome girl slid her hand inside his. She had large, leafy-green eyes and hair the color of goldenrods.

"Blurgamot ah dormor."

Her round face twisted and then she laughed. "You're funny." She stopped laughing and opened her eyes wide. "He took my ribbon and won't give it back to me."

She yanked Roman's arm, and he followed her to the center of a group of children.

"It was him." The gnome girl pointed to a blue-skinned ogre boy sitting on a large rock. Five other children stood around him. Tied to his wrist was a yellow ribbon.

"Bully."

The word came to him as if drifting on the wind. Rowan glanced around. The wind had died down considerably from the previous night. It sounded more like a rood.

"What's up with your mossy coat?" the ogre boy asked him. The other five snickered as if what he said was funny.

Rowan glanced down at his trunk. Moss did indeed cover it

from his roots up to his neck, and moved down his arms. *"Blar-chobat archo defalldor."*

The six children laughed more.

He frowned at them.

The gnome girl sent him a questioning glance.

Having rejuvenated from his stay in the mountain, Rowan stretched his branches and plucked the ribbon off the ogre's arm. He handed it to the smiling girl.

"Hey!" the ogre shouted. He slid off the rock and stepped toward Rowan.

"Thank you, Mr. Mossy Coat Man." The gnome girl skipped off, leaving him to face the group of six alone.

A laugh sounded from behind him. "Mossy Coat Man. Merrow should've named you that instead of Rowan." Torren slapped his claw against Rowan's shoulder.

Rowan took a step to maintain his balance. *"Degrado ma oh frest."* He asked Torren if that was the normal way friends greeted each other.

Torren straightened to his full height and bent over the six children. "All righty then. Is there something I need to know about going on here?"

"No, sir," the ogre boy blurted, his blue cheeks turning red. "It's all good. Right, guys?"

The five others nodded their heads.

Rowan held a finger up to disagree, but Torren interrupted him with another slap to his shoulder.

"Good. Now get ready to go. Horra's awake, and we need to pack up." Torren turned to go back toward the tents.

The five children's smiles instantly dropped. One of them stuck his tongue out at Rowan.

Rowan stuck his tongue out at them.

Two of them screamed and the other three turned and ran away.

Good. Let them run. Children, he was learning, were nothing but smaller, more annoying versions of adults.

He followed Torren to the tents, ignoring the rest of the energetic young ones.

"So, Mr. Mossy Coat Man. How's it going?" Horra asked as he approached her. Torren stood to her right. They both laughed so hard, they snorted.

Rowan scowled at them. He failed to understand the humor in such a name. It wasn't a bad name. Moss could be helpful. And it wasn't exactly a coat, though it covered his bark admirably. So, therefore, it wasn't a bad name. But it certainly wasn't funny.

"Okay, I'm sorry." Horra held up a claw, though she was bent over, tears streaming down her green, warty cheeks. "You have to admit, it's funny, right?" She snickered and spit flew out of her lips.

Rowan scrunched up his face. Such a disgusting display. How did his predecessor Woodsly put up with the girl?

His face made the duo laugh even more.

He grabbed his bag from the ground at Horra's feet. Without looking back at them, he spun and walked away.

How long would he have to bear with these uncouth trolls?

~ *HORRA* ~

Horra was still chuckling about Rowan's new nickname when they tucked the last pole into the tent bag and tied it to her backpack. "Do you think he'll ever forgive us?" she asked Torren.

"Woodsly always did, so probably." Torren said.

Horra stopped and glanced at him. "No, he didn't. He gave

me homework every time I was even close to stepping out of line. I had so much work to do, I'd get cramps from writing." She squeezed her claws into fists for emphasis.

Torren finished tying his tent onto the top of his pack. "That's not how I remember it. You always got away with everything. I mean, I got in trouble for the arrow that almost hit you in Archery."

Horra flung her arms out. "You shot at me on purpose."

"Yeah, I did, didn't I?" Torren guffawed. "I've never seen you move so fast."

She smacked his arm.

"*Ow*! I'm telling the king how you've been beating me up." Torren walked over to the edge of the trees. "Are we going to look for Nimble?"

Horra made a face at his back. "My father will laugh that you got bested by a girl half your size. You'll be the laughing-stock of Oddar." She followed him to the trees and glanced around, but seen neither scaly hide nor a gray boulder that could be her pet. "Nimble? Here, boy."

"What if we don't find him?" Murda stepped up beside her.

A fiery ball of fear roiled in her gut. She couldn't leave Nimble out here. But she couldn't search for him forever. Or even for a little while. They needed to get away from the Erlk-ing's headquarters.

"We can't stay long to search. He's on his own out here." Bile rose in her throat and threatened to spill over. She gulped back the nausea, praying she'd find her pet and that he was safe until she found him.

Though it wasn't a great idea, she split the group into three. She, Murda, and Torren led ten of the children and Rowan in lines spread out to search for the gulgoyle. Rowan went with Murda, probably because she hadn't outright teased him. For a druid, he was an awfully sensitive creature.

Secretly, Horra hoped to find Nimble herself. She didn't want anyone to scare him more than he already would be out here on his own.

"Here, Nimble." She called out softly.

"Can she hear us?" a little hobgoblin boy asked, his eyes scanning the ground as if Nimble were an ant. She wasn't sure what he thought he'd see beyond the layer of snow they trudged through.

"He's a he, and yes. Gulgoyle's ears curve like a bat's ears, allowing them to hear most sounds easily. They use echolocation with their clicking and screeching calls. It helps them in the dark so they don't run into anything they can't see."

Horra had never actually seen a pure breed gully dragon. However, she'd seen pictures of them in Oddar's library. Serpentine, their wide, rounded ears, resembled their broad, feathered wings. She'd always loved the photos and often wished she could find an actual dragon.

He kicked at the snow. "Oh, okay."

"And he's huge. So, unless you're looking for footsteps, you won't find him on the ground like that." She leaned down and pointed into the distance. Snow-covered pine trees were dark against the gray clouds. "He's charcoal in his gulgoyle form but gray when he turns to stone. So, look for a black dragon or an enormous boulder with smoke from his fire, all right?"

The boy happily slogged away through the snow, his gaze now on the horizon instead of the ground in front of him. Energetic as he was, snow caked his clothes, soaking through them.

Horra knew they would have to stop in a few hours before it got too dark and set up camp again. They had slept in their clothes the last eve, but today would be different. They hadn't traveled far enough yesterday for frostbite. That might not be the case this evening.

The space between her shoulders pinched. She shifted her knapsack, hoping to relieve the discomfort. She contemplated all the sicknesses they could suffer from being out in the frosty cold. Her mind settled on the worse one—the Crud. Horra tried to shake that thought from her mind, but it didn't go away.

They had no food, were miles from home, and there were worqs and traps set up everywhere. She could be leading them all to their death.

The portrait of her mother popped into her mind. The painter finished it before she'd gotten sick, before the Crud had diminished her. Horra admired her kindness and the regal way she had moved. Her thoughts turned to her grandmother, Queen Petra, who'd bested the first Erlking. How had her grandmother found the strength amid the plague to face and then defeat him? Horra didn't have the first clue of how to begin. Not when so many people's lives were at stake.

All of this bombarded her mind, blanking out all other noise.

"Princess Horra." A little hobgoblin girl jerked her claw hard.

Horra snapped out of her ruminations and glanced down at the girl, who resembled Sageel, minus the wrinkles and age spots. "What is it?"

A wide smile bloomed across her tawny face. "They found your thimble."

CHAPTER 43

~ *HORRA* ~

"Thimble?" Horra frowned before she realized what the girl meant. "You mean Nimble. Show me."

The girl tugged her toward Murda's group to their left, closer to the mountains and near the doorway. She squeezed the girl's hands and bent over to her. "Can you go run to the other group and let them know we may have found Nimble?" She emphasized the letter *N* on her pet's name.

Wide-eyed and eager, the girl nodded and hustled back toward Torren's area.

So far, Horra couldn't see anything resembling Nimble. Pine trees were dark against the watery sunlight. The snow, once pristine, was now mussed with all the searching. Horra rounded a large, blue spruce tree and came upon several children gathered around a boulder with no snow on or around it.

Murda stepped from the other side and grinned at her. "It's warm. It must be Nimble. How do we get him to turn back?"

Horra shifted her pack, wishing they had another horse to

encourage her gulgoyle to change back. "He's very skittish for a mighty half-dragon. We usually have to use another horse to encourage him out of his stony state."

She patted her claw across the hard surface, noting it was indeed quite warm. Had he been here the whole time? The area was farther from the mountain than she had left Nimble and Torren. Suddenly, the children surrounded her, patting and leaning against the heated stone. Many of them *ooh'ed* and *ah'ed* at the warmth.

One of the woodgoblins glanced at her. Horra could tell he had a question. "You can ask me questions. I won't bite."

His eyes popped. "Um," his voice squeaked. "You look like a tree with a troll's head. Some say you're the troll princess, but you don't really look like it."

Horra glanced down at herself. All she saw was a wooden-cloak with the symbols etched on it. "Well, the roods gave this cloak to me to help me stay hidden from the Erlking." She pointed to Rowan, who stood off to the side, looking awkward. "This cloak helped me get his seed to the Weald safely so he could sprout into the next druid warrior. I couldn't have done it without the roods' help."

Sadness pinched her heart at the memories of their last day in the Weald and of the fire. Kryk had been frustrating some times. But he had helped save her too often to count. She would miss him. Her smile was wobbly as she attempted to cover her grief so the child wouldn't sense her thoughts. Luckily, as with most children, his attention waned quickly, and the rest of the children drew him to Nimble's side.

Though the sun was out, and the wind had died down, it was still cold out. Possibly freezing, which sometimes happened during Winterlude. Troll's hide could handle it. But the hobgoblin and dwarf children were so fragile looking, Horra feared for their health.

A crack resounded, scaring the children who ran away from Nimble.

"It's okay." Horra stepped back and waited while scaly shards fell off of Nimble. Smoke curled from his nostrils as he unfurled his long, black wings and stood up.

He made a sound between the meow of a shadow cat and his normal dragon rumble.

"That's a good boy," Horra softly called to him. She stroked his leathery wings. "You've got new feathers. What a pretty boy."

Nimble tucked his legs beneath him and preened. No longer scared, the children rushed back and petted him. A low purr hummed out of the gulgoyle.

"Wow. I wasn't sure if we were going to get him back without another animal." Torren's voice came from behind them. His children rushed to the others. Nimble was now surrounded by attentive boys and girls.

"Well, he's loving this. I wish we had a sleigh or something to drag behind him. It would be much easier to transport everyone." Horra grinned at the giddy group and her pet. A glance at the position of the sun dimmed her joy, however. Having gotten little sleep the previous eve, she was more sluggish than she wanted to be. "Now that we found Nimble, we need to get going. There's a lot of ground to cover to get back to the castle."

Horra turned to the group and whistled softly. "The smallest ones get to ride the big gulgoyle. Won't that be fun?"

They cheered and Murda rushed to shush them. The panic in her eyes sobered Horra.

"Rowan first. Then smallest to biggest. Line up starting here." She ignored the knowing glint in Torren's eyes. Woodsly had done this to her endlessly in the past three years, and she had always been the smallest of the trolls to line up. Maybe she *had* gotten some preferred treatment from her gnarled, old instructor. She would never admit it to Torren, though.

When they all lined up, Rowan shivering at the head of the group, Murda and Torren helped him and then three of the smallest get into her saddle. The four of them were so small that it took all of them to make up for one of her. She couldn't help the sensation of pride that cracked open in her heart. She'd grown so accustomed to her new size since she'd broken her mother's inadvertent wish to keep her little, that she had forgotten how much she'd grown. Comparing herself now to the smaller creatures, she realized how big she'd gotten.

Horra thought of her father, who had been cold and protective of her in the years since her mother died. Understanding why he was that way had her blinking her eyes against the moisture. He'd only wanted to keep her safe, not let on to her the burden of all the issues he dealt with daily. It was just like her desire to keep this group safe, yet unaffected by the danger they faced. She was unprepared for the responsibility of so many children. Her stomach dropped, and then she rallied.

Woodsly had often lectured her about heroism. His sermons on how being a heroine came from overcoming your struggles or doing the right thing despite the cost. She'd thought he'd been attacking her because she'd whine about the disadvantage of her small stature. Now she realized he meant it for situations like this. He'd been trying to prepare her, but how could she prepare someone for something so unexpected? "You have to go through it and do your best. Rise to the occasion," she recited her former instructor's well-worn phrase to herself.

A child bumped into her, snapping her back to the present.

Luckily, they weren't paying any attention to her, nor was anyone else. She righted the playing child and brushed her trembling claws down her cloak for something to do with them.

Finally, they had the last child situated and strapped in. It wasn't perfect. They were quite small and bundled together tightly, but it should help keep them stable on the top of the gulgoyle.

Rowan didn't glance her way, and she made a mental note not to tease him again. She grabbed the rein hanging down Nimble's neck and went to gather the other one. She dug a compass out of the saddlebag and checked it against her instincts. North was straight ahead. "Let's go."

Moving through the snow with so many small creatures was slow, and the afternoon stretched out before them. At least two feet of snow had fallen during the past week, and with the cold temperatures, there was no melting in sight. The top of the snow had crusted over, and their footsteps crunched, making her more alert to anything that might track them.

She was glad to see there weren't any mice, rats, or other vermin in sight. It was a relief. She knew Nimble hadn't eaten lately, though, and he'd need sustenance if he were to continue. "Torren, can you scout for skeeze or any other small creatures for Nimble? Possibly for a dinner too? Take two children with you."

He'd been walking with Nimble on the other side, watching to be sure the riders were comfortable and safe. He'd adjusted the straps more than once. "Okay, I'll take your bow and arrows."

It wasn't hard for him to move ahead of their ambling pace. Two hobgoblin boys went with him. They crouched down as they hurried away, mimicking Torren's stance.

Her grin didn't quite make it all the way across her face.

Minutes spread to hours, and Horra's body became numb to the cold. Her nose no longer ran, though some drippings had to be frozen to her face from being swiped at with her sleeve so often. A glance back at the rest of the group assured her Murda was in place at the back and keeping everyone in line—not a simple task.

They were getting tired. She could tell by the way the children's backs bowed and how they hunched over. Cold and exhausted. That's what they were. But there was nothing she could do about it.

Torren's whoop in the distance had her jerking her head up. "What now?" was all she could say.

CHAPTER 44

~ ROWAN ~

Rowan disliked riding the gulgoyle. Not only did it remind him of the moment the curse hit him, but it was far too uncomfortable. The only good thing about it was that it kept him warmer than he had been since he'd left his home. He longed to go back to the Weald. However, not to the one that was burned and without the roods. No, he wanted to go back to the one he unrooted in.

He glanced at all the trees as they strolled idly past them. None of them reached out to him in his mind. Even if he were to sink his roots into some soil, he doubted there'd be a reception here. The residue of evil was everywhere, sitting on the area like dew on a leaf. If the roods had been here, the Erlking's presence would've driven them away.

The dwarf girl sitting behind him picked at some moss lining his trunk.

He leaned sideways and made eye contact with her.

"*Blanful.*" Though he knew she wouldn't understand his plea to stop, his tone was firm enough to startle her into stopping.

Turning back ahead, he took in whatever stimuli his roots could give him while dangling from the top of the gulgoyle. The air was thick with magic. It itched and made his root hairs tingle in a numbing sort of way. It wasn't as bad as it had been near the mountain. However, he could tell by how heavy the coverage was that the Erlking had been here recently. Possibly within the last day or two.

Did the troll princess notice it? Though troll females were immune to most magic, her instincts suggested she detected it on some level.

Torren called out to them in an excited voice. A wagon came into view. It laid wrecked against a fir tree. It would be large enough to hold most of their group if it was still functional.

He glanced down at Horra's tangled mass of red hair. She grumbled low enough he couldn't catch what she said. "*Plat-gondis,*" he added, a tone of encouragement to his voice.

She ignored him. He sighed. Merrow didn't warn him about this. Feeling useless in situations. It was quite humbling. Nothing that had happened so far had been close to what he expected. Being a druid, he realized, was harder than he thought it would be. His instructor had warned him, but he hadn't understood the wisdom in the seedkeeper's words until that moment.

Maybe not being able to communicate effectively wasn't such a bad thing. It gave him perspective he might not have otherwise had.

They clomped up to the tree where the wagon leaned precariously against the trunk. Branches had broken off where it landed, but snow covered it. The two hobgoblins with Torren dug into the snow, trying to get it loose from the snowbank.

It was a sturdy-looking vehicle, well-made with solid wood. The children who had been walking pitched in along with Horra and Murda and, in no time, they had it unburied. Rowan was glad to be left out of this chore.

Torren walked around it, examining the damage. "This looks familiar."

Horra stepped around him. "It should. This is Balk's. I was riding in it when the fairies hijacked us. They got him, but I escaped. Then later, you and a couple of worqs were using it to search for me."

The cringe the male troll made was slight, but Rowan didn't miss it. It was something Torren wasn't proud of. It must've been when the Erlking had mesmerized him. The troll princess had teased him about it while they were in the Weald, but Rowan hadn't known what she was referring to. It didn't affect him, so he wasn't sure it mattered now.

Murda squealed. She lifted a cloth sack out of the snow and held it up. "Frozen skeeze," she announced.

"Thank the Creature God." Horra grabbed the other girl and hugged her.

Watching their interactions was curious. So many emotions. And the speed with which they changed from one to another confused Rowan. Yes, he was at a loss when the Weald burned. But it hadn't impaired his reasoning capabilities. He decided that's what emotions did—impeded clear thinking.

"One, two, three," Torren yelled as they rocked the now loose wagon. Children scattered when it fell.

Rowan held out his arms, ready to tell them what they'd done wrong when they all screamed as it teetered and leaned in the wrong direction.

Horra and Torren ran for the wagon as it wavered and started tipping in the opposite direction. Between the two of them and Murda, who dashed in to help, they swiveled the wagon against the slick snow. With another push, it landed on its wheels.

He shook his head. He could've told them an easier way to do it. Their first failure didn't seem to dampen their moods, however. They were all congratulating each other. He scoffed silently at them. They could all use some physics lessons.

Boredom crept upon him as they inspected the wagon and set it up to be tied to Nimble's belly straps. Rowan hoped this would allow them to move faster. He was more than ready to be done with this wilderness adventure. What he was ready for was finding a cure for his hexed tongue. Then he could share his knowledge freely once again.

~ *HORRA* ~

Horra couldn't believe her luck. The Bocan's wagon was big enough for the children to crowd into and ride behind her pet. It meant they could travel so much faster without waiting while they walked behind the gulgoyle. She muttered a quiet prayer of thanks to the Creature God.

"Horra, do you have any extra rope?" Torren called out from his perch beneath the front of the wagon.

She took her pack off, dug out the bundle, and handed it to him. "It's not much, but hopefully it will be enough." The adrenaline from finding the wagon and then tipping it over dissipated, leaving her sore and tired. She leaned against the splintered pine tree, wanting to rest while Torren fixed the ropes. Her eyes drooped.

The next thing she knew, Murda was shaking her arm. "We got it set up and fed Nimble."

Horra rubbed her freezing claws across her chilled face. She yawned and then choked on the cold air. "Great. Thank you." Her body was stiff, and it took a moment to adjust and walk normally. They had backed Nimble up to the wagon. It took her longer than it should to get there. Even though her boots were some of the best around, her clawed toes were numb, as were the fronts of her legs. Her backside, which had warmed at least a little against the tree, chilled instantly. The wagon looked small against the large gulgoyle. Torren jerked at a knot, testing it.

"I had to put the wagon on top of the tip of Nimble's tail. I hope it doesn't damage it, but I don't have enough rope otherwise." He glanced at the sun and back at Horra, concern clear in his clay-colored eyes.

She nodded. "I'll check to be sure. But, good work." Horra bent down to look beneath the wagon, which bounced with the movements of the children loaded in it. The wagon's enormous wheels gave the gulgoyle's tail space to move. She wasn't sure how smooth the ride would be, but it was still better than walking. With a nod to Torren and Murda, who sat with the children in the wagon, it was time to move out.

Horra climbed up the ladder, taking her spot in front of a cross-looking Rowan. The children who had ridden with him before were currently in the wagon. Torren settled in behind Rowan, and with a slap of the reins, they were moving. The wagon rumbled behind them.

Squeals and laughter resounded against the gulgoyle's trotting steps.

Horra wanted to get as close to Bough Valley as she could. That would leave one day's travel to the castle. And they'd be able to find food in the village. Air washed over her as they moved, clearing the sleep from her groggy mind.

She kept an eye out for creatures and any movement, but everything was clear as they crashed through the crispy top layer of snow. After several minutes, the children quieted down, and it was only the rumble of the wagon and the plodding of Nimble's feet.

Everything became hyper-focused in Horra's mind. If she spotted a movement, she'd jerk her head to find what it was. She kept Nimble on the smoothest likely paths, which he navigated like a professional. Once or twice, they crawled over something, making the wagon bounce around and the children scream with delight.

The sun was getting low by the time she got to an area she recognized. They were near Hobgoblin Pass. "I'm heading to the bridge," she shouted over her shoulder.

They came out of the fields and hit the road that would take them to Bough Valley. There weren't many cart marks, though she spotted some areas where horses must've traveled. Her intuition pinged inside her mind. Even though it had snowed, there should be more tracks.

"Halt." A voice came from the side of the road. It was male, gravelly, and threatening.

Horra snapped the reins. "Hold on," she screamed. She was under no illusion that Nimble, along with the wagon full of children, could outrun a single creature on a horse. That didn't stop her from trying.

Rowan clutched her sides tight, all the while muttering things she couldn't understand. Torren had grabbed her cloak on the left side. By the weight of his body against it, he was either almost falling off, or twisting around to watch out for the wagon. Either way, she kept going.

"Horra, stop! It's Balk." Murda's voice carried on the wind, obscuring the last word.

"What?" Horra called back.

Torren tugged at the other side of her cloak. "It's Balk."

She pulled on the reins. "*Whoa.*"

It took Nimble a few feet to stop. She was panting by the time they did. Balk, on the horse her father had given him, rode up in front of them.

"Sorry for yelling. I thought you were the worqs who stole my wagon." He gazed at the wooden wagon full of children. His head was no longer shaved, but dark hair hung down in a curtain around his tattooed head. He looked less menacing than he had the first time she'd met him. However, his attitude was not as friendly as she expected, even if he mistook her for a thief. "I should warn you about the bridge."

"We found the wagon wrecked against a tree. It came in handy." She nodded back at the others. Surely, he wouldn't object to her using it if it kept children safe. "What's wrong with the bridge?"

He grunted but didn't demand to have the wagon back. "Hobgoblin Pass is blocked off. No one's allowed past." His horse danced sideways.

"By who's orders?" She stared at him, incredulous. Though the bridge had been damaged when Grendel, the giant girl, had thrown rocks at it, it was always open. It was one of the oldest landmarks they had.

"By the king's orders."

CHAPTER 45

~ *HORRA* ~

"Why would my father order the bridge closed?" she gaped at him. This had to all be a misunderstanding. The only other way through to Oddar would be through the old Witch Lands. She'd already tried that route once, and she wasn't eager to try it again.

"Why else?" Lines covered his tattooed face, as if he'd aged since she'd seen him last. Dark shadows circled his eyes. Horra knew without asking that his search for his daughter Floke's killer, or his daughter, as he believed she was still alive, hadn't been going well.

Though her heart went out to him, she had many responsibilities now. A whole wagon full of them. "The Erlking. But he isn't near here. He's back in the lower Iron mountains. Surely, we can get across the bridge."

Balk perked up and leaned over his horse's head toward

her. "You say he's in the mountains? How do you know this?" His gaze went past her to the wagon.

Horra pursed her lips. If she told him she'd found these children there, he'd want to go find it so he could search for Floke. It was a fool's mission. And she knew his dedication enough not to doubt he'd go there and possibly get killed for it.

"She's not there. We got all the children out. We're headed back to my castle now." She stopped speaking when he pulled his sword from his scabbard and held it up.

His narrowed eyes took on a crazed glow. "How do you know you got all of them?"

"Because we were all over the mountain before we escaped. There weren't any children left there to save." Torren's voice was gruff. He obviously sensed the same thing about the bocan mercenary.

"I'll be the judge of that." Balk lifted his horse high, and then, without looking back at her, was off at a gallop. He raced in the direction her group had come, following their tracks.

Nimble shuddered. "Blast it all, you stubborn bubble-headed bocan!" she grumbled.

"Don't worry about him. He can take care of himself." Torren squeezed her arm.

"I know. But that doesn't mean he's not being stupid by riding right into the Erlking's trap." She straightened her shoulders and motioned for Nimble to move once again. "I hope he wasn't right about the bridge."

She directed Nimble to keep going. Around another twist in the road and beyond several tall trees came the entrance to the bridge.

Horra yanked on Nimble's reins and stared. Boulders and obstacles such as broken wagons blocked their entry onto the bridge. There wasn't even a small area to crawl over.

"What does he think he's doing?" Horra stared, astounded.

There was no way around the bridge. The one and only bridge that united the northlands with the southern region. Wind whistled up from the valley beneath the stone bridge, throwing loose snow around as it circled. She clutched her hood closer to her chin.

"Isn't there some other way around?" someone whined.

Murda shushed them, but not before others sniffed and cried.

"Let's look." Horra slid down off Nimble. Torren was close on her heels. "Keep the children in the wagon, please."

They walked to the edge of the ravine. Snow covered it, and only the tops of weeds and trees stuck out. It was twice as far down as it was across the bridge, which was quite long.

"It's been cold enough that the river should still be frozen over." Torren sounded dubious. "But that snow is deeper than any of us can get through."

"I know." Horra's eyes skimmed across the narrow river and up the other side. It wasn't a sheer drop, but it was close to it. They'd need ropes and pickaxes.

It was impossible.

"There's no way we can go that route." Horra glanced past the bridge toward the Riven. The wind picked up, carrying some of the loose snow with it. She covered her face with her arms, but the icy gust bit at her, sending shivers through her body.

"*The Riven.*" A ghostly voice cracked in her mind. Like two sticks grinding together.

Like Woodsly's voice. She glanced at Rowan atop the gulgoyle. He tilted his head in concentration. Had he heard the voice too?

"Horra?" Torren waved a claw in front of her face.

When she refocused, Horra's eyes were pointed directly toward the cursed land. Dangerous, her mind argued with her.

Glancing back at the river's dropoff, Horra considered her options. None of them were good. She knew her father must have a good reason for shutting down the bridge. But even if she knew why, that wouldn't help her get across to Bough Valley and then get back to Oddar.

It was their best shot at making it home fast. She ground her tusks together and gave Torren a heavy look.

He understood without her having to say a word. "*Nuh-uh.* No way. We're not going that way."

"The only other road around is over a day out of the way and goes straight through the old witching lands. And the last time I checked, worqs filled the fields." He didn't need to know it was only a half dozen. That number would be enough for an army to deal with on a good day.

"How could you even think of going there? No one ever returns. It's probably full of more dark elves. And if we run into them? That's worse than dying outright by a worq's hand." Torren stomped away from her and then paced back. "No."

"What if there isn't anything there, and we just skirt it to get around the river? It's closer to the castle that way. And will probably take a half of a day off our ride." Stomach roiling with her unease, Horra turned back at Torren, who was shaking his head. "I promise at any sign of danger, I'll turn back. It's getting dark. We have to make camp somewhere. Let's camp close to it tonight, and we'll reassess in the morning."

"Horra, there's a reason everyone avoids it. Even your mercenary wouldn't go in there. We won't come out alive," Torren shouted the last sentence.

Rowan made his way over to them, the snow up to his chest. He waved his stick hands and pointed them toward the Riven. Then he nodded his head.

What? He was agreeing with her? Horra hadn't seen that

coming, but she'd use it to her advantage. "See? Even Rowan thinks it's a good idea."

"He has leaves for brains, then." Spit flew out of Torren's mouth. He was as mad as she'd ever seen him.

But though her gut was twisting with fear, she knew it was the right thing to do. There was no such thing as a path without danger now. It was the best option to get home the fastest.

Rowan wrote *Riven* in the snow with a stick finger. And then *Go*. He motioned for Torren to come.

"I can't believe you both want to go there. You're crazy. Our blood is on your claws." Torren stomped back to the wagon and got in. The children moved to give him space. He plopped down, his arms across his stomach and his face stormy.

Horra glanced at Rowan. He didn't look excited or fearful. She wasn't sure what his motivation was, but at least he was finally on her side. "Well, let's get going then."

~ ROWAN ~

Sensations tickled Rowan's roots as he sat high upon Nimble's back behind the princess. Unlike the silence he'd been suffering since leaving the Weald, obscured voices whispered to him. They grew stronger as the gulgoyle drew closer to the Riven. They were nearing the spot on the map that had perplexed him. Something about that cursed land was important. It was as clear to him as the gray sky above them. But he was used to facts and information, not hunches. And this was undoubtably a shot in the dark.

But the quickening in his heartwood and the murmur of voices pushed him to back the troll princess. It was good he couldn't communicate, for he couldn't explain why they needed to go there.

He shook his head. Woodsly had imbued some of his memories and knowledge on Rowan's seed. He'd implied as much in their discussions in the Weald. But since the seed had experienced trauma, the information that should be crisp and concise was murky, like a word just beyond his recall. It left him with only an intuitive surety.

The sun was an orange smudge across the horizon when the buzz hit him. Heavy magic.

"Do you sense that, Rowan?" Horra's voice held a note of uncertainty. Her red curls whirling in the wind as she glanced around, navigating Nimble as close as she could to the edge of the ravine that bordered the river.

"*Glafog*." He tightened his hold on her. The magic rolled across him like ants crawling under his bark. A shiver wracked him.

"Hold on. Don't let go of me. I'll keep to the edge, but I'm not sure where the Riven's borders are exactly. Say something if you see or sense anything troubling." The gulgoyle kicked at a rock, which rolled over the edge and fell. Horra stiffened.

Rowan laid his head against the woodencloak on the princess's back. It gave him some comfort as the voices changed from subdued to a hissing resonance. Dark magic had seeped into the trees and land here. It vibrated off everything. Tall weeds stuck out of the snow in great tufts, creating mounds. There was no sign of any kind of path. Trees were taller, their trunks dark black as if charred. One stretched toward them as if it had attempted to flee the area but failed. The sap in Rowan's system thinned and rushed around, making him dizzy. Every fiber in his being told him to flee and run in the opposite direction.

Nimble's head twitched. He tugged against his reins. A

ripple passed beneath Rowan as the creature sensed the danger as well.

Horra crooned to her pet in soothing tones. No doubt her concentration was on keeping the animal from getting spooked and turning to a stone.

"Leave here." Boomed an ethereal voice. *"Turn back."*

"You are entering your doom!" another voice called.

Lights bloomed behind Rowan's closed eyes. This magic was different. Darker. Like a black hole waiting to suck him in.

He jerked, his arms flailing. He was wrong. They shouldn't have come here.

CHAPTER 46

~ *HORRA* ~

Rowan pulled away from Horra. She couldn't concentrate on keeping Nimble soothed while the woodgoblin behind her was doing his best to fall off. "Sit still, Rowan." Reaching around, she grabbed his branchy arm and yanked him to her back. "Grab hold and don't let go."

The children in the wagon behind them were uncharacteristically quiet. The hush in the dusky forest was weighty. Horra's heart thumped hard in her chest, making it difficult to breathe.

Magic was everywhere. It zinged her nose and prickled in her ears, popping and snapping. The air was almost alive with it.

"What in the name of piggle's feet is going on?" she screamed as Nimble balked.

A flash of blue light whizzed above her head. Icy particles rained down upon them. She held the reins tight, pulling back on her pet and praying he didn't go into protective mode.

Getting stranded here without Nimble was not something she wanted to contemplate.

The blue light flashed. Horra closed her eyes to the brilliance.

"Princess Fyd, is that you? What are you doing here?" The tinkling voice was one Horra didn't think she'd hear again. And it wasn't so much tinkling rather than accusatory.

Horra opened her eyes. There, before her in a regal carriage, was Queen Stella Toppenbottom. Fairy guards stood on each corner with two at the head. The queen stood, proud and fierce, the static of her magic snapping around her in sparkling flashes. But it was her face, creased and grim, that made Horra hesitate.

Better to deal with her carefully. "Your majesty." Horra bowed in reverence. Her father would've been so proud.

Queen Stella stepped down from the crystal carriage. Her silver-white dress with a spotted-gray fur collar blended in with the background. Gray peppered her flowing blonde hair, and small lines crinkled from the edges of her eyes and mouth. Four guards stepped down in the snow beside her, their weapons raised. The queen didn't order the guards to lower them.

Why was the queen so uptight? They'd left on good terms. "Is something wrong, Queen Toppenbottom?"

The woman's right eye twitched. "I could ask you the same thing. We both know where we are. Why are you here, of all places?" She clipped her words sharply, suspicion clear in the tilt of her eyes.

Horra wasn't sure what had set her on edge so badly. Horra needed an act of goodwill to make the queen relax. "I was coming back from the Weald with Rowan, the new druid." She leaned aside so the queen could see the woodgoblin behind her. "And we got sidetracked. We ended up in one of the lower

Iron Mountains where we found these children. We believe the Erlking abducted them using his magical music. The way through Hobgoblin Pass is blocked, so we're skirting the Riven to save time getting back to Oddar."

"I see." She flicked a finger, and the guards lowered their weapons. Though they relaxed their stance, her own posture showed no signs of relaxing. In fact, she seemed to bristle at Horra's words. "You mentioned the Erlking? Which mountain did you find the children in?"

Curious. Why is the queen so interested in the Erlking now? They'd been quite content to leave him and the trolls behind when they left for their Shining Land. "Why?"

The queen's lip trembled. She schooled her face, but not before Horra witnessed the tears.

And then it hit Horra. "Has something happened to the princesses?"

The guards snapped to attention and bared their weapons again. Queen Stella seemed to wilt before Horra. Her face scrunched, and she curled into herself. She emitted a high-pitch moan that would have made anyone think she was a banshee. When she was done, she wiped her glittering tears with an equally sparkling cloth. "She's gone."

"Who's gone, your majesty?" Horra didn't have to pretend to empathize for the queen. The pain in her eyes was too real to not affect her.

"My darling daughter, Glory." The queen referred to her blonde daughter, the one the Erlking had cursed and disfigured. "She was most distressed even before we left your castle. Nothing we did or said eased her troubled spirit. I fear she has come here to search for the Erlking to get him to turn her back to her beautiful self. I am desperate to find her." She daintily dabbed her nose with a cloth given to her by one of her male fairies.

"Did she say she was coming to the Riven?" Horra asked.

The queen sniffed. "Not in so many words. She has been so closed off, you understand. Not speaking with anyone. But the servants overheard her mumbling to herself about wanting to find the Erlking to reverse the spell."

"How would she do that? Is she strong enough to face him?" Horra was shocked the princess would be so bold. The girl had shown no sign of wanting to do anything when she'd seen her last.

The queen pursed her lips. "She has something, an artifact, that may help her get what she desires—her beauty back. It is why I believe she's come here specifically to find the Erlking. There'd be no other reason for her to take it."

"I see." Horra didn't fully see. She did not know what the fairies could possess that would entice the Erlking. If they knew they had something that would make the Erlking reverse his magic spells, why hadn't they already used it? "I have not seen your daughter, if that helps in your search."

"But you have seen the Erlking." It was a statement, not a question.

She couldn't lie, but was it wise to send the queen after the Erlking? She'd already given too much information away to Balk, who may or may not be dead by now. "I have, yes. I don't wish to alarm you, but several worqs accompany him along with the piskies. It would be foolish to go after him in that dark maze of a mountain."

The queen stuck out her chin. "Princess Fyd, you have shown yourself as exceedingly brave. As heroic as anyone I've come across in many years. Your hesitation does you credit. But I must find my daughter. The Erlking must not get his hands on her. It would be the end of my kingdom if that happens." Lips trembling, she sent Horra a desperate glance. "It would be the end of me."

Horra ignored the queen's flattering compliments. She was desperate, after all. However, the tone and emotion behind what she said struck Horra to her core. "I understand, your majesty." She closed her eyes to gather her courage and then reopened them. "If you must go, then I will tell you, and I pray that no danger will befall you because of it. Follow our path back to Hobgoblin Pass and then through the border forests along the highway. The Erlking hides inside the fourth mountain. You will know it when you see it. We have been all over the mountain and our marks are there. You will find a smooth surface, a trapdoor of sorts, on the outside of the mountain. There is a latch, find it and it will open. Take something to light your way, for it would be easy to get lost within its dark depths. And plug your ears so you will not fall prey to his music magic once again."

"You do honor to your foremothers." Queen Toppenbottom raised a fist to her chest and saluted Horra. "Thank you, dear one, for the glimmer of hope you have given me." She turned her head as if hearing something and turned back to Horra. "This place is not safe for children. I give you a gift to transport you home safely in exchange for your valuable information. May we have peace between us now and evermore." With a wave of her hands, she sent a gleaming ball at Nimble.

An effervescent cold washed over Horra. It bubbled and tickled along her hide.

The magic lifted Nimble and the wagon behind them as if it weighed nothing. The gulgoyle snorted and fought against the spell, but when he realized he was safe, he relaxed. Rowan clung to Horra tightly. Nimble released his wings, flapped them, and snorted. Fire crackled along his throat, glittering a fiery red between his scales.

Perhaps her pet was having a wish come true, for he certainly looked happy. He was aloft, or at least the closest he would ever come to it with his clipped wings. Horra couldn't help but smile at the sight of her pet *flying* as the fairy's magic suspended and moved them.

She waved down at the queen. "Thank you, Queen Toppenbottom. May the Creature God protect you and yours from the Erlking now and forevermore."

The children screamed and cheered. Nimble flapped his wings as they rose over the treetops. The fairy spell glittered around them in the moonlight. Horra prayed silently for the queen's success in finding her daughter.

Now she had to find out why her father blocked off the only major thoroughfare that went through the center of the Wilden Lands. It couldn't be good news.

THE COUNTRYSIDE PASSED beneath them in a blur. Though Horra didn't condone using magic, it was truly a blessing to get from one place to another so swiftly.

The castle was dark and quiet when they dropped onto the courtyard. The spell winked out as they landed in the slushy snow. Mud and water splashed around her pet and the wagon as it rolled across the open area. Awakened by the racket of their landing, alarmed horses nickered from the recesses of the barn.

"Everyone out. Murda, can you alert the maids and have them get some food for the children? Torren, can you take care of Nimble? I'm going to go find my father." Horra climbed down the ladder and waited for Rowan to dismount before she ran off into the castle.

Smells lingered in the kitchen from the last meal, orange-red coals of a dying fire remaining in the large hearth. Horra rushed past the dining room and through the Hall of

Monstrosity where several paintings still awaited rehanging. She took the stairs two at a time, her legs wanting to give out when she reached the top.

Down past her room, then her former instructor's room, she arrived at her father's door to his private bedchambers. She knocked and waited. A few seconds later, she knocked louder, fearing he couldn't hear her if he was asleep. When he still hadn't come, she turned the door handle and entered. He would forgive her this once, she was sure.

"Father? I need to speak with you." She rushed through his sitting area, where his hearth was dark and cold. Up the stairs to his bedroom where she found only the bed, which showed no signs of being slept in. "Father? Where are you?"

"Princess Horra?" Sageel's voice echoed into the room.

Horra rushed back through the sitting room and out into the hallway. "Sageel, where is my father? I need to speak to him."

"He sent a message to you. Did you not receive it?" Sageel was tying her housecoat as she spoke, her head turned to her task.

"No, we had some trouble at the Weald and have been on the run ever since. What was in the note?" Horra stepped closer to the hobgoblin maid.

Sageel frowned. "He's gone. Headed to the swamplands to gather some important supplies."

Hora's heart hit a painful beat that radiated through her chest. "The swamplands. But the worqs have taken them over. What supplies could he possibly be getting there?"

"I don't have the specifics. You'll have to ask Ambassador Rindthorn. The king placed her in charge of the castle in his absence."

Horra stared dumbfounded at Sageel. This could not be happening.

CHAPTER 47

~ *ROWAN* ~

Hobgoblin maids bustled about in the kitchen. Rowan stayed well out of the dashing back and forth, lest he get trampled. They gathered leftovers, putting together the makings of a hasty breakfast for the children. He longed for Merrow's lifesap to restore his branches and bark. Though he'd merely ridden the last hours of his journey, he was strangely depleted of energy.

It could be the dark magic his roots had detected in the air next to the Riven when they'd encountered the Fairy Queen. The voices had been reaching out to him even as they scared him away. The voices hadn't been the queen's, so whose voices were they? Their resonance was akin to the roods, which confused him.

He wasn't thinking straight. Possibly some of the Erlking's mesmerization remained in his trunk. He hadn't been the same since hearing the music and seeing such wondrous sights, or visions, as he came to realize they were, when he'd finally roused from the spell.

Rowan stood by idly as Murda and the maids rushed to take care of their new charges. The castle was unfamiliar to him, and he wouldn't know what to do even if he was acquainted with it. A keen sense of uselessness sparked inside him. Finally, Murda left the children and came over to him. "Rowan, what can we do for you?"

"*Ach*, he'll be wanting to hole up in the Conservatory, I imagine, miss. That's where Woodsly always went to get refreshed," one maid stated as she patted his arm. "Take 'im there. We've got the young'uns well in hand 'ere now."

Murda took Rowan's hand and led him through a large dining hall. Long marble tables had stone chairs tucked tightly beneath them. They passed several rooms. He shrunk when he entered a long hallway featuring portraits of red-haired troll queens. Fearsome animals were displayed on the walls. Trophies gleamed from glass cases.

He was glad when they left that room behind, entering a darker, bare stone hallway. Though it was dark, Murda didn't need light from the unlit lamps to find her way. Rowan stayed close to her side, not trusting the dark space.

"Here we are. The Conservatory. You'll find many rare plants and animals here." She stood before two large glass doors. Moonlight trickled through their surface, shining across the stone hall with blessed light.

Murda took the key from the wall and held it up. "We lock the doors because Horra's pet pudge wudgie will get out if we don't. Not only is she curious, she's quite intelligent for a bird." She swung the first door open. The instant the air—full of loam, plants, and life—hit him, he dropped to his knees on the stone entry. His limbs trembled and his sap sang in his stem.

"Rowan? Are you all right?" Murda shrieked, bending over him.

"*Druboldolog,*" he hoped to assure her with his tone. She helped him stand and took him inside before closing the door.

"You must be exhausted. I know Horra would show you around, but I want to get back and make sure the children aren't giving the maids a hard time. There's water over there." Murda pointed to where he could hear a small trickle of a stream. "And there are many kinds of nutrients on the tables around the end over there." She pointed to a table where bags of fertilizer and other items lay opened next to pots.

He rested a hand on her arm and bowed his head. It was the best he could do to show his gratitude.

"I'm going to lock you in, but I'm sure you'll be fine. Horra will likely come to check on you later. She comes here often to feed Pidge. Rest. I'll see you soon." She turned and left, the keys jangling as she locked it back up.

He stared across the grand expanse, soaking in the humid atmosphere, rich with so many of the essentials he needed. Whispers of slumber leaked from the sleeping trees. Though winter didn't touch the ground here, they were still subject to the yearly winter cycle. They weren't dead or spiritless. Magic lived in this space. It seeped from every leaf. It was as light as the Riven had been dark. Joy and relief intermixed in his heart-wood, making him giddy.

A screech rent the air as a tree's branches rattled. A large, dark bird leaped from the tree and reached out great, dark wings. It was a grand bird, massive and dark as oil.

Ah. This must be Horra's pet pudge wudgie.

He closed his eyes, used his druid ability to connect with her spirit right before she landed in front of the stairs leading up to the landing where he stood. "*Bergardiam,*" he called to her. His words didn't have to relay their meaning, birds didn't understand words. She would understand his meaning through their connection.

Imprinted by the magic of a rood already, she accepted his presence without suspicion. He reached out to touch her head, a common first greeting. He'd performed it many times in the Weald's garden with the whimsy birds that chittered endlessly.

Pidge stepped up and rubbed her head across his mossy trunk. The moonlight glowed down on her ebony body, highlighting a single small feather suspended on top of her head. He stroked her neck, and she preened beneath his touch.

Pidge stepped back and gave him a curious golden glance before fluffing her feathers and clucking at him. She'd accepted him. They were friends. Her head darted sideways, and she let out a sharp note.

He opened his mouth to reply, but she swooped in with her beak before he could make a sound. Mouth wide open, he gagged as Pidge grabbed hold of something and tugged. And tugged. And with one last pull, yanked something out.

Rowan stumbled back, shocked.

Suspended from her beak was a plump worm. With a fling and a snap, the insect twirled in the air and disappeared down her gullet. She cluck-purred at him, her eyes glowing against the dark garden.

"What did—" Rowan slapped a hand over his mouth. He hadn't been tongue tied after all. The Erlking had unleashed a magic grubby worm on him when they'd jumped over that downed tree. It had settled into his mouth—the largest spot in his body and the best place to siphon off his magic. That's what had caused him to speak so oddly. And possibly why he'd become so tired.

He grabbed hold of Pidge and hugged her. She *scree'd* in offence, but that didn't stop him. He let go of her and stared into her golden eyes. "Noble pudge wudgie, you are a genius."

She chirped her agreement and fluffed her feathers.

Rowan laughed. He couldn't believe his fortune to be rid of the impediment. And to think it had not been an actual curse after all. Had Pidge not removed it, the results would've been dire. Grubby worms were ravenous, sucking their prey dry within days or weeks. He'd have been a withered stick in no time. "Thank you for saving me."

Freeing herself from Rowan's grasp, Pidge spread her wings wide and took off back to her nest in the large Yew tree in the center of the Conservatory. Once there, she screeched down at him, still unhappy with his actions.

"This is wonderful." Rowan turned and took it all in. New plants dozing in the dirt. Herbs slumbering in pots. Wetness trickled from his eyes. He ran a finger over it, surprised. "Druids don't cry," he said to himself. He shuffled down the stairs, stepping onto the rich soil with a loud sigh. "Maybe the trolls aren't so bad after all."

He dug in with his roots, naming all the plants to himself as he took in the boundless nutrients the Conservatory offered him.

~ HORRA ~

Exhausted as she was, Horra's mind whirred with the implications and complications of her father leaving the kingdom in non-royal claws. Not that she hadn't done the same thing with Balk after her father had become incapacitated when he'd been mesmerized. However, her agreement with Balk had had several stipulations to it that guaranteed the throne would go automatically back to her.

"Princess?" Sageel shook her arm.

"Wha—yes?" she stammered, trying to gather her shaken thoughts into order.

"You look like something dragged you up from the bottom of the bog and left you to dry. And maybe slung some dung at you for good measure. You need a shower and some food. You do the first and I'll get the second sent up to your room. There'll be time to worry about the king's mission tomorrow." Sageel strode off without another word, her mind on her task ahead.

Stubborn maid.

Horra should be thankful for her steadfast friend, but she couldn't shake the dread seeping into her heart. Sorsha Rindthorn had always been the epitome of a professional. She'd seen no sign the woman would try to overreach and take over the throne. But still. Horra shook her head, and a twig fell to the clean hallway floor.

Reluctantly, Horra headed to the bathroom. Sageel was right. She needed to clean up. There'd be no saving her clothes, possibly her boots. She did her best thinking in the shower, anyway. The water was cold and revolting, but she had a clearer mind when she finished.

Back in her room, Horra munched on broiled frog legs and a wild yak stew with bracken bread and bacon grease. Sageel had brought more than she needed, so she placed the tray on her dresser for a snack later.

She ran through all the things she knew about the old swamplands. It wasn't much. Her foremothers reviled their vulgar history. Her forefathers weren't much on recording history, either.

Though there were legends of trolls who remained in the

swamps, officially the record showed no troll residence there. Most settled in the villages to the south near the old Witch Lands, or they came further south to Oddar to live in the mountains like civilized trolls. Her eyes drooped, and she shook her head to stay awake. What she needed was to go to the library to research her forefather's history. There had to be something in their vast library.

A yawn escaped her. She'd just close her eyes for a moment. That was all.

~ *HORRA* ~

Horra woke to the noise of arguing outside of her door. She smacked her lips and realized Sageel had put coocoo powder in her food the night before. How much had she put in it? Horra closed her eyes and drifted off again before a thunk woke her.

Her feet touched the ground before she realized she was moving. Every part of her body protested and ached. Slowly, she moved to the dresser and then the door. Rubbing her eyes, she yawned widely.

The arguing became heated. Voices raised.

Horra sagged.

Who in the world would be arguing outside her door in the royal hallway? Claw on the doorhandle, Horra opened the door and gazed blearily out into the hallway.

Sageel stood sprawled in front of her door, her thin arms up shielding the entry. The maid turned her head to glance at Horra when the door opened. "See what you done? You gone and woken up the princess. She needs her rest, she does. She's a growing lady." Sageel's voice was a shriek, which was quite unusual. The woman was always calm and collected.

On the other side of Sageel stood Torren's mother, Sorsha, who was rusty-faced and angry as a bungbee. She let out a sound quite similar to *pfth*, which put Horra instantly on alert. Proxy or not, she didn't get to *pfth* at a princess.

"What is going on?" Horra demanded. "And what time is it?"

"It's daybreak. Time to get ready for school. That's what time it is." Sorsha huffed at her. A severe bun pulled at the woman's green face and displayed her pointed ears. Horra didn't think she'd ever seen the woman's ears before. She stood business-like in a suit and heels.

Horra's eyes widened. There'd been no classes since the Erlking had taken over the castle. Woodsly had been their only instructor since before Horra was born, so there was no one to replace him when he reverted to his seed.

"What do you mean, school? We have no instructor." Horra struggled to sound alert. Her body ached and her clawed feet were still raw from blisters. She was in no mood to be told to go to school this morning. Or do anything but go back to bed.

Sorsha lifted her head and huffed. "I will be your instructor. Now, go get dressed and come down to the lab. We have much work to catch up on. You've missed months of classes." With a snap of her heels, she turned and strode away back down the hall as if she assumed Horra would do as she asked without question.

Had the woman completely lost her mind?

Sageel stepped away from her threshold. "I'm sorry, Princess. She's been a tyrant, that woman." She clicked her tongue. "I don't know what's got into her. She's always been so kind to us maids. But now." Her tawny head dropped and shook in sad disgust. "She woke those children up before coming here to get you. Most of 'em are down there crying now like they've lost their last toy."

Horra put her claw on the woman's shoulder. Something had to be done about this, and she was the only one who could do it. She dug deep and mustered enough energy to deal with this fresh crisis. "You survived the Erlking. You can survive Sorsha Rindthorn. Let me get dressed and see what's going on."

CHAPTER 48

~ *HORRA* ~

Sorsha had lined the children up, smallest to largest, along the center tables in the lab. Horra chewed the last of the frog legs, her leftovers, as she entered the room.

Torren sat at the end of the lab at a table by himself, his head hanging in defeat. Murda was nowhere to be seen. Horra frowned. Neither was Rowan. If anyone should be here, it would be him, able to speak or not. He was a virtual informa-pedia, after all.

Sorsha had several potions noted on the green chalkboards along the far wall. "Good of you to join us at last, Princess Fyd. Please take a seat long the far wall there. No talking while I go over my lesson plan, please."

Horra dragged her bare, clawed feet across the cold floor. She'd wrapped them in fine gauze to help the blisters to heal. She glanced around. The fairies had done a fine job of fixing the skylights and the cupboards. New jars gleamed from the shelves, their contents full again. Terrariums were bursting with plants and critters crawling everywhere.

It brought a sense of nostalgia back until she scanned the scared faces of the children.

She considered objecting and overruling Sorsha for a moment. However, she needed to get down to why her father was gone and had left Sorsha in charge.

The seat next to Torren was empty, so she climbed onto the stool and flopped onto the table, mimicking him.

Sorsha stood at the front, writing on the board.

Horra squinted. Was that some kind of potion? It wasn't anything she recognized.

Torren gave her an apologetic glance. "She got you too?" he whispered.

Horra rubbed at her nose, a side effect of coocoo powder wearing off. "Sageel wanted to stop her, but your mother seems a bit determined to teach us something."

"This isn't like Ma. Something's wrong." Torren's low voice sifted through the crack between his arms.

Sorsha turned to glare at them. Horra sat up and acted the part of an eager student. Woodsly would turn over in his grave to see her behaving so attentively to another instructor, even if it were fake.

"That's stating the obvious," she spoke out of the side of her mouth. "But what do we do? And where is Rowan?"

Torren moved his claw in front of his mouth. "I don't think Ma knows about him."

"Let's not tell her then. In the meantime, let's try to figure out what's happening." Horra glanced meaningfully at the textbook in front of them.

He nodded, and together, they started their search.

By the end of the hour, Horra kept track by the clock on the wall, Sorsha was still rambling on about potions. Half of the children had nodded off, and she and Torren had found no leads in their books.

Horra shut her manual with a frown. "Cover me," she whispered to Torren.

His eyes widened. "What? No," he mouthed back.

"I'm going to check on Rowan," she uttered back in a low tone.

"Can I help you with something, Princess?" Sorsha had turned and was glaring at her and Torren.

"I was just telling Torren I need to use the restroom." She smiled as innocently as she could manage. It had always worked with Woodsly. And then she'd slip away to the passages.

Sorsha pursed her green lips. "Fine, but don't be long. I'm getting to the important part next."

Horra glanced at the board. Nothing Sorsha had written made sense, but Horra didn't point it out.

Torren raised his claw high. "I have to go to the bathroom too."

"After the princess returns. Now, on page one hundred-thirty-five," Sorsha droned on.

With a shrug at Torren, Horra hurried to grab a jar of torentula eggs and hustled out the door and into the hallway. She headed straight for the Conservatory.

~ HORRA ~

Keys in her claws, Horra flung the doors wide open. She inhaled a deep breath of her favorite scent in the Wilden Lands —loamy earth. The warmth inside the Conservatory beckoned her in. Her shoulders instantly relaxed. "*Ah*," she breathed out.

"Princess? Is that you?" Rowan's clackity voice came from somewhere in the middle of the garden.

"Rowan? You can talk again?" She shut the doors, pocketed the keys, and meandered down the steps. "Where are you? I need your help."

Pidge squealed, and the center Yew tree shook as her pet took flight.

Horra unscrewed the jar. She took out an egg, threw it in the air, and smiled as Pidge darted and gobbled it up.

"Oh, yes indeed. Your incredible bird freed my tongue last eve." Rowan stepped from underneath a branch and came into view.

Horra's eyes widened. He'd grown. Not only taller, but wider. She stood staring at the druid, her mouth hanging open.

Rowan tilted his head, his beady eyes now shining a polished mahogany brown. "Is something wrong, Princess? Or are you surprised that I am finally coherent?" His hands were no longer twigs, but fully developed. His arms that had been mere sticks had filled out. Moss still covered his bark, but it didn't look like an invasion taking place, but more of a fashion statement.

"You need to look at yourself." Pidge cried out above her head. Horra tossed a couple of eggs high and grabbed Rowan's branchy arm, running for the pool.

They zigged and zagged to get to the hidden gem of a waterfall. Sun shone in from the glass above, allowing her to see fish dart about. "Look," she told Rowan.

Rowan blinked at his reflection. He reached out to his twisted crown atop his head. Bending over, he squinted to study his face. Finally, he opened his mouth and examined his tongue. Everything looked normal for a woodgoblin.

Horra brushed a claw across the plushy willows growing

out of the bank, loving the velvety softness. "How did you do it?"

He glanced up at her and stood. "I do not know. Murda brought me here last eve and after I made friends with your pudge wudgie, she removed a grubby worm from my mouth." Rowan stuck a foot into the water. The hair-like roots were no longer there, and the appendage resembled an actual foot now. "After that, I could speak coherently once more. Then, I settled my roots deep into the soil to replenish my strength."

"And?" Horra asked, impatient to know what had occurred.

He shrugged his broad shoulders. "And that is it. I woke this morning refreshed and reinvigorated. Where did you get your soil from, Princess? It is far superior to anything I've found outside of the Weald so far."

"As it should. It's from the former Elven Lands of what we now know as the Weald. My foremothers took some of their enchanted soil to build it." She held a claw up. "Don't worry, the elves had already deserted it. We didn't steal it. Anyway, Queen Calcy, our first queen, wanted to conserve the magic found in the soil, so they built the Conservatory. Now we use it to keep rare plants and animals safe."

Understanding spread across Rowan's face, but quickly puckered into confusion. "I see. Why didn't Merrow inform me that the Weald used to be elf land?"

"To be fair, the elves used to inhabit these mountains as well, along with some of the witching lands as far south as the Darkling territory of the dark fairies. Their kingdom had wide borders across the whole of the Wilden Lands. Perhaps, because of this, it didn't seem to be a necessary fact to teach you?" She was grasping but had found Merrow to be more than honest in all of his dealings with her. If he kept something from Rowan, she could only believe there was a good reason for it.

Rowan got a far-off look, and he stared into space.

She placed a gentle claw on his arm. "I need your help in something else, actually. It appears as if Torren's mother has something controlling her. She is not acting normal, and I was hoping you might help me figure out what has happened to her."

It took a moment for Rowan to shake himself free from whatever musings had taken over his mind with their discussion about the elves. "Yes, of course." He raised an arm and allowed Horra to lead him.

Pidge squealed and flew above their heads. Horra tossed the rest of the pickled eggs, the juice dripping down her arm, as they made their way to the doors. Ravenous as always, Pidge chattered at her when the jar was empty.

"I'm sorry, Pidge. That's all I have. You'll have to wait until lunchtime now." Horra sat the jar along a ledge that held gardening tools.

Pidge sent her a sideways glance. With a squawk, she barreled straight for the doorway, which Horra realized too late that she'd left closed, but not locked.

Talons out, Pidge clasped the handle, jerked it, and opened the door. She was gone before Horra could yell her name.

CHAPTER 49

~ ROWAN ~

Horra dashed after the ebony bird, screaming and yelling for Pidge to come back. Rowan trailed them, using the sunlight shining from the skylights in the castle's roof to see. He was in no hurry. The other troll female had shown him the way there, and he recalled the path clearly.

Horra's shrill shrieks were as noisy as the bird's joyous exclamations of freedom. pudge wudgies, he knew from his Critter Guide, were high-maintenance pets. They needed to hunt and chase or they would get bored and obstinate.

Rowan worked his way through the hall with the portraits. With more light to see by, it wasn't near as scary as it had been at first. Each fierce painting showed a fiery-haired woman. He studied them all, setting them into the fibers of his memory. Merrow did not have books on the troll's genealogy, so he found this quite interesting and helpful.

He hesitated when he came upon the door to the dining room. The sounds of Horra chasing the bird came from a different direction, so he turned and headed along a narrower hallway. Children ran through an opened door at the opposite end of the hallway. Horra's screams and Pidge's squawks came from the door closer to him.

"Get her off of my mother." Torren yelled at Horra.

A harried Horra stood over Pidge, who perched on another creature. They were positioned so he couldn't get a good look because the princess was tugging at her pet bird. Meanwhile, high-pitch shrieks came from the creature below the pudge wudgie.

The chaos didn't surprise him, even if he'd found new respect for the princess and her friends. Trolls were not cultured, not in a refined way. "Princess?" he called out, hoping to be helpful.

"Not now, Rowan. Can't you see I'm busy?" Horra battled against her bird, feathers flying in their struggle.

Torren grabbed Horra's stomach and pulled. Together, they flipped Pidge off the third creature, who Torren had called his mother.

Pidge landed on her tail feathers, a greasy black grubby worm in her beak. With a snap, the bug was gone.

Horra, having landed on top of Torren, shuffled off him and with her arms wide, shooed the bird out of the room. "Someone close the other door."

Hair askew and cheeks a ruddy mud color, Horra escorted Pidge into the hallway and slammed the first door behind her. "What's gotten into you? Bad bird. You don't attack trolls."

Rowan held out a finger. "If I may, Princess?"

Horra brushed feathers off her shirt and straightened her clothes. "What is it, Rowan?"

Her distraction and indifferent tone of voice didn't dampen

his enthusiasm. "Pidge has done you a favor. She has removed a malignantly magical bug from Torren's mother, possibly rescuing her from a terrible fate."

Horra stopped what she was doing and stared at him. She swung her head back toward her pet, who was now fluttering around in the hallway, looking for her next prey. Scared, the children bolted, screaming.

"Pidge did what?" Horra asked, panting.

Rowan bent down to get a better look at her mud-colored eyes. "Did you hit your head? You're acting dazed."

Her face screwed up. "I'm fine. I was asking for clarification in case you didn't understand the question."

"*Ah.* I see. This grubby worm, called malignatitis parasitica, is what Pidge pulled from my tongue last eve. They are a parasitic strain of magical beetle larva that feed upon a creature's magic. This leaves the victim weak, or mad, possibly killing them if they remain for too long." He smiled down at the troll, who's mouth was still open wide enough for him to see her back teeth.

He had to wonder at his forebearer's ability to impart etiquette to these trolls. Either Woodsly was incapable or the trolls were more obstinate than he first considered.

The door behind the princess opened. "Horra come quick." Torren waved her back inside the room.

She rushed to his side and in front of another female troll. This woman's green hair was darker than her skin, but her features resembled Torren.

"Sorsha, are you okay?" Horra asked, sitting on her knees.

The woman rubbed her head. "I am now. It was as if I were walking through some strange dream."

Rowan nodded. "The grubby worm's toxin. It can affect certain creatures with hallucinations."

They all turned to look at him.

"Grubby worm?" Sorsha repeated in a sharp tone. She paled. "I had a grubby worm on me?"

"It has to be the Erlking's work." Horra glanced at Sorsha and back at him. "How do we get rid of them, besides having Pidge attack everyone who's infested? Better yet, how do we prevent them?"

"I am not versed in insecticide or pest prevention. Only the actual pests themselves. It seems, however, that you have a vast library with which to do research." He waved an arm for the room across the hall.

Horra grinned.

* * *

~ HORRA ~

With Torren absent and taking care of his mother, Horra yanked at the rope she'd hastily created to wrangle Pidge back to the Conservatory. The bird was too smart for her own good. She'd balked when Horra had tried treats alone. It seemed she understood when she was being bribed now. So, along with some roasted roaches, Horra was going to have to drag her unwilling pet back to her home.

"Rowan, stop yammering and open the door, please." The druid had done nothing but talk the whole time Horra was wrestling with her pet. She was certain he was trying all at once to make up for all the days he couldn't speak.

"Certainly, Princess." He sauntered over to the door, his newly acquired rootless legs gliding against the stone floor. Woodsly had walked like that—effortlessly.

She tossed the last roach into the Conservatory and let the rope go when Pidge dodged for the treat. Horra had made a slipknot, which would loosen when let go, so Pidge would be fine. "Close it now," she squealed at Rowan. When he'd shut the door, she hastily locked it, hanging the keys on the wall.

"Whew! That bird is a clawful." She leaned against the wall. Her body was still stiff and sore, the bandages long gone from her feet. They throbbed now, but she didn't have the energy to go upstairs to get more bandages.

Rowan steepled his fingers in front of him. "pudge wudgies are indeed handfuls. Avid hunters, their species will eat well over twice their weight each day. Given that kind of intake, they also need to be exercised regularly so they don't become anxious, rambunctious, or overweight. I can help you work out a schedule if you'd like."

Horra glanced at him. Her father was missing, grubby worms had infested the castle, and he was worried about Pidge's schedule? She pushed herself from the wall. "We can do that later. Now we have to figure out how to get rid of these grubby worms, and then I have to figure out why my father went to the swamps. C'mon." Horra headed to the library without looking back.

Oddar's library was organized by subject and then by alphabetical order. Horra headed for the Critterology section and searched for grubby worms. One book rested in front of the others on the shelf, the Critters from *GR* to *GU*.

"*Uh-uh-uh.*" Rowan's words stopped her.

She stiffened and rested a claw on the book. He sounded so like Woodsly that she automatically bristled. "What is it?" she asked through clenched teeth.

"Look under *M* for *malignatitis parasitica*," came his reply, as if he owned the books she was looking at. She liked him better when he talked nonsense.

"You look under *M*, I'm looking under *G*." Horra yanked the book down and took it to a table near to the shelf. She searched in the index and ran a claw down the list of critters. "Groose..."

she murmured, "Ah, here it is. Grubby worm." Horra flipped to page one hundred and ninety-eight and read.

"Grubby worms, (order *magilapaeda*) *malignatitis parasitica*, are the larvae form of the morphological, *blah, blah, blah*." She drew her claw down the page. "There are several types, the most toxic being the bright red blister beetle and the next being these greasy black ones."

She looked up to catch Rowan watching her. "They siphon off the magical aura of creatures, but when no magic is found, as in the case with trolls, it often leads their victim to become crazed because of their toxicity."

"Does it state how to get rid of them or prevent their infestation?" Rowan blinked brown eyes at her.

It all clicked in Horra's mind. She knew her father wouldn't just leave their kingdom. "Swamp sludge, but only a certain kind. That's why this book was already pulled out some from that section of informapedias. My father must've been researching it too. That's why he left the kingdom and barricaded Hobgoblin Pass. He must've realized there was an infestation, and since he'd lived in the swamp once, he knew exactly where to get the sludge."

"Do we wait for the king to return?" Rowan asked.

"No." Horra slammed her book shut. "We're going to exercise Pidge."

CHAPTER 50

~ HORRA ~

"Rowan, you'll ride with me." Horra buckled the last strap of Nimble's cinch. She eyed the sun, realizing how late it had already become. It was past lunchtime already. "Has anyone seen Murda?"

Hobgoblins raced around the sloppy courtyard, preparing horses and supplies they would need for a trip to find the king. The swamp was at least two day's ride from the castle, according to her trusty map, and she planned to ride as far as she could before night fell.

"Is there no other conveyance?" Rowan asked. He stood stiffly off to the side, his handmade bag clutched to his trunk.

"Would you rather ride Pidge?" Her question was only partially serious. Rowan had gotten too big to fit on Pidge. However, the hopeful look in his eyes made her laugh. "I was just kidding, Rowan. I doubt you'd find her a better *conveyance* than Nimble, anyway."

"Here's some food, Princess." Sageel handed Horra a basket full of wrapped goodies.

She dumped them into the side saddle unceremoniously and disregarded her maid's *harumph*. "Thank you. Any spruce juice?" she asked hopefully.

Another hobgoblin ran up with three canteens dragging in the mud. "Here, Princess."

There wasn't time to frown. They had to get moving. The last thing she needed to do was get Pidge.

Shouts echoed against the stone castle. Everyone turned toward where the sound originated.

"*Ach*, who could that be?" Sageel wrung her gnarled hands in her apron.

"It's the king." Rowan said, a brightness in his voice that hadn't been there before. "It's the king! He's coming in fast. Make way." He rushed over to Horra, his eyes wide with earnestness. "The trees told me."

Horra didn't hesitate, understanding the implication. She drew Nimble over out of the way. The shouting grew louder, and at last, they could see a rider on a tall horse coming from the north. His cape whipped at his back. She strained to hear what he was shouting. "Can anyone hear what he's saying?"

Rowan's gaze drifted off as if listening. "Danger, they're telling me. Something, something, the worqs." He turned to her. "The worqs are coming."

Horra's heart dropped and pounded hard in her chest. "Get in the castle. Everyone, get back in the castle."

"What about Nimble?" Sageel's wringing hands were the only giveaway to her apprehension.

"Get Torren to open the throne room doors. They are the only ones big enough for a gulgoyle to go through. I can't leave him out here for them to mistreat. Get a move on, Rowan," she screamed at the transfixed druid.

Like marbles on a stone floor, the hobgoblins ran around in a panic. Rowan jerked the kitchen door open and ran inside.

Nimble dug his feet in and pulled his head back. Smoke curled out of his nostrils and his eyes were open wide with fear. Horra stopped to pet and reassure him. "It's okay. We're just going into the throne room. Somebody get me some oats, please."

Her father was finally close enough to hear. "Get in the castle. Lock all the doors." His voice rang, though she lost sight of him around a corner.

Someone handed her a pail of cracked corn and oats. "Here you go, Nimble. Just a little treat." She walked backward, coaxing her pet around the front of the castle. By the time she got him to the entry, her father crested the hill up to the castle.

"Open the doors," she barked at no one in particular.

Her father darted straight for her on a horse she'd never seen before. He was riding bareback, and his clothes and hair were wild. He'd tied several canteens and containers to his chest and they bounced around at his legs.

"Get inside," he yelled.

His frenzy made fear catch like fire on kerosene inside Horra. "I can't open the door and coax Nimble in at the same time."

King Fyd jumped off the horse before it fully stopped and ran for the doors. Blood ran down his side, his shirt torn where some weapon had injured him.

"Father, are you all right?" She clutched Nimble's reins tight.

"I will be if we get into the castle in time. The Erlking is not far behind me." With a last shove, the doors slowly arced open. "Get in." He ran back to the horse.

Horra led Nimble in. Luckily, the doorway was tall enough

the gulgoyle didn't have to duck or he might have balked at going inside. "Good boy."

Her father blew past her and Nimble once they cleared the entryway, the horse behind him. It clopped away—toward Nimble and the oats. The king unstrapped the containers, and the smell hit Horra's nose.

She coughed, recognizing swamp sludge. It was rank and pure by the noxious scent of it.

Sorsha ran through the doorway. "What's going on?" Her hair hung down her back, and she wore a robe. She must've been resting after her ordeal with Pidge.

Torren quickly followed. "You've recovered!" His glance at Sorsha was brief.

"The castle is under attack. Follow emergency protocol," her father bellowed. "Horra, take the windows. Torren, gather as many sacks, bows, and arrows as you can from the Armory. Sorsha, check the rear of the castle to make sure it's secure, then come back. We need everyone. The Erlking is coming."

Horra rushed for the windows, yanking down the iron bars that slid between the stones and locked them in place. It had been her job during their emergency drills since a child. Now, she'd grown enough that she didn't have to crawl up the wall to get to them. It took her no time to set the bars and lock them into place.

"Not that one. We need firing positions both in front and in the back. Keep three windows free on each side." Her father drug the mighty lynchpin over to the entry's double doors and set one side in place.

"Got it." Horra ran to the other side and secured those windows, leaving two more open.

Torren ran in with his arms full of items. He dumped them on the table next to the thrones. Six bows of varying sizes and several dozen arrows, along with some cloth and burlap feed sacks. "This is all that I could find. Is there anything else you need, sir?"

"Gather the containers I brought in with me. Horra, unscrew the tips of the arrows and get some string. We're going to substitute them for mud bombs."

"Mud bombs?" she asked.

"The Erlking's using grubby worms to control the worqs. It's how he got to the trolls who disappeared. It doesn't take long for the toxin to turn a troll mad. For the others, such as the worqs, we might still have a chance of removing them, and freeing the victims."

———

HORRA HURRIED from the lab with some spoons, scissors, and string, almost giddy with anticipation. It had been years since she'd last been involved in a mud fight. She hesitated before her mother's portrait, which the fairies had repaired and rehung.

Her mother had been an ace at mud-slinging. She'd taught Horra everything she knew. The week before her mother died, they'd had her last epic Mud Crawl in the swamps at the base of the castle's mountain. Tears gathered in Horra's eyes. Their team, the Royal Hogs, had won claws down. "I'll make you proud, I promise." Her mother smiled down at her.

Determined, Horra entered the throne room to find the children and hobgoblins, along with Murda and Sorsha. The female trolls lined the children up and were giving them instructions from their Wartime Protocol manual. "Here, Father."

"Thank you, Daughter. *Ah,* I forgot we might need scissors and spoons. Good catch." He took the items and added them to the table. "Everyone gather around. You will each have a job.

First, cut a hunk of cloth, roll it in the mud, and get it good and messy." He demonstrated the first one for them. "Just like this. Tie it off and then attach it to the arrows like this."

Music filtered through the stone walls. It wasn't just one instrument this time. The Erlking had a virtual symphony going with tweeting high notes and jangling low beats.

"Everyone, stuff your ears," Murda yelled above everyone's voices.

As one, the hobgoblins and children shoved cloth and cotton—whatever they had—into their ears

"What are you doing?" the king asked, perplexed.

"We found if you stuff your ears, the music magic doesn't mesmerize you." Horra took two chunks of burlap and handed them to him.

"You are as smart as your mother and grandmother." The king took the cloth and put it in his ears. With a wave of his arms, he drew everyone together around the table.

The children tore the cloth, dunked it into the sludge, and then tied it off. The hobgoblins were next, finishing off the mud bombs and attaching them to the arrows.

Horra gathered the arrows at the end of the table, where Sorsha and Murda waited to line them up. "Where's Rowan?" she asked them.

Murda glanced around. "Is he in the Conservatory? That's been his favorite place so far."

"That makes sense." She was torn. Should she go warn the druid? He was with Pidge, which might be the safest place for him. For a moment, she considered putting him inside the passageway, but the warning her mother had sternly given her as a child stopped her. Only royal female trolls could step foot inside that holy ground without losing the Creature God's blessings.

But could she make an exception? Rowan was the newly

crowned druid warrior, after all. She glanced around at the other's activity and decided. If they were overcome and the need arose, she would escape to the Conservatory, find Rowan and Pidge, and take them into the passages. They could escape when the time was right if needed. They'd be perfectly safe there behind the barriers.

The music grew louder the closer the Erlking came. It tingled along Horra's hide, the heavy pulling of the dark magic like breathing in smoke. It was cloying and choking.

"Take your positions," King Fyd yelled as he stood watch at the windows.

Sorsha and Murda gathered a dozen children and moved to the rear of the castle, their backup should they need it.

Horra took her position in the center, between her father and Torren. The king waited by the last window, his gaze focused on the front yard.

A dozen worqs riding harried beasts clomped up the road toward the castle. Their metal armor clanked along, joining the clomping of their beasts. Piskies flew around them, their lights glittering even though the sun was still shining. Behind them and riding in the fairy queen's crystal carriage was the dark figure of the Erlking.

Horra's heart sunk to the ground. The fairy queen was nowhere in sight. Neither were her guards. However, her disfigured daughter sat slumped next to the grinning Erlking. He waved a bony hand in the air in a strange gesture. The music stopped, and so did the army.

He stood with a grand flourish of his black cape. The fairy princess didn't move. "I've come for the troll princess."

CHAPTER 51

~ ROWAN ~

Information zinged along Rowan's roots, which had dug deep into the elven dirt in the Conservatory. The trees informed him the Erlking had arrived with a small group and the injured fairy princess. He couldn't tell what was happening with the trolls or the others inside the castle. There were no plants with which to communicate.

Pidge screeched from her branches high in the Yew tree, clearly distressed. The pudge wudgie's connection to the roods had opened the bird up to root transmissions. He assumed it was necessary when the princess had been on the run with his seed. Without a rood to rescind that gift, the bird was sensitive to the tree's mood and messages.

"Come," he called to her. It would do no good to have an anxious bird flying around while he figured out what his part would be. Merrow had versed him in tactical and strategic plans, but violence wasn't something he was comfortable with yet.

Pidge swung a wide arc in the air before settling down next to him. The windows on the west provided a small glimpse of the front lawn. More of the view was of the small swamp at the base of the castle, but that was a drop-off and probably not something the Erlking would incorporate into his attack.

He stroked the bird's neck to calm her. Her earnest desire to help vibrated off her in waves. "Yes. If I can come up with a plan." Somehow, he needed to get out of the castle. However, the king had ordered it to be sealed. There wasn't a way to get out.

Pidge crooked her head at him and chirruped. She blinked golden eyes at him.

"You know a way out?"

She let out a rumbling purr and took off toward the center of the garden.

Rowan followed her to a section of gnarled, knotty trees. His roots detected fresh air. Pidge skirted a wide tree, which moved ever so slightly to let the bird by. It greeted him warmly. The moss across his trunk moved as if by wind and then settled.

Sap sang in his inner fibers. There was a rood left, a very old and wise one. Which explained why Pidge was so attuned to his kind.

"I see," Rowan said. "Thank you, Master Knurl, for your help and information."

Together, Rowan and Pidge crawled out of a hole in the castle's fenced wall. He was going to make sure the pudge wudgie got her exercise and saved them all.

~ *HORRA* ~

Horra was glad her father couldn't hear what the Erlking said. No one besides her could. But even if they could, she wouldn't give herself over to the fiend, hostage or not. However, she worried about the other princess's safety. Would they be able to get to her before the Erlking did something else to the poor girl?

The king held his fist up, a signal to hold. He focused on the Erlking and the carriage.

"Come now." The Erlking gestured toward his small army of worqs. "You're surrounded. Give me the princess, and no one else gets hurt." His hood covered his despicable head, but Horra was sure he was smiling as he said it.

"Liar." Horra glanced at her father, a frown on her face. He smiled at the defiance he must've seen in her expression.

King Fyd began the countdown. "Five ... four ... three ... two ..."

With a fling of the Erlking's gaunt hand, the music started up again.

"One ..." The king waved.

Torren was the first to shoot. He was always over-zealous in archery. Horra took the second shot at the biggest worq in front. The one she owed for a few bruises.

It sailed true, hitting him on his temple. The mud bomb splattered, covering the side of his head and half of his face, dripping down to his chest in a thick layer of black goo.

She grabbed another from the quiver in front of her and aimed again. Arrow after arrow, she let loose. Five worqs were down, clawing at their heads as the toxic mud smothered the grubby worms.

Piskies darted in between the sailing arrows. One flew by Horra's window, intent on getting in. She jabbed the arrow at the creature, knocking it out of the air in an explosion of mud. Two piskies zagged down to catch their fallen comrade, only to get dirty in their haste to save their friend. All of them fell to the ground, rolling around. Grubby worms fell off the dazed piskies.

The Erlking stood tall, his arms moving as if conducting a symphony. Possibly he was, because the music changed as he moved. However, the shouts and noise of the worqs coming out of their music-siphoned stupor rose to drown out the notes. Mud caked their ears, inhibiting the music magic from penetrating the once loyal group.

Suddenly, from the side of the castle, came a black blur.

"Pidge!" Horra screamed. How did her pet get out of the castle?

Rowan stepped out from the side of the castle. Green foliage covered his body and limbs. Moss and liverwort covered his face in a thick, green bush.

What did he think he was doing? He wasn't even armed. "Rowan, get out of there," she shouted down at him, but he didn't hear her. He kept a straight path toward the Erlking.

Pidge darted and attacked one of the worqs, like she had with Sorsha. The pudge wudgie was a force to be reckoned with. She tugged and pulled until, finally, the grubby worm came loose from its victim. With a gulp, the worm was gone, and Pidge was onto the next worq.

Horra had no arrows left. Torren also was out of ammunition. Her father had the last of his arrows nocked and ready to send flying.

The Erlking reached down and grabbed the princess by her long hair. Holding her up, he chuckled. "Not a step closer, druid, or the princess dies." He formed a dark, swirling sphere in his free hand and held it to the princess's head.

Rowan stopped.

The king's arrow loosed and flew directly at the Erlking.

Startled, the Erlking ducked. Mud splattered as it hit the fairy princess right between her eyes. It covered her head and oozed down the front of her body. A black blob fell from her neck.

Pidge swooped in and it was gone.

A scream rent the air, and the princess awakened, realizing she was covered in toxic, smelly sludge. She wrestled out of the Erlking's hold and fell over the side of the carriage to the ground. Mud dripped down the side of the crystal carriage.

Rowan's branches reached out toward the Erlking.

"Yes!" Horra screamed. Rowan had him. They'd won.

With a blinding flash of blue light, the carriage lifted out of Rowan's reach. A streak of cold magic burst. The carriage was gone, sailing over the treetops, disappearing from sight in mere moments.

"No!" Horra fell to her knees.

He'd escaped them again!

CHAPTER 52

~ *HORRA* ~

Horra stared out the window down at the front courtyard, unseeing. Her eyes stung with unwanted, angry tears.

"Daughter," her father's deep voice pulled her out of her bewilderment. "Are you okay?"

She snapped her mouth shut and sniffed. "No. You saw it. He got away again." She couldn't help the whine that filled her voice. "He was right there." She gestured with a claw. "Right there."

Her father wrapped her in a tight hug. "I know. I saw." He held her while she sobbed on his shoulder.

"Why?" she asked, only half expecting an answer. She wanted to stop crying, but the dam that was inside her wouldn't be stopped. All the last few months of waiting for the seed to grow, the trolls going missing and ending up dead, the trek from the Weald back home—she'd shoved every emotion down and pressed so hard to keep them bottled up that once they came up, they refused to stop.

Finally, after several minutes, Horra pulled away. Her father's shoulder was damp and snotty. "I'm sorry, Father."

He chuckled. "I'm covered in sludge and sweat and you're worried about a little snot? Come, sit with me." He led her to their thrones. After she sat down, he took her claw in his. "You were so very brave today. You need to know that war is not just one fight that gets won. Sometimes you win minor battles, but the war continues on. Even your grandmother, Queen Petra, didn't win the War of the Warts in one grand battle. She won in increments, learning as she went."

Horra sniffed and ran a sleeve across her nose. "She did?" The victory had been such a big deal. Horra had only focused on that last battle.

"Of course. They knew nothing about that Erlking. They had to learn how to fight him and what to do to end the plague all at the same time. There were different fighting fronts, different armies doing separate tasks." He frowned. "War is not simple. But we won this one. Take it as the win it is and rejoice, for there will be other dark days ahead."

He squeezed her arm. "Now, let's go see to the casualties."

Horra followed her father to the entry, where they removed the barricades.

Pidge was flying around, searching for more food, when they finally found their way outside.

Rowan was helping the fairy princess to stand. She looked like a swamp swine with the black smudged across her hair and body.

"What were you thinking, coming out of the castle like that?" Horra plodded over to the druid and faced him. Up close, she could see the plants growing along his trunk and limbs. If he laid down on the ground, she'd think he was part of the scenery.

"Pardon?" he removed a tuft of green leaves from his ears. "*Ah*, princess. I'm so glad you're safe. You won't have to exercise your pet today. I took care of it for you." He looked quite proud of himself.

"Do you still have a grubby worm in you, because you're absolutely crazy for doing what you did."

"Not at all. I had faith in Pidge."

Horra blinked at him. "What is all of that greenery?" She waved a claw over his trunk.

"*Ah*, yes. Master Knurl, your Conservatory rood, informed me it would protect against the Erlking's magic. You're quite lucky to have such a wise rood in your midst." Rowan stood with his hands linked in front of him.

That took the wind out of her bluster. "We have a rood in the Conservatory?" Why did she not know this?

"Indeed, yes. I believe he's been keeping Pidge company for quite some time now." The greenery split, possibly in a smile, but Horra couldn't see the bark beneath, to be completely sure.

As if hearing her name, Pidge flapped over them and landed a few feet from Horra. She preened.

Horra scratched her pet on the neck. "So, the roods are not all gone? That's great news." She turned toward Princess Glory, her ire at the druid now gone. "How are you? Did the Erlking hurt you?"

Glory made an ambivalent noise and swiped at the muck on her face. "Not as much as this rank substance has." She shook her hands, flinging it around.

Horra jumped back to avoid the droplets and ignored her rudeness. "By the way, your mother was searching for you. Did she—"

"Yes, I know," Glory interrupted her with a sharp tone. She

stomped her foot, her hands covered in black mud from peeling it off of her face. "What is this stuff? Why am I covered in it? And why does it stink so terribly?"

"You don't know?" Horra asked. She needed to find out about the queen.

"If I knew, I wouldn't be asking you." Glory bent and wiped her hands on the damp, winter-dead grass. It didn't fully remove the heavy sludge, and she squealed with distaste. "Why won't this come off?"

Horra counted to ten before answering. "It's swamp sludge, a trick we trolls use to remove grubby worms. It's thick and won't come off easily. You can wash up in the castle. But first, did you see your mother when the Erlking took you?"

"It figures you trolls would use something as disgusting as this. Why can't you use magic like everyone else in the Wilden Lands? You're uncouth and undeserving of being called a princess." Ending her high-pitched tirade, Glory stomped over to the doorway and into the castle. Mud dripped behind her, leaving smudges on the smooth, stone floor of the entry hall. The same entry hall the girl's mother and sister had worked tirelessly to clean.

Though the princess had been through much, Horra struggled to find any kind of empathy for her. Kryk's words about bitterness came back to her mind. She could already see it taking hold of Glory's heart, which saddened her. She hadn't even seemed concerned about her mother.

"Pleasant girl, that one." Sageel *tsked* and stood next to Horra. The children all came out with the hobgoblins. Murda and Sorsha came from the backside of the castle, two worqs following them. Mud dripped down the sides of the blue creature's heads, their greasy hair pinned to their necks.

"We got these two trying to break into the back of the

castle." Sorsha said, shoving one worq in the back toward the king, who had joined them.

"Any injuries?" the king asked, eyeing the worqs dubiously.

"None that we can see. They aren't talking." Sorsha answered. "Torren might help if he remembers any of the Worqen from before."

King Fyd nodded. "Let's get everyone rounded up, cleaned, and then maybe we can sit down to eat. I'm starving. I've had nothing to eat since I left two nights ago."

FOUR HOURS LATER, the castle had been cleaned, though a faint scent of the sludge remained. Horra had taken Nimble and the new horse to get settled into the barns and returned Pidge to the Conservatory. Now, the king had assembled everyone in the dining room. The hobgoblins raced around, putting together a hasty meal for the added guests.

The king sat at his regal throne at the front of the room, an empty plate before him. Piskies flickered above them. Sageel had assured her they'd been fed honey instead of pollen that they normally feasted on. Horra had been reluctant to allow them inside the Conservatory where Pidge rested. It was not only for her pudge wudgie's sake, but also the safety of the piskies who resembled a bite-sized snack to her pet.

King Fyd tapped a spoon to his glass goblet, gaining everyone's attention. "Thank you, everyone, for attending this meal. We welcome you." He raised his glass.

The worqs glanced at each other but made no sound or movement toward their glasses or plates. They seemed ill at ease, and Horra could understand why. She was reluctant to sit and dine with them as well. Besides, they still smelled like worqs, regardless of how long they'd been hosed down to get the sludge off.

"As a goodwill offering, I have had our staff prepare some of your native food to restore your health." He nodded toward Torren, who sat on his right side.

Torren scrunched his face and then spoke in heavy, consonant-laden words. Waiving his claws over the trays, Torren worked to explain to them what the king said.

When he finished, the worqs once again glanced at each other. One took a fork and studied it as if it were something new to him. Damp still, they'd been hosed off behind the barns where the stable hands cleaned the livestock. Horra had never seen a clean worq before, and they resembled damp rats.

"We hope to make peace among your kind," the king continued, hope making his voice lighter. "After all, we have the same enemy now."

Torren translated, stumbling on some of the words. He nodded when he was done.

The biggest worq grunted, and the others followed suit.

Torren sent the king an unsure look. "I believe that's a good sign."

"Tonight, let's eat and rejoice in the small victory in setting the Erlking's war back. May the knowledge we gained be used to defeat him fully in the coming future." The king raised his goblet once more and then drank from it.

The children all drank from their juice glasses, and the worqs gulped down their frothy wheat hash drink.

Horra grimaced and sipped from her spruce juice. She delighted in its cold tartness.

Hobgoblins marched in with the main course—barbequed wildebeests. Two of them—a fresh one for the worqs with the head and feet still attached, and the other roasted over an open fire for everyone else.

The worqs all roared.

Apparently, food was a universal barrier breaker, which brought to Horra's mind her forever hungry pet pudge wudgie. She made a mental note to take her pet some treats later. It would be a relaxing end to a disconcerting day.

The king pointed his knife at the ravenous worqs, who had already dug into their wildebeest with gusto. "Minor victories. You see, daughter? This is how allies are made. Oddar will be stronger due to an alliance with them." Her father's smile was indulgent, the gleam in his eye one she hadn't seen for too long. He stood to carve the first chunks out of their golden carcass with radish flowerets and pickleweed garnish around it.

Horra glanced at everyone talking and eating, even Rowan, who drank a milky substance from a tall glass. Nothing seemed like a victory to her. Children were still missing. The Erlking was still out in the wild, doing whatever he could to take over the Wilden Lands. And the fairy queen was still unaccounted for.

CHAPTER 53

~ *HORRA* ~

Light shone in from the stained-glass ceiling of the sanctuary in the castle's chapel. Horra sat quietly on a carved bench as she'd seen her mother do countless times when she was a child, 'seeking Divine inspiration,' as her mother would often say.

The fairies had cleaned it until it sparkled. No one would even know the king had sealed it off for three years following her mother's death. Gold gleamed from the holy sword which rested on pegs nailed to the stone wall. Sigils carved along the blade's side threw shadows across the gray stone. Horra had always thought them to be decorative. She now realized they were magic sigils carved into the weapon.

"Princess?" Rowan's crickety voice called from outside the chapel. "Your father said I'd find you here?"

She let out a pent-up breath. "I'm inside."

Rowan's crown brushed the sides of the door. He had grown much in a short time. His trunk was as big around as a twenty-year-old spruce now. "Am I interrupting something?" he asked.

"Not really. I needed the peace and quiet." Horra shifted so he could sit next to her.

He sat down, the bench creaking beneath his weight. "Did you find it?"

She glanced at him, golden light turning his bark a lustrous brown. "Did I find what?"

"Your soul is in turmoil, is it not? You were uncharacteristically quiet at dinner this evening." His hands were no longer stick-like. He'd outgrown Woodsly already, and no longer reminded her of her old instructor.

That thought wrapped her heart in sadness. "The kingdom is a mess, Queen Toppenbottom is still missing, and the Erlking is once again on the loose. We may have won the battle of the grubby worms, but what's next?" She dropped her head and sniffed back unwanted tears. "I always thought when the time came for me to step into my mother's shoes, to become a great warrior, I'd feel more capable. Everything has been overwhelming. Nothing has been easy."

"I see." Rowan stared at the colorful glass depicting her foremother Calcy placing a cornerstone on the castle. "Do you think all heroes are brave, Princess?"

"Yes. Fearless and fierce. I try to be fearsome, really, I do. But I'm so far from it. I'll never measure up to my ancestors." She rubbed an arm across her leaking nose.

He glanced back at her. "I think you're wrong about that. Merrow said that bravery is simply fear taking a stand in the face of adversity. Since you came into the Weald, I've seen you do just that." He laid his branchy hand on her arm. "I may not like how impulsive you are, or how loudly you slurp your soup, but I never doubted for a moment that you were fierce, Princess."

Tears blurred his face as she smiled at him. It was exactly the thing that Woodsly would've said to bolster her. Somehow, deep down inside the new druid, her old instructor remained. It gave her comfort and strength. "Thank you, Rowan."

"You're welcome." He removed his hand and stood. Horra noted how regal he already looked, a credit to his kind. "Now, Master Knurl has given us a new quest. He's received a message through the roots. The Erlking has set up camp in a forest north of the Riven. The roots say the forest has disappeared as if it were never there. We must figure out what he's up to before it's too late. Are you up for this new task?"

Horra rose, a new courage sparking in her heart. "Absolutely."

TO BE CONTINUED ...

Acknowledgments

I thank God for the gift of seeing stories in my mind, and then giving me the courage to figure out how to write those visions down and make a book out of them. And to husband and family who root for me, lift me up on those dark days, and help me brainstorm when I need help, I will always love you more. For my friends who have supported me even when my writing was cringe-worthy, thank you and I love you for it. Thank you Scrivenings Press and ScrivKids, I'm so blessed to know each and every one of you. To my readers, I want you to know how much it means to me that you take precious time our of your lives to read this story. I hope it doesn't disappoint.

ABOUT THE AUTHOR

Winner of the 2016 ACFW Genesis Award, Dawn has been recognized for her published and non-published works. Her flash fiction stories have been published in *Havok* magazine under both her real name and pen name, Jo Wonderly.

As a child, Dawn often had her head in the clouds creating scenes and stories for anything and everything she came across. She believed there was magic everywhere, a sentiment she has never outgrown. Nature inspires her, and her love for the underdog and the unlikely hero colors much of what she writes.

Dawn adores anything Steampunk, is often distracted by shiny, pretty things, and her obsession with purses and shoes borders on hoarding. Dawn lives in Iowa with her husband, a chef and food service business owner.

ALSO BY DAWN FORD

Woodencloak

The Band of Unlikely Heroes - Book One

Thirteen-year-old troll princess Horra Fyd's life changes forever after
an unexpected visit from the fairy queen and her two daughters.
Tales of fairies gave Horra nightmares as a young troll. Before
evening falls, however, a real nightmare unfolds. Horra's father, King
Fyd, goes missing. Her woodgoblin instructor is poisoned and uses
his magic to revert to a seed. And a mysterious, gaunt man wearing a
cape and playing a panflute joins the fairies in trying to capture her.

Horra flees but is instantly lost in a world she's never had to travel
alone. A letter hidden in her knapsack from her late instructor
informs her that a power-hungry Erlking seeks revenge against her
kingdom and their allies for a two-generation old war. She is tasked
with getting his seed to the Weald, a magical forest. There it can
regenerate into a druid, the only creature with the power to hold the
balance between good and evil, and who is able to defeat the Erlking.

However, the Erlking is always one step behind her. Horra must fight to protect herself, but she has no magic. She accepts a gift from a dead druid spirit of a charmed woodencloak to disguise her. But magic failed her mother, how can she possibly trust it?

Can Horra have faith and courage enough to trust a power she can't see, and become a warrior heroine her foremothers can be proud of? Or will she allow fear to rule over her and lose everything that matters—including her life?

Get your copy here:

https://scrivenings.link/woodencloak

The Girl with Stars in Her Eyes

Firebird Series—Book One

Eighteen-year-old servant girl Tambrynn is haunted by more than her unusual silver hair and the star-shaped pupils in her eyes. Her uncontrollable ability to call objects leads the wolves who savagely murdered her mother right to her door.

When she's fired and outcast during a snowstorm, her carriage wrecks and she's forced to find refuge in an abandoned cottage.

There, her life is upended when the magpie who's stalked her for ten years transforms into a man, Lucas. He's her Watcher and they're from a different kingdom. His job is to keep her safe from her father, an evil mage, who wants to steal her abilities, turn her into one of his undead beasts, and become immortal himself.

Can they make it to the magical passageway and get to their home kingdom in time for Tambrynn to thwart her father's malicious plans? Or will Tambrynn's unique magic doom them all?

Get your copy here:

https://scrivenings.link/thegirlwithstarsinhereyes

The Girl with Fire in Her Veins

Firebird Series—Book Two

Former servant girl Tambrynn struggles with her new firebird abilities, especially the internal fire she cannot control. So, she, along with her Watcher Lucas, and her grandfather Bennett journey to a hidden mountain keep to find the answers she seeks before she sets the kingdom aflame.

But there's a new dragon who's targeting Tambrynn, a mergirl who wishes to manipulate her, and the froggen king, Siltworth, who hasn't forgotten that Tambrynn destroyed his watery reign. When her father, the evil mage Thoron, attacks someone she loves, Tambrynn's group is separated and she has to face another powerful foe alone.

Is she strong enough to withstand the deluge? Or will she drown in the fire and the flood?

Get your copy here:

https://scrivenings.link/thegirlwithfireinherveins

The Girl with a Dragon's Heart

Firebird Series—Book Three

After being injured while reversing the froggen's flood on Anavrin, Tambrynn travels to the depths of the mysterious Bloodthorn Forest for a cure. There she finds what she's looking for, but she also finds more trouble than she can handle. Thoron, her dark mage father, has found her and he's brought the Hulda, a villainous spirit Guardian, along as well. Tragedy strikes during the ensuing magical battle, leaving Tambrynn reeling from one loss closely followed by the death of a loved one. Shaken, Tambrynn barely manages to escape to her grandfather's mountain sanctuary to hide.

Burgeoning with power siphoned from dragon bones, Thoron is only a few steps behind her, making that sanctuary a prison. When unrest spreads across Anavrin, threatening all the Anavrinians again, Tambrynn must race to unlock the hidden power of her firebird abilities in order to defeat her evil father. But time is of the essence, and there's no way out of the mountain in sight.

With time running out, and hidden dangers around every corner, will a fairy tale and a secret pathway lead Tambrynn to find a true dragon's heart, the only power pure enough to take on Thoron's enhanced malevolent magic? Or will her father do what he set out to do since she was born—steal her abilities and destroy all that the Kinsman has created?

Get your copy here:

https://scrivenings.link/thegirlwithadragonsheart

ExpanseBooks.pub and ScrivKids.com are imprints of Scrivenings Press LLC.

Stay up-to-date on your favorite books and authors with our free e-newsletters.

https://scriveningspress.com/join-our-email-community/

Made in the USA
Monee, IL
27 June 2024

60747153R00177